A fiercely addictive crime thriller

CRIME IN THE GALLERY

(Detective Markham Mystery Book 6)

CATHERINE MOLONEY

First published in Great Britain 2019
Joffe Books, London

ISBN 978-1-78931-233-1

For Percy

PROLOGUE

Gemma Clarke was saving the best till last.

With tantalizing deliberation, she walked through all the rooms on the first floor of Bromgrove Art Gallery until she reached the wing devoted to Pre-Modern Art. There the poet's elaborately calligraphized paean greeted visitors at the entrance to the collection:

Full of great rooms and small the palace stood,
All various, each a perfect whole
From living Nature, fit for every mood
And change of my still soul.

But Gemma barely registered the periwigged and powdered notables gazing down at her from their gilded frames; scarcely turned her eyes towards the idealized landscapes, family portraits and ponderous allegories. Instead she forced herself to walk slowly, alert with anticipation as she approached her goal.

And finally, there they were.

Room 9. The Pre-Raphaelites.

Those vast colour-drenched canvases with their strange titanic forms whose impact struck her with a shock to the solar plexus.

With a feeling akin to being in church, Gemma sank onto one of two high-backed pine benches and gazed greedily around her at the jewel-like masterpieces glowing against burgundy silk-clad walls.

Nervously, she smoothed her neat blue skirt and jacket and adjusted her badge. No other security attendant was in sight, owing no doubt to yet another leaving do downstairs in the gallery staff room. But she knew she could only count on a quarter of an hour. Even though Sunday afternoon was generally the gallery's quietest time, Mr Bramwell, the director, would likely go ballistic if he found out about staff sloping off. What with those demonstrators from the university out the front protesting against 'Imperialist Art.' She wasn't even sure what that meant, only that it had something to do with pictures being racist. There was a little black pageboy in one of the paintings down the corridor . . .

Thoughts of gallery security faded as the painting directly in front of Gemma exerted its familiar hypnotic pull.

In the left foreground was a statuesque woman with alabaster complexion and rippling copper tresses. Clad in sinuous white drapery, its folds pooling at her feet, she held a book in one slender hand while the other lay on a stiffly jointed figure in full armour, the casque drawn back to disclose a pensive face. Behind the couple was a square building with an arched entrance, decorated in gleaming mosaics, like a little church with a tomb inside. The right foreground depicted beautiful gardens with exotic creatures bathed in pearly light, and above them hovered a cluster of angels in pastel robes and swallows diving with mystical intent. In the background was a shimmering golden citadel.

The two figures with their air of grave courtesy fascinated Gemma, as did the strange little building from which they had emerged. Mr Carstone, head of Conservation, had explained the story behind the picture. It was meant to be symbolic, he said. The ethereal lady and the thoughtful gentleman in armour represented a person's soul leaving the body after death. They were coming out of a mausoleum, not a house, and the angels were directing them towards Heaven, the far-off city. It was called *Life and Thought Emerging from the Tomb*, he told her, and there were coded messages in it. About resurrection and eternal life.

Gemma wasn't really interested in all that intellectual stuff, though she liked the way Mr Carstone treated her as an equal and never talked down to her — as though he saw something more in her than just indifferent qualifications and job prospects. Not like some of the other curators who looked through her like she was invisible.

She couldn't really say why she felt drawn to this one painting more than the rest. Perhaps it was something to do with the way the woman seemed to be looking right out of the canvas directly at Gemma, almost as though she wanted to tell her something.

Or perhaps it was the fact that she looked like Helen Melville, the gallery's willowy auburn-haired acquisitions officer. Gemma thought wistfully of the young director's graceful undulations and romantic aura. However hard she tried, however carefully she studied that languid elegance, it was a look that she, with her stubby sandy-haired ordinariness, could never in a million years hope to reproduce.

Reluctantly, she tore her eyes away and looked around her, wave upon wave of intense colour flooding her senses in the half-light like the magic-lantern images of a trance.

She knew her colleagues scoffed at her fascination with the paintings of Room 9 — their strange archaic themes, medieval heroes and sorceresses. But to her, the pictures spoke of a magical world vibrating with mysterious harmonies for which, did she but possess the key, she could exchange her daily humdrum reality — the crowded terraced house on Bromgrove Rise, her worn-out mum and the three grungy older brothers who somehow seemed to suck up all the oxygen. The knights and ladies, with their queer beckoning eloquence and cryptic gestures, seemed infinitely more vivid — more potent in their suspended animation — than the pallid specimens of humanity who populated everyday life.

The silence of Room 9 lapped about her, enveloping her.

She felt a curious reluctance to move. As though there was a spell laid upon her.

Voices floated up towards her, signalling the end of her reprieve. The shrill giggles of the café staff struck her ears discordantly like a blasphemy. God, that Julie one sounded tipsy.

Gemma sighed. Time to make her way back to Craft and Design on the ground floor. She'd hoped to start the Christmas rotation on Old Masters or Victorians, but her request had met with a level stare from Rebecca Summerson, the haughty blonde facilities manager. 'Security staff don't get to choose rotations until completion of their probation period,' she observed in frigid tones which left Gemma in no doubt that she had committed a major faux pas. 'Take no notice of that snotty cow,' her co-worker Barbara said kindly, but Gemma felt nevertheless that she had got off to a bad start.

Tapestries and musty old fabrics just didn't do it for her, she thought with a last wistful look at the samite-robed figure emerging from the tomb. Still, if she minded her Ps and Qs, she'd get taken on full-time, and in the meantime she'd have a look at the adult education brochures Mr Carstone had given her. Perhaps one day it would be *her* giving talks to visitors and looking at her wavy-haired heroines whenever she chose. The mere thought was like having a grape when her mouth was dry.

Craft and Design was located on the ground floor of the gallery to the left of the black and white marble floored entrance. On the right-hand side of the lobby was the Sculpture Gallery, whose smirking nudities made Gemma feel uncomfortable, unlike the scantily clad nymphs and shepherds of the Victorian pictures which oddly enough didn't bother her at all. Behind the Sculpture Gallery could be found the small exhibition centre and offices for senior staff. To the rear of the lobby were the gallery shop and café with cloakrooms, storage lockers and staff room in the basement. An imposing staircase, continuing the black and white theme, led from the front hall up to the first floor which housed the paintings. The cupola-roofed first-floor landing had an echoing, cathedral-like air of hushed devotion which seemed to have risen up like incense from the cavernous gloom of the foyer below.

Bromgrove was proud of its art gallery. A small, compact building in the neoclassical style with majestic pillared portico, it was situated right in the centre of town next to the Central Library and boasted thirteen rooms (an unlucky number some might say) spanning art from medieval times to the present day. Chronologically arranged, a wander through the collection would give visitors a whistle-stop tour of art through the ages, though, like Gemma, most visitors seemed to have their particular favourites. There were some big names too, she was wont to boast — Monet, Turner, Gainsborough and Lowry — but nothing could dent her allegiance to the Pre-Raphaelites. 'Dunno what you see in 'em,' her boyfriend, Jeff, had yawned on a visit one rainy day in October. 'Jus' letchy old gits with a thing about redheads. Give me Banksy or the Matchstick Man any day.' After that, she had kept her raptures to herself.

Now, outside, the November afternoon was already getting dark. She started as she passed the ceramics desk and caught sight of her white face reflected in the long sash window behind it. Moving swiftly through displays of jewellery, pottery and glass, she passed finally through a door marked Textiles, her station for the day.

It was a long narrow space lined with wall-to-ceiling cabinets containing mannequins in crinolines, bustles and breeches for which Gemma found it difficult to work up any enthusiasm. Wispy grey-haired Miss Crocker, Assistant Textiles Curator, was squinting myopically at a swatch of fabric in a packet on the counter in front of her making the little beaver-like noises which, with her, generally indicated puzzlement.

'Who could have left this? The label seems to have come adrift. I wonder what—'

Then her face cleared.

'Oh, *I* know what it is!'

The girl waited for enlightenment.

'It's from that tapestry Mr Traherne was worried about. He thought it might have mould.'

None the wiser, Gemma did her best to look alert and intelligent.

The diminutive older woman smiled kindly at her.

'It needs storing in the freezer, then Conservation can have a look. I wonder if you'd mind taking it down for me, Gemma,' she said, looking rather distractedly at the untidy work service strewn with a variety of labelled garments and paperwork. After rummaging in the capacious pockets of her corduroy skirt, the curator located a swipe card. 'That'll unlock it for you.'

''Course, Miss Crocker.'

For some reason that she couldn't explain, Gemma felt fidgety, restless, as though impelled to keep on the move. Normally she had no difficulty subduing such outbreaks of cabin fever when she was in Textiles, but today was somehow different.

The textiles freezer was accessed by a narrow black-railed spiral staircase at the very far end of the room.

Just as she put her foot on the first tread, Gemma felt an uneasy sensation. A kind of prickling between the shoulder blades as if someone was stood behind her.

But there was no one there.

She gave herself a little shake. No chance of impressing the likes of Rebecca Summerson if she came down with an attack of the heebie-jeebies any time someone asked her to do an errand.

At the bottom of the stairs, she flipped on the light switch and there it was, the walk-in freezer.

Again, that feeling of unease. But this time it was an almost unconquerable reluctance to swipe the electronic lock.

The stairwell was cool and musty, but she felt beads of sweat breaking out along her hairline and at the nape of her ponytail.

God. What was the matter with her? Too much time spent drooling over pictures of fairyland, she told herself grimly, vowing to ration the dose on her next trip upstairs.

Another little shake and then she raised the swipe card, her hand steady now.

The freezer door swung open.

But Gemma Clarke stood as though turned to stone, the packet dropping from her nerveless hand.

Curled up in a foetal ball at her feet was a woman, the hands like claws at her side.

A woman with auburn hair.

1. THE PALACE OF ART

At last Bromgrove Art Gallery was silent. The pathologist had been and gone, Helen Melville's pitiful remains wheeled away on a gurney, and the building left to an army of technicians and SOCOs.

Now DI Gilbert Markham, 'Gil' to his friends, and DS George Noakes were taking stock in a small windowless office adjacent to the exhibition centre behind the Romanesque Sculpture Gallery.

Noakes was clearly relieved to be away from the impersonal alabaster busts and statues which lined the route like a sinister praetorian guard, their blank stare reflecting the light of some fathomless alien world.

'Freakin' creepy that lot,' he grunted, jerking a thumb towards the passage they had just traversed. 'Like horrible wax-works jus' watching and waiting to make a grab at you. Always hated it when they dragged us here on school trips and whatnot.'

The stolid DS not being noted for his imaginative disposition, Markham found this an interesting reaction.

'I take it you're not a fan of the gallery then, Sergeant?'

Noakes looked sheepish. 'Not really, guv.' He struggled to frame his thoughts, his pudgy hangdog features corrugating with the effort. 'None of it feels like it's got anything to do with real life. I mean, all them angels and folk lying about outdoors picnicking . . .'

The DI suppressed a grin as his subordinate consigned centuries of Judeo-Christian culture to the dustbin.

''Course we took our Nat here a few times,' Noakes ploughed on, evidently anxious that his boss shouldn't regard him as a complete philistine.

Natalie Noakes, undisputed doyenne of Bromgrove's flashier nightclubs, struck Markham as unlikely to have profited much from the experience, but he kept such thoughts to himself and smiled non-committally.

'I imagine it's not everyone's cup of tea,' he commented mildly, making no mention of the many rainy afternoons he had passed in the gallery, eking out the time till he had to return to the home that was no home at all, desperately escaping into a parallel universe of grace and enchantment before encountering the sordid reality of a stepfather's abuse.

Something close to compassion flared in Noakes's piggy eyes, so that the DI had the feeling his sergeant knew exactly what he was thinking.

The two men's rock-solid relationship was an object of mystification to most of Bromgrove CID, and to slimy DCI Sidney in particular, it was nothing short of incomprehensible. Indeed, Sidney's jeremiads against 'dinosaurs' and 'detectives out of step with modern policing' were now so routine that the DI regarded them pretty much in the light of an occupational hazard and went his own sweet way regardless. George Noakes was one of his non-negotiables: not only had they come through many adventures together, but he knew the other always had his back and, by some strange attraction of opposites, understood him better than anyone else. The shambling, uncouth DS and his darkly handsome boss with a reputation for impenetrable reserve made a decidedly incongruous pairing, but their clear-up rate had so far rendered them impregnable to all assaults on their partnership. Markham intended it to remain that way.

'I take it we've got full contact details for everyone who was in the gallery when the alarm was raised?'

'Yeah, guv. Burton and Doyle are on it,' came the prompt reply. Then with a sly grin, 'Burton went round with the facilities manager securing the area. Prob'ly boring the pants off her oohing and aahing over every two-bit daub in the place. You know what she's like.'

Markham smiled wryly. Keen-as-mustard, DS Kate Burton was a university graduate, the team's acknowledged 'culture vulture' and Noakes's polar opposite, so it had been a case of dislike before first sight. Notwithstanding which, the two detectives had settled into an uneasy truce. Along with a grudging respect for each other's abilities, they shared a fierce devotion to their boss. With Burton, this had gone much further than professional regard, though Markham had never suspected her hopeless crush on him. Noakes guessed but never betrayed his colleague's secret, confining himself to the occasional knowing glance. Since Burton was now engaged to an up-and-coming DS in Fraud, the danger looked to be long past, though Noakes suspected she would never be entirely 'over' the guvnor.

'What about the young girl who found Ms Melville?'

This was another quirk of Markham's. No victim was ever just 'the body' or 'the deceased' to him, and woe betide any junior officer who thought to indulge in gallows humour. On such occasions, the DI's tongue could cut like a lash.

'Security attendant name of Gemma Clarke,' came the reply. 'Poor little bint. All snot and tears. Burton did a mop-up an' called this lad Jeff to come an' collect her.' Noakes scowled. Clearly he had not hit it off with the boyfriend. ''Bout as much use as a J-Cloth. More interested in squeezing his blackheads than anything else.'

'Hmm.'

A pause and then, 'What did you make of the rest?'

The DS had surprisingly sharp instincts when it came to sizing folk up.

'The facilities woman,' he consulted a dog-eared notebook, 'Ms Summerson — definitely a *miz* that one — looked like a stuck-up piece of work. Kept looking me up and down like it was *Downton Abbey* or summat and she expected me to use the servants' entrance.'

Noakes's sartorial instincts lagging markedly behind his inquisitorial skills, this was hardly to be wondered at. Today's ensemble consisted of baggy mushroom-coloured cords, scuffed brothel creepers and hideous emerald-green jumper topped off with a Columbo-style mac. It didn't even have the merit of being a considered fashion statement, but was rather a combination of total indifference to how he looked coupled with his ongoing battle of the bulge. With his brick-red complexion and haystack of salt-and-pepper hair, the DS hardly conformed to anyone's ideal of the gentleman detective. A blot on the artistic landscape if ever there was one.

'But efficient, I'll give her that,' Noakes conceded grudgingly. 'Got a roll call of the staff organized in double quick time, so Doyle could tick 'em all off.'

He frowned, 'You could see it hit her hard, though. Turned white as a sheet when we told her who it was. Pulled herself together sharpish, but there was a moment back there when I thought she was going to pass out.'

Interesting.

'Oh, and get this, guv.' Another look at the notebook. 'The boss is Helen Melville's ex-husband, well, separated, any road. Lemme see . . . yeah, that's it: Benedict Bramwell,' Noakes declared with a flourish.

Benedict Bramwell. Markham recalled meeting the gallery director at some civic bunfight or other. Tall, balding and adept at meaningless bonhomie. The epitome of a useful committeeman.

'Has he been informed?'

'They're trying to locate him? He's at a meeting in Birmingham today.'

'What about the rest of the command structure?'

'Well, there's the Board of Trustees — they're only around now and again, for meetings and that sort of thing.' More riffling through the notebook. 'The Treasurer and Secretary share an office behind the exhibition thingy, but nobody sees much of them.' Noakes gave an eye-roll. 'Too grand to mix with the plebs if you ask me.'

'Get that chip off your shoulder, Noakesy. Tact and diplomacy are the order of the day here.'

'If you say so, boss.'

'I do.' Markham was firm, grimly recalling his sergeant's less than subtle approach during their most recent murder investigation involving the local ballet company.

With a long-suffering sniff, the DS continued down his list.

'With it only being a small outfit, there's not that many chiefs . . . leastways they all double up. Helen Melville was responsible for paintings and sculptures, as well as buying stuff. Then there's the head of Craft and Design who handled textiles too, name of,' Noakes squinted at his untidy scrawl, 'Marcus Traherne. His deputy's the one who took us down to the freezer—'

'Miss Crocker?' The assistant curator, with her air of the world being too much for her, had reminded the DI of DCI Sidney's much put-upon PA, Miss Peabody.

'Yeah. She was in a right state, poor old biddy. Seemed to think it was all her fault. The facilities manager's PA made her a cup of tea, nice sensible woman, Cathy Hignett. God knows how she copes with Ms Bossy Knickers.'

'Anyone else from the top brass?'

'Silver-haired gent, Head of Conservation Aubrey Carstone.' Noakes just couldn't help himself. '*Marcus*, *Aubrey*, I mean, I ask you!' At a steely look from Markham, he subsided and resumed his recital. 'Thin, weedy, spectacles . . . getting on a bit. But kindly, you could see the staff liked him. Prob'ly lets 'em get away with all sorts.' Noakes flicked over a page. 'He's got a youngish deputy, Daniel Westbrook — crew cut, tough-looking, doesn't miss much, related to some art collector.'

'Did Ms Melville have an assistant?'

'Nah, she was one of them ball-breakers, er, executive types,' Noakes hastily amended, 'didn't like to delegate. Got the feeling it may have got up folk's noses.'

'Anyone else I should know about at this stage?'

Noakes snapped his notebook shut.

'That's all the main players, guv. We're trying to get hold of Bramwell an' the two trustees. Apart from that, it's jus' the café and cloakroom people, security attendants and such like.' He screwed up his features sagaciously. 'I think there's one or two researchers floating round the place as well. Postgraduate types from the university.' This was said with an air of profound suspicion. 'Mr Carstone's giving Doyle the details.'

'What about those demonstrators who were outside? What was that all about?'

'Oh, jus' the usual rent-a-mob lot.' Noakes looked disgusted, no doubt recalling their entanglement with Bromgrove University 'activists' in a previous murder case. 'Usual snowflake shite, guv. Summat to do with paintings being nasty about black people.'

'Thank you for that neat paraphrase, Sergeant.' The DI's tone was dry. 'Somehow I suspect the reality may be more complex.'

Noakes grinned, not at all abashed.

'Well you know what they're like, boss. Never happy unless they're taking offence.'

'Do we know if there was any trouble with gallery staff? Any run-ins with Helen Melville?'

'Right, now I get you.' The DS was suddenly serious. 'I'll get Burton on to it, guv.' With an air of magnanimity, 'She'll be on their wavelength, if you get my drift.' With her poncey psychology degree and MA in Gender Studies he meant, though the words were left unsaid.

'Quite.'

Markham leaned back in the tasteful ergonomic chair which was already giving him a back ache.

'Any obvious oddballs jump out at you? Other than the university lot,' he asked hastily before Noakes resumed his denunciation of Generation Snowflake.

'A couple of the security guards seemed a bit gormless.' Then, in an unusual burst of empathy, 'But that's cos they're looking at the same stuff day in day out.' Clearly the notion of there being any art-fanciers amongst their number never crossed Noakes's mind. 'Mind, there's one bloke definitely looked like he'd got a screw loose.'

'Oh yes, who was that?'

'Fella called Bill Hignett—'

'Hignett? Isn't that—'

'Yeah, Cathy Hignett — the facility one's PA — she's his mum.'

Noakes did an expressive eye-roll.

'I heard one of the others call him "Quasi."'

'"Quasi?"' Markham wondered if he was being exceptionally dense.

'You know, short for Quasimodo, guv, like the Hunchback of Notre Dame — you know, creepy bell-ringer from that Disney film.'

'Ah. And how did Mr Hignett react to this term of endearment?'

'Oh, he seemed used to it . . . like a nickname,' the DS replied warily, antennae suddenly alert to what he privately termed his boss's 'sarky' tone. 'I think he's jus' a bit simple, learning disabled or whatchamacallit. One of the café girls said his mum got him the job.'

'Any issues with his fellow workers?'

'He could be a bit, well, intense if he got a thing about someone, he'd follow 'em round like a dog.'

'Helen Melville?'

'Oh, she slapped him down early on and Mum made sure to keep him out of Melville's way. Nah,' Noakes shook his shaggy head, 'Reckon he's just a big harmless lummox, guv . . . part of the furniture. Bit of a nuisance sometimes maybe, but that's about it.'

As the DI sat digesting this information, there was a tap at the door and DS Kate Burton appeared. Smartly attired in a charcoal trouser suit and immaculate white shirt, conker-brown pageboy swinging, she was visibly energized by the start of a new investigation. Head on one side, she regarded the DI with the air of an intelligent beagle.

Not exactly pretty, with her retroussé nose and solemn eyes like enormous lollipops, there was something undeniably appealing about Burton's earnestness. She had faced tough opposition from home when she decided to join the police, but rapid promotion and Markham's interest in her career had done much to smooth ruffled parental feathers. 'She'll be safe with him,' was her father's verdict after meeting the DI, and Markham had fully justified that faith, though there had been a moment in last year's investigation into a series of murders at the Newman Psychiatric Hospital when the team thought they had lost her. It was a close shave, but Burton came through the crisis with flying colours and somehow the whole experience bound the little unit even more closely together. 'Markham's groupies,' others in CID were wont to mutter sotto voce, but the same cavillers would have killed for a chance to work with the legendarily austere DI whose reputation as Bromgrove CID's rising star made him an object of intense interest.

'All secure, Kate?'

'Yes, sir.' Shooting an apprehensive sideways glance at her fellow DS, she cleared her throat. 'It's an amazing place.'

Markham's smile was kind.

'People think it's all whipped cream and sponge-cake style paintings, but there's a decent section on contemporary art,' she elaborated, her tone defensive.

'You mean folk being angry with splattery paint,' Noakes grunted.

There was something almost ritualistic about their sparring, Markham thought with amusement. The preliminary skirmishes before they got down to the serious business of finding a murderer.

'Where're we up to with initial statements, Kate?'

'Doyle and the uniforms are just winding things up downstairs, sir. He'll be along in a few minutes.'

'Good.'

Markham's keen grey eyes were fastened on her face.

'First impressions?'

'As you'd expect, sir. Everyone shocked. The facilities manager, Rebecca Summerson, looked badly shaken up. I mean, she took control — snapping out orders left, right and centre — but when we were checking the rooms, I caught her leaning against a wall like she'd been sucker-punched.'

It chimed with what Noakes had noticed.

'She didn't like it when I said she should take a moment, sit down, have a glass of water. Got pretty sharp with me. So I didn't push it.' Burton's expression was thoughtful. 'She seemed like the kind of person who's afraid of looking weak.'

Afraid of looking weak or afraid of something else? Markham wondered.

'When was the last time anyone saw Ms Melville?'

'No one's entirely sure about that. Funnily enough, though, Gemma Clarke said she'd been spending a lot of time in the Pre-Raphaelite room.' Seeing Noakes looking mulish, she elucidated, 'The one with the Victorian paintings. The same room Gemma visited shortly before she found the body.'

'Oh aye, what was the big attraction, then?'

'Well, the pictures in there are very dramatic and brightly coloured — lots of myths and legends, biblical stories, if you like that kind of thing.'

It was clear her colleague didn't.

'But we're not just talking escapist fantasy,' Burton persisted. 'Apparently they're full of in-jokes and coded messages—'

'Messages?' She had Noakes's interest now.

'Yes, for people in the know.'

The DS cogitated.

'P'raps there was a symbol in one of them pictures which meant summat to Helen Melville . . . summat *dangerous.*'

He caught himself up short, beefy features mottled with embarrassment, and looked belligerently at Burton as though he would accuse her of luring him into flights of fancy.

'I think you may be onto something there, Sergeant,' the DI observed quietly.

Mollified, Noakes proceeded to develop his hypothesis.

'Which painting was it she liked best, then?' he asked Burton.

'The same one Gemma Clarke liked. *Life and Thought Emerging from the Tomb.*'

'Eh?'

'It's what they call an allegorical painting.' Burton was careful not to sound patronizing. 'It shows two figures leaving a kind of little house . . . a sort of grave monument—'

'Like the ones down the municipal cemetery,' Noakes put in, 'the tombs for the posh families. Proper fancy some of 'em.' He shuddered slightly, doubtless recalling an earlier case when he and Markham had ended up exhuming murder victims from the waterlogged neighbourhood of one such mausoleum.

'That's right. Well, the idea is that the figures represent Life and Thought leaving the body and setting off for heaven.'

'Is that all?'

Markham did his best not to smile. Clearly Noakes had been hoping for cabalistic clues worthy of the *Da Vinci Code*.

'There are all kinds of symbols of life after death,' Burton persevered gamely. 'The painter included a peacock, a butterfly and a bird hatching out of an egg.'

Noakes did his best to meet her halfway.

'It's weird all right.' He scratched his frowsy thatch. 'But why would any of that stuff have spooked her?'

'We don't know that it did,' Markham observed before Burton had a chance to embark on a discussion of nineteenth-century iconography. 'The painting might not have anything to do with her death. She could just have been in a morbid state of mind. Or perhaps she simply felt drawn to it like Gemma.' Observing his subordinates' disappointed faces, he added, 'But it's part of the background to her murder . . . part of the context. So let's not discount it.'

Suddenly there came the sound of an eerie rhythmic rattling which took them by surprise.

Sleet.

To Markham the moment felt disconcertingly sinister, as though they were trapped in some sort of kettledrum.

'It's not the first murder to have happened here,' Noakes blurted out.

He had their full attention.

'Well, last time was more a *disappearance* than a murder.'

'You're full of surprises, Sergeant. Tell us more.'

Knuckling his forehead as though by this means he could assist his memory, the DS duly obliged.

'It wasn't long after I'd joined the force, guv. A little lad wandered away from his mum down one of the corridors upstairs. There'd been a power cut or summat like that an' she kinda lost sight of him for a moment . . . got distracted . . . Afterwards she said she remembered him walking away from her but then he seemed to sort of, well, *blur* into the shadows.' The DS shifted uncomfortably in his seat. 'Like he was there one minute and gone the next. It was quite dim and gloomy with the lights being off, so at first she thought she could still see him. But then she called out an' he didn't answer. By the time she got to the other end, there was no sign.'

'I'm with you now, Sergeant,' Markham said slowly. 'The Carter abduction.'

'That's the one, guv. Never solved. Big Jim McLeod an' the rest bust a gut on it, but nada.' Noakes's face was grim. 'It was a Sunday afternoon . . . bit like today. The poor cow only really came in to get out of the rain and see some nice bits 'n bobs. Never got over it an' ended up on the sauce.'

'You don't think there's a connection with Helen Melville do you, sir?' Burton looked troubled. 'I mean, a cold case . . .'

'Could just be a tragic coincidence, Kate, but I'll want to review the Carter files asap.'

She nodded, her face sombre.

There was a rap at the door and DC Doyle appeared.

The tall, gangling ginger-haired detective was the fourth member of the unit and, after a rocky start, had proved himself a valuable member of the team. Something of a sharp dresser, his Hugo Boss suit struck just the right note of professionalism, so that he looked perfectly at ease in his surroundings. As with Noakes — his mentor when it came to football and affairs of the heart alike — it had taken time for him to jell with Kate Burton, but they had developed a solid mutual respect which seemed proof against any 'arty-fartiness' on her part.

'We've got all the statements and contact details now, sir,' he announced cheerfully. 'There were only a few visitors in the building on account of it being a Sunday, but they're all accounted for.'

'Thank you, Constable,' Markham said crisply, rising to his feet. 'I'd like a word with Ms Summerson, but the rest of the staff can go. With the gallery being a crime scene, we'll do interviews in the library next door. I'd like you to get that set up for tomorrow morning please.'

Clicking his heels smartly, Doyle disappeared into the corridor.

Outside the sleet had ceased its insistent thrumming.

Burton felt curiously reluctant to leave the safe space of the office. But Markham was motioning towards the door.

Time to hear what Rebecca Summerson had to say.

2. BIRDS OF PARADISE

Now that the staff had left the building, the front entrance seemed more cavernous than ever, its hollow acoustics heightening the gallery's resemblance to a place of worship.

'Jus' like the swimming baths,' Noakes observed more prosaically. 'Everything sounds like it's a long way off.'

Dream-like and somehow unreal, thought Markham, watching strange aqueous shafts of light strike the chilly marble floor from the cupola high above.

The facilities manager's office was located to the rear of the gallery café. Not particularly prepossessing, there was nothing to distinguish it from any other executive office. Save for one unusual feature.

A reproduction which the DI immediately recognized.

The famous *And When Did You Last See Your Father?*

He contemplated it with pleasure, temporarily oblivious to the other occupants of the room.

The little boy with feathery blond hair, clad in powder-blue breeches and lace-collared jacket, confronting Cromwell's Roundheads with his hands clasped nervously behind his back as they interrogated him about his Royalist father's whereabouts. Perhaps it was the fact that the child was depicted standing on a footstool which made the portrait so poignant . . .

'It was moved down here some years back. No one remembers where it hung to start with. The original's regularly on tour, of course. On loan to Sudley House in Liverpool right now.'

This was a whippet-thin nervy-looking blonde with sharp angular features and cut-glass accent to match. Expensively dressed in what looked like a vintage coral dress and jacquard tapestry jacket, hair drawn back in an elaborate pleat, she appeared composed, though her features were bleached with strain.

'Just as well CID's budget doesn't run to high art,' Markham said lightly. 'No chance of our being distracted by *Halsbury's Laws of England* or *Spilsbury on Blood Stains*, eh, Noakes?'

And a good thing too, was the DS's private conclusion, though he forbore to voice this aloud, preserving the inscrutable stolidity which he considered an essential antidote to the guvnor's intellectualism.

At their entry, Rebecca Summerson had been standing with two men in the centre of the room, flanked on one side by a mahogany partners desk with smaller adjoining desk, and on the other by a brown leather chesterfield and three button-backed armchairs. Ugly central heating pipes ran along the scuffed white-painted skirting but they at least had the merit of ensuring the room was several degrees warmer than the marble lobby. The uneven hardwood floor was almost covered by a somewhat faded crimson Aubusson carpet while a ceramic jardinière in one corner held some forlorn sprays of winter jasmine. Two fussy chandelier floor lamps and a low wooden cabinet crammed with art books failed to soften the room's rather oppressive atmosphere. All in all, it was a curiously impersonal space which gave no clue to its occupant's personality. Perhaps that was the intention.

The room had no windows, but there was a large square skylight on which the darkness of the November evening seemed to press down like a pall. For a moment, glancing up at it, Markham thought he saw the outline of a face in the top right-hand corner. Then he blinked, and the fleeting impression was gone.

Introductions were duly made.

The older of the two men was Aubrey Carstone, head of Conservation, who looked to be in his early seventies but held himself ramrod straight. With his double-breasted, two-piece pinstriped suit and waistcoat, fine head of silver hair, patrician mien and round-frame glasses, he exuded an air of courteous formality. Marcus Traherne, by contrast, appeared almost spivvish. Much younger, short and stocky with slicked back dark hair and fleshy, petulant features, he was flamboyantly dressed in a garish Prince of Wales check suit whose calculated Woosterishness seemed almost designed to set teeth on edge. Carstone's voice was mellifluous and cultured, while Traherne's words emerged in a lazy drawl. Vowels optional, one might say.

Markham had the feeling that neither Rebecca Summerson nor Aubrey Carstone particularly cared for Traherne. Certainly, Carstone visibly winced when the head of Craft and Design joked about the gallery being 'jinxed.' Involuntarily, the older man's eyes wandered to the room's sole painting and the figure of the little boy with the golden hair. The facilities manager's eyes followed his gaze, her expression solicitous. Of course, if Carstone was a long-timer, he could have been around at the time of the Carter tragedy, so his colleague's ill-judged levity was no doubt dredging up all kinds of painful memories.

Traherne seemed to realize he had made a gaffe. 'Sorry, bad taste,' he mumbled with what appeared to be genuine compunction.

'It's been a trying day,' Carstone said with magnificent British understatement.

And indeed, all three looked drained, Summerson and Carstone almost putty-coloured with fatigue and distress. As for Traherne, well something was definitely troubling him, thought Markham. Not just the murder . . . something else.

But the DI knew better than to press. Even in the 'Golden Hour' of an investigation, he knew how to wait. Fools rush in, was ever his watchword. The checking of alibis could wait till morning.

So now he simply expressed his condolences. Correctly, sincerely, with the compassionate reserve which invariably characterized his dealings with all those caught up in the maelstrom of a murder investigation.

Taking the hint, Carstone offered Traherne a lift to Bromgrove Station and the two men left the facilities manager's office.

Once the door had shut quietly behind them, the words burst out of Rebecca Summerson with the brittle velocity of machine gun fire. 'I think I should tell you — before you hear it from anyone else — that I was in a relationship with Helen Melville.' Two spots of angry colour burned on the high cheekbones. 'Or rather, I *had been* in a relationship with her until just recently,' she concluded miserably.

Something in the steady tranquillity of Markham's gaze seemed to reassure her. More collectedly, she continued, 'We were having space from each other, if you like . . . Things had got too heavy . . .'

'Was there someone else?' Markham prompted gently.

'A PhD. Fine Arts student from the university. Charles Randall. Tall, dark and handsome, if you like that kind of thing,' she added defiantly.

'Were the two of 'em happy together?' Noakes asked bluntly.

It was a twist of the rack.

'They were thick as thieves all right,' came the bitter reply. 'Forever whispering and passing each other notes about their latest hobby-horse.'

'And what would that be, Ms Summerson?'

'Randall's specialism is *aediculae*. Funerary shrines and monuments. Last I heard, he was writing a paper on the Holy Sepulchre. Helen was helping him with it.'

'That's the cathedral in Jerusalem with the strange miniature church inside it,' Burton broke in excitedly. 'I've seen pictures. It's got a little secret passageway and room with a shelf marking where they think Christ was buried and—'

'Hold on a sec.' Noakes radiated bafflement. 'Whatcha mean *miniature church*? Like in one of them model villages? A toy church?'

'No, sarge. It's a real church but inside a cathedral. People can stand up and walk round in it.'

'Think of it as being like a house within a house,' the facilities manager said kindly, momentarily distracted from the wreckage of her love life. 'As if a mausoleum from the municipal cemetery were to be magically transported from the graveyard and set down in St Mary's Cathedral.'

Noakes's eyes widened, not altogether pleasurably, at the thought.

'*Aediculae*,' Markham said musingly. 'That's an interesting field of study. Isn't there something similar in Italy?'

'That's right. Inside the basilica — the cathedral — in Loreto. A stone house where the Virgin Mary was supposed to have lived in Nazareth.'

'How'd it get to Italy?' Noakes was intrigued despite himself.

'It was supposedly carried there by angels in the Middle Ages to protect it from the Saracens. After a few stops along the way, they eventually set it down at Loreto where a shrine was built over it.'

The DS made a noise that sounded very much like 'Pshaw', but it was clear the idea had a hold on him nonetheless. 'Like those funny stacking dolls — the Rusky ones — that go one inside the other,' he said ruminatively.

'Same principle, Sergeant,' the facilities manager said laconically.

Markham regarded her narrowly. 'You said Ms Melville and Charles Randall were "thick as thieves." Were they up to something you didn't approve of . . . something underhand?'

'Well, they were always in a huddle . . . almost conspiratorial. Then Helen dropped hints about having found something in our archives. Stood right where you're standing now and bragged about finding the key to a mystery from the past. Unsolved crimes or some such folderol.'

'Think carefully, Ms Summerson. This could be important,' Markham said seriously. 'You're quite sure that's what she said?'

The woman looked discomfited.

'Well, she was always prone to melodrama. My attitude was she could keep her stupid secret.'

Perhaps if Helen Melville had confided in her former lover, she might still be alive. As it was, an indiscreet boast had likely signed her death warrant.

'Was Mr Randall in on the secret?'

The DI knew what was on Burton's mind. Charles Randall might well be in danger if their killer believed his girlfriend had shared her discovery.

'Oh no. She made a point of telling me that. Said she wasn't going to tell a soul until she'd fitted all the pieces together.' Her face suddenly anguished, the facilities manager turned to Markham, the muscles of her throat working convulsively. 'D'you think she might have told me . . . if I hadn't been so proud and angry?'

'She prob'ly wanted to do a Miss Marple, luv,' Noakes said sturdily. 'Mebbe stringing you an' this Randall bloke along was all part of the excitement.'

Oddly enough, the DS's gruff common sense seemed to bring Rebecca Summerson a measure of comfort.

'Well, she was always the consummate tease.' Her face fell. 'But this time she got way out of her depth.'

'Yes, Ms Summerson.' The DI's voice was sad. 'I think your friend was playing a dangerous game.'

One for which she might well have paid with her life.

'So, Helen was clear that she hadn't let on to anyone else?'

'Yes, Inspector.'

'But she seemed very caught up in this project on *aediculae*?'

'That's right.' A thoughtful frown. 'She and Charles always had their heads together in front of that second-rate Evelyn De Morgan painting.'

'*Life and Thought Emerging from the Tomb*?'

'Yes, that's the one. Ghastly mawkish tat if you ask me. Not at all the kind of stuff Helen usually favoured . . . but I assumed there was some connection with Randall's paper on funerary aesthetics . . . *Ars moriendi* . . .'

A mutual fascination with the Cult of the Beautiful Death or something more sinister, Markham wondered.

'Do you think there was some connection between that painting and whatever it was Helen had found in the archives?' Rebecca Summerson's voice was hoarse, as though some nightmare grappled her by the throat.

'We're not making any hasty assumptions at this stage, Ms Summerson, but it's definitely a possibility.'

The woman looked almost beside herself at the realization. Markham could have sworn her anguish was genuine but knew better than to rule her out as a suspect on that basis, his experience, professional and personal, having taught him that some words and wrongs went too deep to heal. The facilities manager had undoubtedly suffered intensely from her lover's defection, and it was not inconceivable that this led to murder. Her present meltdown could as easily have derived from a mixture of remorse and thwarted passion as from the dawning awareness that Helen Melville had harboured dangerous secrets.

'When did you last see your mate, then?' Noakes was as imperious to atmosphere as a diver in his bell.

Rebecca Summerson looked startled.

'Yesterday afternoon, around two or three. She was having a coffee in the café.'

'Was she on her own?'

'Yes, Sergeant. I seem to remember she was looking at a notebook or exercise book . . . something like that . . . Then she got up quickly and headed for the stairs. I assumed she was going up to her office or the archives room.'

'How did she look?'

'Now I think of it, sort of happy . . . pleased with herself . . . Sorry, I know that sounds vague, but it was just a fleeting impression. I didn't see her for the rest of the day, but that's not unusual when people have something on . . . and she was very wrapped up in this project on *aediculae.*'

'Were you busy as well?'

At least Kate Burton was subtler than Noakes when it came to establishing a suspect's movements.

'Saturday and Sunday were pretty uneventful for once. My PA, Cathy, was helping out upstairs both days because a couple of staff had called in sick with the lurgy or some such.' Wearily, she massaged her temples. 'There was a send-off for someone or other on Sunday afternoon, but I didn't show my face.' She grimaced. 'It would only have put a dampener on things if management swung by. Ben's quite strict about that kind of thing — likes to run a tight ship — but I don't see any harm in the occasional shindy provided they toe the line the rest of the time and don't take advantage.'

And know who's the boss, Noakes added mentally.

Until the PM results were in, they wouldn't know cause and time of death. But it sounded as though Rebecca Summerson was potentially without an alibi. Clearly, from the way the colour came and went in her face, the thought had crossed her mind also.

Markham decided they'd got enough for one day.

'Can I arrange for one of my officers to take you home, Ms Summerson?'

'No, it's fine thanks. I'll take my own car.'

Outside the rain fell heavily, drearily, with a soughing mournfulness.

'If you're sure,' the DI said.

'Quite sure.' She hesitated. 'How long will the gallery be closed?'

It sounded callous, but Markham knew work was the best medicine for grief.

'As short a time as possible, hopefully. Days at most. We'll be starting interviews in the library first thing tomorrow. I'm also going to want you to walk me through the gallery.' A spasm rippled across her face like the spirit of a sob. 'I know it will be painful,' the calm, cordial tones continued, 'but I need to see things through Ms Melville's eyes as well as get a feel for the place.'

Slowly she nodded. Finally, 'Would it have been quick?' she whispered.

Dark eyes met hers steadily. 'It's likely your friend lost consciousness, and once that happened she won't have been aware of anything much.'

But before that, blind terror and gut-wrenching panic. The brain darkening as Helen Melville froze into immobility, fossilized and mute. Then merciful oblivion.

* * *

Later that night, Olivia Mullen sat opposite from Markham over supper listening attentively to his account of the day.

Their third floor flat in The Sweepstakes — a complex of upmarket apartments and townhouses at the end of Bromgrove Park — overlooked Bromgrove North Municipal Cemetery at the back where Markham had his study. Olivia suspected that it soothed her lover to have this memento mori close at hand, as though it served as a talisman — his mysterious compact with the souls of the murdered dead that he would secure justice for them. Their living room looked onto formally landscaped gardens which wrapped round the whole apartment block, though its heavy damask curtains were now tightly drawn against the gusting wind which made the tall poplars twist and writhe as though whipped up to madness.

An English teacher some years older than her lover, Olivia bore a striking resemblance to the gallery's Pre-Raphaelite heroines, a waterfall of Titian hair framing fine bone structure and luminous grey-green eyes, her pallor as witchily other-worldly as any Circe or Guinevere.

'That poor woman. Was it quick?' An echo of Rebecca Summerson's earlier plea.

'Dimples,' this being 'Dimples' Davidson, the police pathologist, 'said there were pressure marks on her neck. If there was a struggle, she may well have been unconscious when the killer put her in there.'

'D'you think they originally meant it to look like an accident — make everyone think she'd got trapped in there by accident — only something went wrong and there was a struggle?'

'It's a strong possibility, Liv.'

There was silence while the lovers contemplated the crackling wood burner, lost in their own thoughts.

Finally, Olivia roused herself, determined to divert the conversation into more cheerful channels.

'How did George weather his exposure to high art?' she enquired roguishly.

Noakes and Olivia were, somewhat surprisingly, the firmest of friends, the DS having fallen for her ethereal charms hook, line and sinker, much to the chagrin of Muriel Noakes who contented herself with acid reflections on the 'obviousness' of red-headed schemers.

'Poor Gilbert Markham had no chance,' she was wont to sigh with ostentatious commiseration to her cronies at the Women's Guild whenever Olivia's name came up, 'no chance at all.' Normally what 'the missus' said was law to Noakes, but in this instance he showed an unaccustomed independence of spirit, refusing to hear a word against the woman he considered the guvnor's soulmate — the one who had somehow broken through that impenetrable reserve and breached his psychological defences. 'She's good for him,' he told Doyle during one of their confidential sessions in the pub. 'Gets to the parts no one else can reach.' Like Guinness, the younger man smiled to himself, but he knew what the DS meant. Since the advent of Olivia, there had been a gradual thaw, as if Markham's girlfriend had dissolved an invisible carapace allowing glimpses of the inner man.

Noakes's devotion to Olivia both amused and touched his boss, showing his oafish sergeant in an entirely new light, as if this most unlikely candidate had transformed into a paladin worthy to rank with the truest knights of the great days of chivalry.

At his girlfriend's question, he broke into a smile which transformed his normally sombre features.

'Let's just say I didn't dare risk him anywhere near the *Sexuality, Gender and Identity* exhibition. There was quite enough harrumphing, teeth-sucking and eye-rolling as it was.'

Olivia chuckled.

'That puritanical Podsnappery of his is never really far from the surface. I imagine he'd have been perfectly at home in the nineteenth century, covering up piano legs in case they "brought a blush into the cheek of the young person."'

'Oh, the Victorians are full of surprises. The Pre-Raphaelite brotherhood strike me as a pretty lecherous crew . . . nudity fine so long as there's some mythological, moral or historical tie-in.'

His girlfriend gurgled again.

'I take it George wasn't bowled over.'

'It was obvious he thought the place was Perv Central, but mercifully he didn't let rip. The facilities manager will be taking us round tomorrow morning, but hopefully he'll keep it zipped.'

'I bet Kate Burton was in clover.'

'Oh, the seventh heaven.' Markham's expression was wry. 'Couldn't get enough of it, asking all the intelligent questions. At least it helped dispel any impression of the police as philistines.'

'Perish the thought!' she grinned.

'Noakesy was cringing at first, but he got interested in the idea of there being coded messages in some of the paintings.'

His girlfriend too was intrigued by the riddle of *Life and Thought Emerging from the Tomb* with its hovering angels and birds of paradise.

'You think this secret, whatever it was, had some connection with the painting?'

'Well, Helen Melville was taking an unusual interest in it, so there must have been something, though I'm blessed if I can see what.' He sighed, 'Or maybe I'm overcomplicating things. Maybe it was just part of this project she was working on with her boyfriend . . . you know, funerary art and *aediculae*.'

'An odd coincidence nevertheless,' his girlfriend said thoughtfully.

Suddenly, she shivered.

'There's something creepy about that whole house-within-a-house thing. Something . . . Hansel and Gretel-ish . . .' Embarrassed, she forced a clumsy laugh. 'Don't mind me, Gil. You know how I let my imagination run away with me sometimes.'

Markham reached across the table for her hand.

'No, I know what you mean. It's that feeling of there being an optical illusion . . . sliding walls . . . hidden miniature universes.'

She smiled at him gratefully.

'That's just it. I was never much of a one for dolls' houses. They always seemed just like a prison . . . little gilded cages with no way out for the people inside.'

Another shiver. 'Like flies trapped in amber.'

And a spider at the centre, thought Markham.

After they had adjourned to the squashy chesterfield, he told her about the Carter case and the little boy who had vanished from the gallery without trace.

'You don't think . . .' She left the sentence unfinished.

'No.' Markham held her close. 'I don't see how the child's disappearance can have anything to do with Helen Melville's murder. It's more than thirty years ago. Just some tragic backstory.'

‘I suppose the gallery was very different back then.’

‘Well, I’ll be taking a look at the cold case files. They should have photographs showing the layout.’

Markham described the reproduction in the facilities manager’s office. The one with the little blond cavalier. ‘The Carter child and that lad in the painting are somehow fused in my mind,’ he said ruefully.

Olivia squeezed her lover’s hand.

‘How could he have been there one minute and gone the next? Did he pass through the walls or what?’

‘Easier in those days for a child to slip through the net. Now, of course, it’s different with the Child Rescue Alert protocols.’ Markham’s gaze held a faraway look. ‘But you’re right about it being like some kind of conjuring trick.’

Or an optical illusion.

Like the *aediculae*.

Could he be wrong? Was there in fact some link between that decades-old crime and the murder of Helen Melville?

Olivia sensed his tension.

‘You said there was some sort of demo going on outside?’ she observed lightly.

‘That’s right. What Noakes likes to call the rent-a-mob lot from the university taking aim at cultural imperialism.’

An exasperated groan rose to his lover’s lips.

‘Not Leo Wofitt and his barmy army?’ she asked, referring to a student agitator who had crossed swords with Markham in a previous investigation.

‘God, I hope not.’ He grinned. ‘No, he’s probably raking it in as a merchant banker by now.’

‘That’s the thing about your youthful revolutionaries. They always evolve into pillars of society once they’ve got the idealistic fervour out of their systems. “Bliss was it in that dawn to be alive, but to be young was very heaven.”’

‘Trust an English teacher to start spouting Wordsworth at me!’

‘Actually,’ his girlfriend riposted smugly, ‘he was quoting Edmund Burke on the French Revolution.’

'That's all I need. Sans-culottes rioting in the town centre. Sidney'd just *love* that!'

Olivia snorted. 'Talking of your revered boss, have you briefed him yet?'

'I've been putting off the evil hour.' Markham felt his guts constrict at the thought of the DCI. 'No doubt he plays golf with half of the trustees and won't want a breath of scandal to touch the gallery . . . or the university, for that matter. You know what he's like . . . gagging to pin it on our old friend the "bushy haired stranger."'

'I know Sidney's a direct descendant of Judas Iscariot,' she said tartly, mindful of Sidney's deviousness and jealousy of the rising star whose glory risked eclipsing his own. 'He's a treacherous fink, Gil, and the worst of it is you always let him claim the credit when you close an investigation, so he's out there schmoozing the press and bigwigs while you and the team slope off into the background.'

'So long as we get our man . . . or woman.'

'That's typical,' she said with mock irritation. 'Letting Sidney waltz off with the plaudits when all he ever does is obstruct you at every turn.'

'Well, you have to admit it takes skill to play both sides against the middle the way Sidney does,' Markham pulled a comical face. 'Wasn't it Churchill who said anyone can rat but it takes a certain ingenuity to re-rat?'

Olivia burst out laughing. 'All I know is that you'll be down to Doggie's the moment you're done with Sidney tomorrow.'

It was a palpable hit, since she knew it was Markham's invariable habit whenever he went ten rounds with the DCI to resort afterwards to the insalubrious gym in Marsh Lane operated by one 'Doggie' Dickerson where Bromgrove Police Boxing Club had its unofficial headquarters as a favourite haunt of CID and the local criminal fraternity alike. Knocking the proverbial seven bells out of an opponent in the ring never failed as a panacea to the DI's encounters with the higher echelons of the police service.

'You read me like a book, dearest,' was all he said.

Then, as though by mutual consent, they abandoned the subject of the gallery and all its works and snuggled down together to talk of other things.

Outside, the poplars continued their tormented writhing. Eventually the wind dropped and all was finally still.

3. DEMON'S LAIR

Monday morning dawned wild and wet, the wind moaning in hollow murmurs that seemed to Markham like the lament of lost souls.

He had slept badly, chasing phantoms down endless winding passages lined with niches and alcoves, heading deeper and deeper into a subterranean maze.

It was all the talk about those blasted *aediculae*, he thought, idly googling details about the mysterious stone house of Loreto on the computer in his study as he waited for his coffee to cool.

It certainly looked as though researchers would be spoiled for choice when it came to this most famous *aedicula*, there being innumerable true-to-scale copies of the Holy House scattered across Europe, and around two thousand in all throughout the world . . .

Despite himself, he was fascinated by all the maps, plans and 3D models slotting inside each other as perfectly as an egg in an egg cup or those nesting dolls Noakes had mentioned.

Olivia looked over his shoulder.

'What's with the archaeology?' she enquired, gazing at a complicated line drawing.

'Oh, that's the shrine Rebecca Summerson was telling us about.'

'The one in Italy?'

'The very same. Apparently, this diagram shows how it fits perfectly between the walls of some Jewish-Christian grotto in Palestine that they've pinpointed as the site of the Virgin Mary's house, going to prove that it must, at some stage, have been miraculously transported to Europe.'

'By angels?'

'Well,' Markham brought up some text, 'according to legend, it visited a few places but kept being moved when local inhabitants "proved unworthy of the gift from God."'

'Hmm.'

'Eventually it came to rest in Loreto.' Markham took a scalding gulp of coffee while running his eyes down the screen. 'But it probably wasn't carried by angels. Some researcher or other dug around in the Vatican Secret Archives and discovered from secret documents that it was the members of a Byzantine noble family, the Angeloi, who rescued the remains of the Holy House of Nazareth and brought them to Italy.'

Olivia laughed. 'A rather more prosaic explanation than the original legend.'

Markham's tone was sardonic. 'That's probably why the reigning pope didn't allow the researcher to publish his findings.'

'Ah, to preserve the miraculous tradition.' His girlfriend smiled. 'But I suppose there was *some* truth in it after all, with the Greek word for "angels" being *angeloi*, just like the name of the noble family.'

Markham scrolled back to his line drawing and contemplated it thoughtfully.

'There's something miraculous all right. When an underground passage was excavated beneath its walls in the 1960s, it turned out that the house had no foundations and just stood on a medieval road without any support.'

'Spooky.'

'They found the remains of hedges and bushes between the walls.'

'How romantic.'

'And there were scratch marks on the bricks of the house itself, showing it had been venerated in Nazareth in the fourth century.'

'It all sounds pretty fantastic, Gil,' Olivia said musingly. 'But I suppose science will unravel the riddle.'

'There must have been something to the story,' Markham concluded. 'Builders in the Middle Ages removed a supporting wall of bricks surrounding the original walls . . . which suggests that the house had been held in great honour and no expense spared to preserve it.'

'If it had just been an ordinary pilgrimage site, it would have been torn down and rebuilt more magnificently, I suppose. So it must've been something special.'

'Exactly.' Markham squinted at the image in front of him then turned to face Olivia. 'Spooky's the word, sweetheart. If all these archaeologists and palaeographers are right, then there's an exact correspondence of the Nazareth and Loreto footprints — place to place, site to site, space to space.'

'Easy to see why someone might be drawn to this kind of thing.' Gently, Olivia massaged his neck. 'Archives, hidden documents, graffiti, secret spaces. It's really quite addictive.'

'But what's the connection between *aediculae* and Helen Melville's unsolved mystery?' Olivia could feel the knotted muscles in her lover's broad shoulders. 'And where does that painting fit in?'

'The one with the mausoleum?' she asked continuing her gentle kneading. 'Can you see the interior of the building?'

'Not really.' Markham exhaled ruminatively. 'There's a sort of raised black marble altar or sarcophagus inside this flat-roofed crypt with an arched portal and a flight of shallow steps.'

'No skeletons or festering shrouds, then?'

'No. Just your average squat Gothic mausoleum with this medieval couple — like Saint George and his bride — in the foreground and a bevy of angels waiting for them.'

'Ah, angels again.'

'Yep, and what looks like the yellow brick road leading to the emerald city.' Markham gave an exasperated sigh. 'All it needs is the Scarecrow, Tin Man and Cowardly Lion and you've got the Land of Oz to a tee.' He broke into a reluctant grin. 'Rebecca Summerson called it "ghastly mawkish tat," and I think she may have had a point.'

His girlfriend giggled. 'Now that's no way to talk about sacred art, Gil. Anyway, I thought you said there were exotic birds not munchkins.'

'Well there's a whopping great peacock and a couple of doves or some such.' He reached up to clasp her hands. 'Oh, I know it's meant to be an allegory of eternal life, but it's the mausoleum that dominates the painting . . . like an evil little dungeon. You just can't tear your eyes away. The heavenly stuff's moonshine by the side of it.'

Olivia shivered. '"Here lies the sign that we shall break our prison; Amidst the storm he won a prisoner's rest."'

'What makes you say that?' Markham was startled.

'I hardly know, Gil,' she replied slowly, almost reluctantly. 'Just the idea of life as a prison from which death releases us.'

A dungeon tomb. Confinement. Fetters.

Images far more compelling than the sunlit uplands of heaven promising a good and glorious life beyond the grave.

Markham gave himself a mental shake. Much more of this morbid musing and he wouldn't be able to see his way clear.

Gently, he released Olivia's hands. 'I'm due a tour of the gallery this morning.' He did his best to sound hopeful. 'Helen Melville's office or the archives room may throw up a connection.' Stiffly, he got to his feet. 'And we're bound to get something from the interviews.' His voice rang with a confidence that he was far from feeling. 'Somebody must have seen something. She couldn't have disappeared into that bloody freezer without anyone noticing.'

Neither of them mentioned the little boy who all those years earlier had slipped through the cracks never to be seen again.

Olivia looked at her lover with the tender soulful gaze that seemed as though she could not bear to let him go.

Whatever secrets lay hidden in that gallery, she knew Markham would never rest until he had dragged them into the light of day. The pledge had already been given to the dead woman, just as it had been given to countless others whose ghosts were never far away.

* * *

In the event, the tour didn't prove particularly illuminating, though Markham experienced the same visceral shock as Gemma Clarke on his visit to the Pre-Raphaelite exhibits, their sudden rich colour packing an even greater punch after the miniaturized world of paintings hung on faded blue silk walls with powdered ladies and gentlemen posed decorously amid spindly furniture or pale stags. There was something almost obscene in the contrast between the anaemic tight-laced denizens of an earlier century and those flaunting, fleshly women with their rippling tresses.

He would have liked to linger and drink it all in. But Rebecca Summerson and Noakes padded closely at his heels so that in the end it was all just a glut of confused impressions. Even Helen Melville's favoured painting failed to speak to him.

Likewise, the dead woman's immaculately tidy office next to the staircase leading down from the first floor yielded nothing of significance. With a sinking heart, Markham guessed that the parallel search of her flat in Pelham Crescent being conducted by Kate Burton was likely to prove similarly unproductive. This was clearly an individual determined to give nothing away, though there was always the possibility that something useful might be unearthed in the digital trawl. Next of kin had been informed, but her surviving brother had emigrated to Australia so there was nothing to be gleaned on the family front.

To reach the archives room, the little group retraced their steps through the collection, giving Markham the slightly vertiginous feeling of time travel as they finally arrived at the Renaissance. Noakes was clearly underwhelmed by the room's panorama of Christian art awash with chubby cherubs and colossi, contemplating its array of celebrated biblical characters with the prudish disapproval of a latter-day Cromwell. 'Jus' folk getting their kit off,' he muttered to no one in particular. Before he could start denouncing the degeneracy of artists past and present, however, the facilities manager had whisked them through the door and into a narrow windowless passage. 'It's at the far end,' she said, pointing to the end of the corridor but making no move to advance, as though struggling with some unconquerable aversion.

Markham looked at her curiously then courteously motioned her to lead the way.

There was something undeniably unsettling about the gallery's deserted rooms and corridors, he thought. Like bodies without souls, all individuality and expression had departed, submerging them into one dead uniform repose. The impression of sepulchral gloom was only heightened by marble busts mounted in niches along their route, somehow like living sentinels and yet so unlike in their empty-eyed stillness and silence.

About halfway along was an alcove covered by a grille. There appeared to be nothing behind it.

'What's down there?' Noakes asked, peering into the dusky interior.

'Oh, I think there was some sort of recessed staircase for staff — so they could nip up and down between floors.'

'Very handy,' the DS said thoughtfully. 'Why'd they wall it off?'

Markham sensed the question was unwelcome.

'It was before my time really . . . renovations probably . . .'

And then Markham felt it.

The unmistakeable presence of evil there in that stuffy airless space.

He knew Noakes felt it too. The DS was looking around intently, almost sniffing the air as though to pick up a scent.

The scent of a predator.

Rebecca Summerson shifted uneasily. 'There were all sorts of nooks and crannies. I think the idea was to let the daylight in . . . make the whole place more open plan, more accessible.'

Let the daylight in.

Markham stood very still. In his mind's eye, he saw a figure crouching and slinking its way along the corridor. The image was so clear, he could see the dreadful shadow pausing at the entrance to the alcove. A tall shadow whose eyes looked and ears listened, busying its hands with something.

But he couldn't see the face.

It was a feeling of dim uncertain dread.

The moment passed and they moved on.

The facilities manager paused before a nondescript door.

'Here we are.' Again that strange reluctance.

There was nothing inside which appeared to justify her discomfort.

Just an ordinary room lined on two sides with old-fashioned gunmetal filing cabinets, each of which had a typed inventory taped to its side. A photocopier and recycling bin stood against the third wall, while in the centre of the room was a plain conference table with two chairs.

Nothing to see.

And yet, thought Markham, Helen Melville had apparently dropped hints about finding something in the archives. Something which offered the key to an unsolved crime.

'I wonder if you could take a quick look, Ms Summerson,' he said quietly. 'Give these filing cabinets the once-over . . . just to see if anything's been obviously disturbed.' He nodded to Noakes. 'We'll be just outside.'

Back in the corridor there was that same feeling of things being slow and aqueous and slightly distorted.

'Creepy up here, ain't it?' Noakes observed. '*She's* dead uncomfortable with it an' all.' He jerked a thumb in the direction of the archives room. 'Watcha reckon to this corridor being the one where that little lad went missing?'

'It wouldn't surprise me,' came the grim response. 'The Carter files should shed some light.' The DI raked a hand through thick dark hair. 'But we need to keep an open mind. There may be no connection with Helen Melville.'

'Bit of a rum do though, guv. The two of 'em copping it in the same building.'

It was an uncanny coincidence. And, as his team well knew, Markham mistrusted coincidences.

The air in the corridor was musty and stale. Markham felt a headache starting at the base of his skull. The desire to escape back to reality was overwhelming.

As if in answer to his prayers, Rebecca Summerson's voice summoned the two men back to the archives room.

'There *is* a file missing as it happens, Inspector.'

Markham's pulses quickened.

'Which one is that?'

'The Lestrange papers.' The woman looked genuinely puzzled, the aquiline features puckered. Tucking a stray blonde hair into her otherwise immaculate French pleat, she continued, 'Donald Lestrange was a connoisseur and collector who died suddenly . . . oh, around five years ago. One of his interests was *aediculae*. He wrote a few articles on biblical antiquities that were quite well received.Tthe Holy House of Loreto that I was telling you about yesterday, that was one of his hobby horses. But I can't see . . .' Her voice trailed off uncertainly.

'Could Ms Melville and Mr Randall have been consulting this material for their project on funerary art?'

'Well, yes. But they'd have had no reason to remove the file.' She gestured to the photocopier. 'Staff are meant to photocopy anything they want to take away.' It may have been the airlessness of the stuffy room, but she suddenly looked quite pale. 'As far as I can see, nothing else seems to have been moved.' Another nervous adjustment to her coiffure. 'The gallery's records are mostly computerized now. This room's really just for overspill. Hardly anyone uses it these days . . . just the odd researcher looking for peace and quiet.' Looking from one to the other, she added, 'Perhaps the file's just been misplaced or,' with a happy flash of inspiration, 'it might be somewhere in Helen's office or her flat.'

'We'll carry out a thorough check, Ms Summerson,' Markham replied easily, though the look he gave Noakes told the latter he had no expectation of finding the missing documents at either location.

Helen Melville had come upon something in the missing file which made her a threat. A threat that had to be neutralized.

Noakes ran a finger round the inside of his less than pristine collar.

'I'm coming over all claustrophobic in here,' he rumbled. 'If we're done with these files, is there any chance of a cuppa, luv?'

With alacrity, the facilities manager led the way back to the corridor and the trio once more made their way through various interconnecting rooms until they came to the main staircase adjacent to Room 13 which, so far as Markham could see, was pretty much a hotchpotch of styles in contemporary British art. Even the lure of his beloved Matchstick Man was not enough to distract Noakes from the pursuit of breakfast, however, so Lowry and various other gritty Northern artists flashed by without pause or comment. Rebecca Summerson, still unnaturally pale, looked only too happy to leave the artwork behind.

They reached the lobby and made for the café at its rear. 'I'll just locate the kettle and—' The facilities manager broke off. 'What are *you* doing in here?'

A chunky middle-aged woman with a badly styled butch haircut stood in the far shadows over by the semi-circular display cabinet.

Noakes moved forward. 'This is a crime scene, luv,' he said with ponderous joviality. 'Sealed off for the foreseeable.'

The woman came towards them.

'Hey up, didn't I meet you yesterday?' the DS asked with a sudden gleam of recognition.

'That's right. I'm Cathy Hignett, Ms Summerson's PA.' The voice was a surprisingly shrill sing-song which grated on Markham's ear.

'How did you get in?' he asked.

The woman had a cast in one eye, which made it difficult to tell whether she was looking at him or something over his shoulder. With difficulty, the DI suppressed the urge to turn around.

'Through the back door to the cloakrooms. I've got a key, see.' The tone was defensive.

'I'll have that, luv,' Noakes said cheerfully. Then, eying her denim overalls, 'Seeing as you're here, how about you fixing us up with summat. I could murder a bacon roll.'

Inwardly Markham raised his eyes to heaven, but neither woman flinched at the infelicitous phraseology. Rebecca Summerson sank onto a plastic chair as if oblivious of her surroundings while her PA disappeared behind the front counter into what was presumably the kitchen.

'I expect you'll be needing an office, Inspector,' the facilities manager murmured faintly. 'In the meantime, Cathy can see to hot drinks and so forth if that's all right.'

Noakes looked at her approvingly. 'More'n all right, luv.'

His expression brightened even further when, within a surprisingly short time, a tray with steaming mugs of tea and a plate of bacon doorstops was plonked down on the table in front of them.

'Champion,' the DS thanked the PA through a mouthful of toast. 'Reckon this'll set us up for the day.'

Rebecca Summerson shuddered delicately, darting anxious looks at her subordinate. 'Perhaps Cathy and I should adjourn next door,' she suggested. 'That's if you've finished with us.'

'You've been most helpful. Both of you.' Ever the gentleman, Markham escorted them through the lobby to the entrance and watched as they crossed the paved courtyard that the gallery shared with the Central Library.

'Think they needed to get their stories straight, guv?' Noakes grunted on his return to the café.

'Who can say?' Markham's gaze was brooding.

'That Cathy might be expecting us to pin this on her lad . . . the one they said has special needs . . . Quasimodo.'

'Bill Hignett,' the DI amended repressively.

'That's the one,' Noakes agreed, nothing abashed.

'Well, time to hear what the staff have to say for themselves.' Markham stood up, ignoring his subordinate's reproachful glances at the remaining doorstop. 'Maybe we'll learn something more about this file that's mysteriously disappeared.'

The two men walked slowly towards the entrance.

As they did so, Markham's attention was drawn to a giant tapestry in a glass case hanging above the front door.

With a chill, he recognized the motif.

The Old Testament temptress Jael hammering a spike into the head of Sisera whom she had lulled into a trap.

Markham felt his brain thrill to its core, as though his own temples bled under the impact of that lethal nail.

Who were they looking for? Who had baited the trap for Helen Melville? Man or woman? Was their killer even now stalking another victim . . . sharpening a weapon?

Noakes, predictably, was unmoved.

'Imagine sticking summat nasty like that right over the front door.' He eyed the protagonists with disfavour. 'Flashing her assets while clobbering some bloke through the head.'

Bromgrove CID's answer to Simon Schama, thought his boss with wry resignation.

He looked at his watch. 'Right, Doyle should have got things organized next door by now. We'll see what they've got to say for themselves and then have a debrief back at the station.' He kept his face impassive. 'No doubt DCI Sidney will need updating too.'

The DS looked as though something — not necessarily the bacon buttie — violently disagreed with him. With a last sour look at the biblical homicide, he followed Markham through the revolving door.

* * *

Bromgrove Central Library, by contrast with its neighbour, was blindingly bright, modern and airy. No dark corners or blind alleys. Just acres of freshly polished chrome, carrels and computers.

They headed up the escalator past the Costa Coffee franchise to the first floor where DC Doyle had been instructed to commandeer two meeting rooms.

The young detective was ready and waiting, clipboard in hand. Trying hard not to boggle at Noakes's attire — fuchsia shirt clashing horribly with grease-spotted regimental tie and straining brown flannels — he self-consciously smoothed the lapels of his sharply tailored jacket and cleared his throat.

'Key personnel are all here, sir. I believe you saw Mr Carstone and Mr Traherne briefly yesterday?'

'That's right,' the DI confirmed, recalling the gentlemanly head of Conservation and his distinctly less prepossessing counterpart in Craft and Design. 'Who else have we got?'

'There's Mr Benedict Bramwell. He's the gallery director — and Helen Melville's ex . . . though looks like they hadn't got round to divorcing. He was at a meeting in Birmingham most of yesterday, finished up around two. It all checks out.'

'Hmm . . . doesn't necessarily give him an alibi, though we won't know for sure until the PM gives us a time of death.'

'Oh, Dimples called earlier, sir.' Doyle was clearly pleased to be the bearer of intelligence from the pathologist. 'He said to tell you, *unofficially*, that she died sometime between four and seven o'clock on Saturday evening. Cause of death was myocardial infarction through shock. There was a pre-existing heart condition too, though no one had cottoned on to it.'

'So she died on Saturday evening,' Markham said slowly. 'Time enough for Bramwell to have caught up with her.'

'Same goes for the rest of them,' Doyle put in ruefully. 'Carstone and Traherne were holed up in their offices. Mr Daniel Westbrook — that's Mr Carstone's deputy — was here in the library doing some research in the fine arts section. He had a coffee in Costa with Helen Melville's boyfriend, Charles Randall.' He shrugged. 'Gives them an alibi of sorts.'

'Hardly.' Markham frowned. 'Either of them could easily have slipped over to the gallery at some point in the afternoon. It closes at five on a Saturday, right?'

'Yes, sir.' Doyle consulted his notes. 'They split up at closing time. Westbrook says he went for a jog on Bromgrove Rise while Randall just went back to his flat in Medway and watched telly.'

'Anyone else?'

The DC grimaced. 'Well, there're two trustees in there . . . so far up themselves it's a wonder they haven't disappeared up their own backsides.' He came to an abrupt halt and blushed. 'Sorry, sir, but they're a proper snotty pair. I heard the bloke saying he wanted to speak to the organ grinder not the monkey.'

'Did he indeed.' Markham's voice was deadly. 'We'll leave him till last.'

'I think that's pretty much the main players, sir, apart from the facilities manager, Ms Summerson, and her PA. They showed up a few minutes ago . . . said they were over at the gallery with you.'

'Correct,' Markham said in a ruminating tone. 'Did anyone stand out from the crowd, Constable?'

'Well, Mr Randall looked downright ill . . . Twitchy too, now I come to think about it.'

'Twitchy?'

'Sort of jittery and excited.'

'Prob'ly on drugs,' Noakes intoned. 'You know what them students are like.'

'No, I don't think it was drugs, sarge.' Doyle struggled to put his finger on the cause. 'He was just kind of watchful and frightened at the same time. Like he'd been hypnotized or something . . . like there was a snake charmer in the room.' He laughed as though somewhat embarrassed by this flight of fancy.

'Randall's the boyfriend.' Noakes was having no truck with this tarradiddle about snake charmers. 'He's gotta know that makes him Suspect Numero Uno. Bound to freak him out.'

Unless there's something else, thought Markham. Unless he *knows* something.

Suddenly the DI felt a deep sense of misgiving. A sense of something in train that he was powerless to stop.

As though to mirror his mood, he saw through the library's vast glass frontage a raft of dark clouds scudding towards the building. Fat drops of rain began to fall, and soon the whole complex echoed to an ominous rhythmic tattoo.

He turned back to the DC. 'Where's Kate?'

'On her way back from checking out the victim's flat, sir. Nothing significant to report 'cept lots of art books.' The glance Doyle flashed at Noakes was eloquent in its conviction that they were due an educational blitzkrieg.

Markham ignored the subtext, aware that his colleagues had their own resources when it came to self-medicating against the infliction of too much culture.

'Right, you can wheel them in now, Doyle. When Kate gets here, I want the two of you to re-interview everyone on the admin side — cleaners, café staff, security guards, students, cloakroom people and all the rest of it. See if they've remembered anything new since yesterday.'

'What about the demonstrators from the university, sir?'

'Kate's bailiwick, wouldn't you say?' The DI's expression was deadpan. 'I believe you'll be happy to leave her to it, Sergeant?'

'Ecstatic, guv.'
'Hmm.'

* * *

It was still pelting down outside, and the darkness of an hour seemed to have gathered in an instant. As though the elements warned of further wickedness, Markham thought uneasily. Then, squaring his shoulders, he gave Doyle the signal.

Time to meet a killer.

4. FOR WHOM THE BELL TOLLS

Benedict Bramwell was what Noakes would doubtless call a cold fish, Markham concluded as he studied the gallery director.

Tall and shaven-headed with the build of a useful scrum half, Bramwell gave very little away, though the DI detected a dull deep light somewhere within his gaze like that which reddened the eyes of a wild creature with its back to the wall.

The split from Helen Melville had been handled without rancour, he insisted, though a vein pulsing at the corner of his mouth was a giveaway.

'It *had* to have hurt, mate.' Noakes leaned in conspiratorially, his tone one of leering insinuation. 'I mean . . . leaving you for a *woman* . . .' Left hanging in the air was the implied slur on Bramwell's manhood.

Bramwell coloured, an ugly painful flush which subsided as quickly as it came, leaving his complexion a livid white.

But he had himself well under control, his expression one of chill distaste, his voice betraying no sign that Noakes's words had sent venomous suckers into his soul.

'We were separated *before* Helen took up with Rebecca Summerson.'

The DS looked at him pityingly as though to say, 'There's none so blind as those who will not see.'

And yet Helen Melville's ex-husband refused to rise to the bait. In any disclosure of disappointment or sorrow over his romantic past, Benedict Bramwell would see nothing but a humiliation which would have been vinegar to his wounds. He was therefore well garrisoned against Noakes's barbs, maintaining an air of apparent indifference which made it impossible to fathom whether his one-time love for Helen Melville had curdled to embittered hatred.

'An' now she'd taken up with this student fella.'

Noakes managed to make it sound as though Charles Randall was some sort of toy boy and the dead woman none too scrupulous about where she took her sexual pleasure.

'Naturally Helen was free to live her own life. Mr Randall is a postgraduate student close to completing his PhD,' came the repressive rejoinder.

'Indeed.' Markham decided it was time to turn the conversation along other channels.

Bramwell confirmed that he had spent Saturday evening alone at his hotel in Birmingham, though since it would have been perfectly possible for him to have slipped away unobserved, this meant he was without an alibi for the time of the murder.

'Can you recall anything unusual . . . anything out of the ordinary in your dealings with Ms Melville over the last few days?'

'Well, she was very taken up with this project on *aediculae* . . . suggested the gallery might do something on secret spaces as a tie-in . . .'

'Secret spaces?'

'Hidden rooms . . . the iconography of concealment.'

Noakes looked as though the gallery director was speaking Hindustani.

'What . . . like paintings of prisons?'

Bramwell smiled condescendingly, clearly pleased to have the upper hand in *this* exchange.

'More like places with haunted histories. There's quite a lot of mileage in that kind of thing, Sergeant. The Princes in the Tower, for example. I believe Helen fancied the idea of doing something with their story.'

'Ah yes,' Markham interposed suavely seeing that Noakes appeared none the wiser for this information. 'The two princes Richard the Third allegedly murdered and buried within the Tower of London . . . I seem to recall a picture of two wavy-haired little blond boys in hose and doublet near the head of the main stairs in the gallery.'

'That's right,' Bramwell said approvingly. 'It's a copy of Paul Delaroche's painting. The original's in the Louvre.'

Noakes had rallied.

'Murdered kiddies,' he said speculatively. 'Didn't you have one of 'em right here in the gallery back in the day?'

'The Carter case.' Bramwell's tone was weary. 'Mere coincidence I'm sure.'

But was it?

Was the dead woman's vaunted secret — the one she told Rebecca Summerson she had uncovered in the gallery archives — somehow connected with that long-vanished child? Was it because Helen Melville's thoughts were running on a modern-day abduction that she developed a sudden passion for medieval child murder? Could she have been sending someone a coded message, and was that someone working at the gallery?

The DI became aware that their interviewee was clearing his throat.

'Was there something else, Mr Bramwell?'

'I'm not sure to be honest . . . something and nothing most probably . . .'

'You let us be the judge of that, sir.'

'It was just a throwaway remark . . . something she said when we met for a coffee in the café.' He gave a rueful smile. 'I can't remember how we got on to the subject, but Helen was talking about some true crime documentary or other

— she was always very keen on that kind of stuff, though I found it morbid.'

Markham had the gift of patience. He smiled encouragingly and the gallery director seemed to take heart.

'It was something about the Moors murderers . . . Hindley and Brady. She said . . .' He screwed up his eyes in an effort to remember, 'something like they were only caught because of a doodle.'

'*A doodle*?' Noakes was nonplussed, his features creased like a grumpy bullfrog's.

'Well, some scribble really. Apparently the police were searching Brady's house as part of an investigation into the murder of a local teenager, when they came across a lost luggage ticket in the back of a prayer book. It led them to suitcases that had been left at a railway station. In one of the suitcases was a notebook in Brady's handwriting . . . on one page they noticed the name "John Kilbride."'

'That was one of the kids who went missing.' Noakes's eyes were alert with interest. 'But they hadn't linked the lad to Hindley and Brady till then.'

'That's right.' Bramwell sounded relieved to have been thrown a lifeline. 'Helen said something about the breakthrough being a bit of a fluke . . . that John Kilbride might never have been found but for Brady's slip up.' A shrug of the shoulders. 'For some reason it tickled her. As I say, she had a bit of a morbid streak.'

After the gallery director had left them, the two policemen pondered over the interview.

'D'you think he was trying to send us on a wild goose chase with that Moors murders stuff?'

'Difficult to say, Sergeant. But he sounded genuinely puzzled.'

'So Helen Melville might've come across summat like that . . . like a doodle or graffiti . . . which put her on the trail of little Alex Carter's killer.' Noakes scowled. 'Sounds a bit far-fetched if you ask me.'

Markham pinched his temples, a sure sign of perplexity.

'I can't help feeling there's a connection with the Carter case, Noakes.' The keen grey eyes were suddenly remote. 'Remember when we were standing in that corridor outside the archives room? It felt as though it was imprinted with the child's final moments.'

Perhaps, he reflected, the souls of the murdered dead could never quite separate themselves from the place of their demise. Maybe they experienced for it an unbreakable attachment, like the love that captives were supposed to feel for the cell in which they had been long confined.

Cells, prisons, secret spaces . . .

Noakes sensed they were on dangerous ground. The last thing he needed was the DI going all psychic on him.

'Of course, there could be no connection at all,' Markham said crisply, as though he knew exactly what his subordinate was thinking. 'But it sounds as though Helen Melville was preoccupied with thoughts of child murder accidentally brought into the light of day.'

'Jus' say she *had* found out something about the Carter case, boss.' Perversely, Noakes now sounded willing to be convinced. 'Which of 'em would've been around in the gallery when the kid went missing? I mean, it's only the older gent Aubrey Carstone an' that Miss Crocker who've been here for donkey's years . . . an' I don't honestly see either of them two clobbering a child.'

'No, that's true,' Markham said slowly. 'But I think you'll find most of the senior personnel will have been in and out of the gallery as students or for research purposes in their early careers. And then there are people like Cathy Hignett who've been attached to the place all their working life. So no reason we should just be looking at the oldsters.'

'If it *was* the Carter case, why wouldn't Helen Melville have told the police about it? I mean, a *child killer* for Chrissake!'

'You said it yourself when we were talking it over with Rebecca Summerson. You said it sounded like Ms Melville enjoyed playing Miss Marple, that she was excited by it.'

'Yeah, but you reckon she'd have twigged how serious it was.'

'Maybe she hadn't got that far, Noakes. Remember, she said "she wasn't going to tell a soul until she'd fitted all the pieces together."'

'You mean she might not have been sure, guv?'

'That's one possibility. Or perhaps she felt a strong affinity with whoever it was . . . wanted to understand what had happened . . . hear the killer's side of it . . .'

Noakes whistled. 'Silly cow.' Markham shot him a look. 'I mean, she was asking for trouble, boss.'

'Hindsight's a wonderful thing, Sergeant.' The DI was pensive.

Noakes revolved the possibilities. 'Hey, maybe it wasn't the killer she'd tracked down but someone close to him . . . or an accomplice.'

'Or maybe the crime she uncovered had nothing to do with Alex Carter at all. But one thing's for certain,' Markham exhaled heavily, 'she didn't see the danger she was in till it was too late. I imagine her affair with Charles Randall threw her off-kilter too.'

'Talking of which,' Noakes heaved himself to his feet, 'I'd better get lover boy in here.'

At that moment, the bell of St Chad's rang out the hour with a mournful sound, as if it had grown sad from too much communing with the dead and unheeded warning to the living.

Hear it not . . . For it is a knell that summons thee to heaven or to hell.

* * *

Charles Randall was a dark-haired softly spoken man of Mediterranean good looks who looked to be in his late thirties.

But he was pale under his tan, and Markham recalled DC Doyle saying the researcher had appeared frightened.

He answered their questions readily enough, however, speaking with infectious enthusiasm of his work on funerary art including a forthcoming study of the famous *aedicula* which housed the remains of St Peter in Rome.

'It was a complete accident how St Peter's bones were discovered,' he said with breathless reverence. 'They'd been excavating the catacombs under the basilica when some bones turned up in a box stored in the Vatican Grottoes. Apparently they'd been removed from a burial niche in what was called the graffiti wall — where all the ancient Christians had carved their secret codes and symbols — without the archaeologists knowing.'

There it was again, thought Markham. Secret spaces. Mysteries, codes, symbols . . . and a missing body discovered by chance.

Randall had moved on to the Evelyn De Morgan picture in the gallery. 'There aren't many aedicular paintings, you see.'

Noakes looked as though he could happily dispense with further historical exegesis. The researcher had a slight lisp which was getting on his nerves.

'Never mind about all that,' he interrupted rudely. 'How did you cope with your girlfriend swinging both ways . . . keeping you an' that facilities manager dangling . . . playing you off against each other?'

Randall looked somewhat blankly at his interlocutor.

'Helen was a free spirit,' he said, not without a certain dignity. 'It was an open relationship. I'd never have tried to restrict her. But I think we had something special.'

'So special she never told you about her secret discovery,' the DS fired back with undiminished truculence.

'What secret discovery?'

Watching the young man closely, Markham could have sworn Noakes's revelations came as news to him.

'An unsolved crime,' Randall murmured wonderingly at the conclusion of the DS's recital.

Uneasily, he cut his eyes at the door as though desirous of keeping something on the other side at bay.

'Mr Randall.' Markham's voice was unusually earnest and emphatic. 'If you know anything — anything at all, then I urge you to tell us.'

'There isn't anything, Inspector.' His voice was flat. 'Whatever Helen was up to, she didn't share it with me.'

'Slippery piece of work that one, you mark my words,' Noakes grunted as the door shut behind the researcher.

The DS showed himself more favourably disposed towards their next interviewee, Miss Crocker, exhibiting a degree of solicitude for her comfort which was uncommon for him.

Privately, Markham found Esmée Crocker's wispiness somewhat cultivated. Certainly there was a distinct note of asperity when she mentioned Helen Melville's habit of interfering with the work of other departments. 'She expected poor Mr Traherne to drop everything when she was in the grip of one of her . . . enthusiasms. It could be very tiresome.' And there was a definite whiff of jealousy in an allusion to Gemma Clarke's slavish devotion. 'Helen enjoyed the hero worship,' she observed, thin-lipped, and somehow it seemed to Markham that there was a world of meaning behind her words.

Although the assistant textiles curator had no alibi for the time of death, having been 'in and around the department', this did not appear to bother her. On the other hand, she exhibited a surprising level of unease when they spoke of how Helen Melville met her end. Markham could only guess that the sight of the younger woman's body had elicited a terrified guilt, as though the curator suddenly beheld her own secret vindictiveness — the hidden rites by which she soothed herself — embodied in those shrivelled remains.

Noakes detected no such undercurrents. 'Nice old bat,' was his cheery verdict on her departure. Despite the affliction of 'that toffee-nosed name', he also warmed to Aubrey Carstone, the gentlemanly head of Conservation, who had clearly sustained a shock. After the ghastly discovery of the previous day, it looked as though nothing could restore Carstone's complexion to its natural colour and the slight limp that Markham had observed at their previous meeting was more pronounced.

He spoke of Helen Melville's professional achievements with respect, though the DI suspected from his air of guarded restraint that he had not liked the acquisitions officer.

'Helen raised our profile in the North West,' he observed carefully, 'though she didn't always care whose toes she stepped on in the process.'

Carstone could shed little light on Helen Melville's recent activities, though he confirmed her interest in *aediculae* and haunted buildings, discussing the various projects with a lack of condescension which made Markham warm to him. Clearly this was a man who wore his learning lightly.

'Had you noticed any change in her? Any alteration in her usual routine?'

Carstone looked surprised.

'Our paths didn't cross all that often, Inspector.' He paused. 'Of course, I'm in the twilight of my career.' A self-deprecating smile. 'Not exactly one of the movers and shakers. So you see . . .' The sentence was left unfinished.

Once he had left the room, Noakes finished it for him.

'What he meant ter say was Helen Melville wasn't interested in an old has-been like him.'

The DI laughed. 'Yes, I think that's probably about the size of it, Sergeant.'

'He reminded me of that Sister Wendy from the telly. You know, the nun who lived in a caravan and only came out to do art programmes. Talked about pictures without being all lah-di-dah.'

Markham contemplated his colleague with amusement.

'As ever, you're full of surprises. Olivia's a fan of hers. You'll have to compare notes.'

Blushing furiously, the DS shuffled his feet. 'Who d'you want next, guv?'

'Let's see what Carstone's deputy Daniel Westbrook has to say.'

* * *

In the event, they learned precious little from the conservation assistant. Stocky with close shorn dark hair, shrewd dark eyes and a rather brutal mouth, Westbrook was, as Noakes declared in disgust, 'tight as a clam.'

'He was certainly no fan of Helen Melville,' Markham said thoughtfully, recalling the gleam of antipathy which had flashed across Westbrook's features. 'But I had the feeling something was bothering him.'

'Yeah, he started fiddling with that signet ring on his pinkie the minute you mentioned the archives.'

Without giving any hint of the mysterious secret that Helen Melville claimed to have discovered, the DI had casually led Westbrook on to talk about the gallery's records.

'Weird him being related to that "conosewer," the one whose papers went missing.'

'Hmm. Donald Lestrange.' Markham recalled the furtive, almost shifty, expression which had crossed Westbrook's face. It came and went so swiftly that he almost wondered afterwards if he had imagined it.

'Funny, Rebecca Summerson didn't say owt about Westbrook being his nephew.'

'It probably didn't occur to her, Noakes. The art world's a small one. Westbrook probably got his job on the strength of the Lestrange connection.'

'It rattled him though, guv.'

'Yes, for some reason he wanted to get off the subject of the archives.'

Markham frowned. There had been something off-key with Daniel Westbrook . . . a false note somewhere. But for the life of him, he couldn't pin it down. As with Carstone, there had been no especial consciousness when he touched on the Carter case, both men appearing to take Helen Melville's fascination with the Princes in the Tower as the natural corollary of her research interests.

So, what was it? What was Westbrook holding back?

There was a knock at the door and a buxom woman entered wheeling a trolley.

Noakes's eyes brightened at the sight.

'There's tea and coffee,' she told them briskly, gesturing at her cargo. 'Sandwiches — cheese and pickle, roast beef and chicken salad — and biscuits. If you need topping up, just send someone along to Staff Catering downstairs.'

'Righto, luv.' With that, Noakes duly got stuck in. No point going under for want of sustenance.

The DI was grateful for the coffee which was piping hot and excellent. For a time, he and Noakes talked desultorily of other things, though he could not dispel a deepening unease — a sense of some inexorable process which held them all in its toils, of something brooding across the way at the gallery.

Oppressed by these fatalistic thoughts, Markham walked over to the window which looked out onto Binderton Place. The rain had stopped but, although only early afternoon, it was already growing dark outside. The lights of the surrounding buildings made him suddenly feel quite desolate, for with their help, night and darkness seemed to come on faster. It was always the same at this time of year, he reflected. Always the sense of everything being shrunken stiff, hard and dry . . . just like the corpse of that poor woman.

Oblivious to his boss's inner communing — or, more accurately, being used to it — the DS munched on happily. Eventually, he declared himself replete. 'Good to see they've got their priorities straight round here.'

There was a sharp rap at the door and a thickset jowly man appeared.

Casting a disparaging look at the trolley as if to say, 'Wasting taxpayers' money as usual', he spoke in a high-pitched whine which was strangely at odds with his rubicund appearance. 'James Armitage, Trustee.'

Markham did not bat an eyelid. 'DI Markham, DS Noakes. What can we do for you, Mr Armitage?'

'Ms Watson and I have been waiting more than an hour, Inspector.'

A dumpy unprepossessing figure with glasses and greasy pageboy appeared at James Armitage's elbow. Smoothing the lapels of her dreary sage-green trouser suit, she looked equally disapproving.

'Murder knows no distinctions of rank, Mr Armitage. We'll get to you in due course.'

James Armitage opened his mouth then shut it.

Noakes smirked. It never paid to cut up rough with the guvnor when he used that voice. Immoveable force meets immoveable object.

The stand-off lasted a matter of seconds and then they were gone.

'God that's all we need,' Markham said with quiet resignation. 'What's the betting he has the DCI on speed-dial?'

Noakes's mood of self-congratulation evaporated. There'd be hell to pay back at base with Sidney.

Kate Burton peered round the door.

'Afternoon, sir, sarge.'

'How's it going with the interviews, Kate?'

Bouncing lightly on the balls of her feet, as was her wont when fired up by an investigation, she flipped open her notebook. 'Nearly sorted, sir. I'm just on to Gemma Clarke. Then there's Cathy and Bill Hignett and we're more or less done.'

'Okay. We'll take Marcus Traherne and Rebecca Summerson. After that, let's compare notes.'

Burton nodded vigorously.

'I take it you drew a blank at Helen Melville's flat.'

'Nothing significant, sir. No sign of those papers missing from the gallery. I'd say the lifestyle was high-maintenance.' She looked as though she would like to have said more but subsided at the sight of Noakes's jaundiced expression. Clearly the last thing he wanted was an inventory of Helen Melville's art purchases. With a bob of the head, she reversed into the corridor.

'Right, Noakes. Now for Traherne.'

Half an hour later, the two detectives regarded each other wearily across the table.

'Nothing to take us forward,' Markham concluded.

'Well, at least Traherne admitted he'd made a pass at Helen Melville, guv.'

'She swatted him away like a fly, though. No hard feelings on either side.'

'Yeah,' Noakes agreed, 'he's the kind that'll always try it on. All in a day's work. Like Slick Willie in Vice.'

'There was something else, though, wasn't there? Something Traherne wasn't telling us. He seemed almost *relieved* when we zeroed in on the sexual approach to Ms Melville.'

'As if he was afraid we'd found out about summat else.'

Markham brought his hand down on the desk with a thump.

'They're hiding secrets, the lot of them.' His voice was hoarse. 'And secrets *kill*.'

'D'you think Summerson could've snapped, guv? Melville was messing with her head . . . an' all this stuff about mysterious secrets could jus' be a blind. I mean, we've only got *her* word for it that Melville said she'd discovered something in the archives.'

'I'd say she was telling us the truth about that. She sounded genuinely disturbed by it. And it fits with Ms Melville's sudden interest in child murder.' Markham stood up and began to pace the room. 'Which isn't to say that Rebecca mightn't have lost it. We can't exclude the possibility of a *crime passionnel* coexisting with something else.'

Something evil that had lain dormant for years.

'Right,' Noakes said glumly, 'time to see where Burton's up to with Mrs Mop and Quasi.'

'Sergeant.' It was a warning note.

'Well, God knows we need a bit of light relief after that lot, guv,' the other grumbled.

* * *

In the event, laughs were thin on the ground.

Bill Hignett appeared a good-humoured and harmless man, somewhat gone to fat, with a lopsided grin and habit of chuckling at inopportune moments.

His mother watched him like a warder, lips tightly folded, as though continually apprehensive of what he might say and do. But beyond a lumpish slowness, there seemed nothing to justify alarm. He admitted to wanting to please Helen Melville but said she'd 'told him off for hanging around.' After that, he'd kept out of her way.

Markham made a mental note to check Bill's social services records for any indication of sexual pathology, but detected no unusual self-consciousness or signs of evasion. He had no alibi for the time of death having been engaged unsupervised on some joinery in the gallery workshop adjacent to the main building before leaving with his mother.

Mother and son didn't socialize much with gallery staff, though it came as no surprise to learn that Aubrey Carstone had been instrumental in finding them jobs after Bill's father had been killed in a work accident when he was a child. Other than that, it appeared nobody had much time for them except for Gemma Clarke. 'That's a nice girl,' Cathy Hignett told them. 'Always respectful to Bill, unlike some of them.'

Markham's eyes rested on her thoughtfully. How far would she go to protect her son, he wondered.

'We need to do some digging into the background,' he said after they had left.

Burton snapped her notebook open. 'On it, sir.'

You're welcome, luv, Noakes thought to himself. After their nightmarish experiences in the Newman Psychiatric Hospital on two previous investigations, he figured he'd had enough of 'crazies' to last him a lifetime.

Then a sobering thought struck him. What if their killer was a sicko? What if Alex Carter's killer had come back to his old stomping ground? There had to be some twisted agenda behind stuffing that poor cow in a freezer. The thought sent a surreptitious shudder down his spine.

'Greetings all. Hope you haven't scoffed all the sarnies, sarge.'

DC Doyle breezed in, and with him a blessed blast of normality.

* * *

An hour and a half later and Markham rose stiffly to his feet.

'I've had enough of this place. Let's get over to the gallery. I want to take another look at that Textiles room . . . see how easy it would have been for someone to lie in wait without anyone noticing.'

At the top of the escalator, he paused as a thought struck him.

'What about the gallery staff? Where are they now?'

'We packed them all off, sir.' Doyle sounded anxious. 'Was that all right? Didn't see any point in them hanging about seeing as they couldn't go next door.'

'The senior bods said something about working in the library for the day. They usually use the study carrels on the third floor,' Burton put in.

'That's fine.' Markham surveyed the peaceful space with its subdued hum of purposeful activity. 'Liaise with the Head Librarian once we've checked the gallery, will you, Kate? We need to give this place a sweep, especially any areas where Helen Melville was known to work.'

'Will do, sir.'

Noakes exhaled stealthily, vastly relieved that the task of library liaison hadn't fallen to his lot. He hadn't much liked the look of the gimlet-eyed tartar who ran the place.

'Right, time to make Cosmos out of Chaos.'

The DS eyed his boss warily. The guvnor must be all right if he was cracking them weirdy jokes, but then with Markham you could never be sure.

They headed for the library exit.

* * *

All was quiet as Burton unlocked the main door with her passkey, the trio having ducked under what seemed like acres of crime scene tape cordoning the pavement area from the entrance.

The SOCOs were gone for the day, but protective equipment and other paraphernalia showed they weren't yet ready to re-admit the general public.

The entrance lobby felt more like a mausoleum than ever, waxy holy families, scriptural pictures and baroque masterpieces staring down at the visitors like figures in some dismal allegory.

To the left of them lay Craft and Design, while to the right was the Sculpture Gallery.

Burton noticed that Markham was standing unnaturally still, his gaze riveted to something at the far end of the right-hand corridor as though whatever he saw barred his way like a phantom.

'What is it, sir?'

For a moment the DI remained motionless, then, instead of turning left towards Textiles, he led them past blind Roman busts and friezes with strange foreshortened figures.

Noakes glowered at the marble guard of honour, as though he half expected the various emperors and antique deities to descend from their pedestals and issue a gladiatorial challenge.

'Creepy as fuck,' he muttered under his breath.

Doyle looked as though he heartily agreed.

Burton, meanwhile, gazed apprehensively about her as though oppressed by the sheer weight of human history.

Then she saw it.

The monument in front of which they had halted — replica first-century sarcophagus said its plaque — was covered by a tarpaulin or dust sheet under which the outline of a figure was visible.

'Workmen . . . conservation . . . restorations,' Burton muttered desperately, as though the words were an incantation to ward off evil.

Markham stepped forward.

With a single commanding gesture, he whipped off the makeshift counterpane.

Charles Randall, glassy-eyed, stared up at them, beads of crimson embossing his neck like the delicate tracery of an imperial collar.

His throat had been cut.

5. FOREBODINGS

Early Tuesday morning found Markham tucked away in a corner of Waterstones with Ned Chester, the arts correspondent from the *Gazette*.

The open-plan café, surrounded by books, was located on the first floor of the large store. Markham liked its homely laid-back atmosphere, friendly staff and the feeling that he was just like any other customer.

Between sips of steaming chai latte his friend watched him with eyes that were at once shrewd and kind. Typical of Gilbert Markham to imagine he could just be another face in the crowd. With those dark good looks and sensitive ravaged features, he was already attracting admiring attention, the youthful waitresses taking surreptitious peeps at him as they bustled about their duties. All in all, the most unbecoming companion, the journalist mused wryly, suddenly acutely conscious of his own rumpled lankiness. He suppressed a sigh at the thought that in the charisma stakes, Markham would always lead him by several lengths.

'How's your cappuccino, Gil?'

'Excellent, thanks.' Markham gestured at their surroundings. 'I see they're playing around with the seating again,' he observed with some amusement. 'Red leather moon chairs . . . whatever next.'

'Yeah, a bit avant-garde for your average shopper. Can't see Noakes going for it. More a greasy spoon man, I'd have thought.'

'It's Greggs or bust with Noakesy,' Markham laughed.

'How is the old devil?' Chester shot his friend an appraising glance. 'Running interference for you this morning?'

Another mirthless bark.

'Pretty much. When I need the DCI keeping at bay, Noakesy's worth his weight in gold . . . a past master at laying false trails.'

'I'll bet.' Chester grinned. 'Unlike that girl guide DS . . . the priggish one . . . what's her name . . . Burton?'

'Oh, Kate's coming along nicely.' Markham smiled his rare charming smile. 'She'll be as devious as the rest of us in no time.'

'If she wants to survive at Bastards HQ, she'll need to be.' Then, seeing Markham's smile fade, 'C'mon, Gil, what's up? Why're we here? Is it that death at the gallery?' He looked his friend squarely in the eye. 'Whatever you say stays between us, you know that.' He couldn't resist adding hopefully, 'First dibs on the inside story of the investigation, though?'

Markham nodded. Ned Chester had never betrayed his confidence. Bromgrove CID might leak like a sieve, but Chester would remain 'utterly oyster.'

He looked round cautiously, but there was no one within earshot, only another elderly couple sitting on the far side of the café. The two servers were taking advantage of the lull to exchange news and gossip. There was no danger of being overheard.

Quietly, soberly, he recounted the events of the last forty-eight hours, finishing with the dreadful discovery of the night before.

By the time he had finished, Markham was very pale.

Chester could see that the discovery of Charles Randall's body had hit him hard.

'I could so easily have missed it, Ned,' he said very softly. 'But when we were standing in the entrance hall, I just knew something wasn't right. It was that dust sheet on the sarcophagus . . . as though someone had made up a bed.'

Chester's gaze was keen. He was one of very few people who knew that Markham was tormented by the last glimpse of his younger brother, shrouded and still on a hospital gurney, irrevocably lost to drink and drugs. While one brother had hauled himself out of the failure pit, the other never managed to slough off the legacy of childhood abuse. In some ways, Markham's entire career in CID was a never-ending quest to make amends to his lost sibling.

The journalist made his way over to the service counter for fresh drinks and toasted teacakes.

By the time he got back to their table, Markham had recovered his composure. Having skipped breakfast, the hot milky beverage and food put new heart in him.

'The awful thing was the parents turning up,' he said.

'What?' Chester was startled. 'You mean the victim's parents?'

'They'd arranged to meet him outside the gallery.'

'*Jesus.*'

'When they arrived, they saw all the commotion, never dreaming it was their son.' Markham bit his lip hard enough to draw blood. 'Mum collapsed screaming. The paramedics had to give her a shot to knock her out.' He shuddered. 'It was awful. Dad was this big strong man who just stood there in shock, asking politely if we were sure we'd got the right person because their lad was meant to be taking them for a meal.'

There was a long silence.

'How'd your victim get into the gallery in the first place, Gil?' The journalist frowned. 'Hadn't the SOCOs secured it? Wasn't the place alarmed?'

'We let ourselves in with Kate Burton's passkey. I only registered afterwards that the alarm had been deactivated.'

Chester's frown deepened. From the way he was fidgeting, Markham could tell he was itching for a nicotine fix.

'So, there must be some staff keys floating around.'

The other's face was grim. 'We thought they'd all been handed in, but clearly not.'

'D'you reckon he met the killer by appointment, then?'

'Well, we were doing interviews in the library next door.' A spasm of anguish crossed Markham's face. 'There seemed no reason to keep them all corralled together, though with hindsight . . .'

'Don't go there, Gil, else you'll drive yourself mad.' The journalist was thoughtful. 'If not in the gallery, it would have happened somewhere else. Randall must've had something on him.'

'Or her.'

'You think a woman could have done it?'

'Dimples says yes . . . if Randall was taken by surprise.'

'Wouldn't there have been lots of blood? I mean, it's not as if they could just walk out the front door after something like that.'

'There were signs someone had been in the kitchen at the back of the café . . . that's where they must've cleaned up. Did a thorough job by the look of things.'

'Forensics?'

'The SOCOs aren't holding out much hope . . . but in any event, everyone and their mother's been through that café, so there'll be trace evidence from the whole caboodle.'

'The killer took a hell of a chance, Gil,' Chester's finger-rubbing increased in tempo, 'waiting for the SOCOs to clock off before sneaking inside . . . And even then, there was a good chance you lot might rock up in the middle of it.'

'At least it means we can be positive about time of death.' Markham's voice hardened. 'The SOCOs finished in the gallery one-ish. We rounded off interviews in the library around the same time. After that we spent about an hour and a half reviewing what we'd got,' his face twisted, 'and planning how to bypass the DCI. By the time we went next door to the gallery it was half two or thereabouts.'

'I still don't get it, Gil. Okay, so an hour's enough time to cut someone's throat and get cleaned up, but how could they count on you not walking in?'

'I'd asked DC Doyle to tell the Assistant Librarian we'd be needing our conference room till at least two for the team debrief. Anyone in the vicinity would have known that was their chance.'

Chester's face was intent as he visualized the scene. 'So, you think that's when the killer arranged the rendezvous?'

'Yes. I think they checked the lie of the land, clocked the SOCOs had gone home and told Randall to meet them at the gallery in five minutes . . . something like that.' Markham's eyes narrowed. 'Presumably at some point that morning, Randall must've let something slip, some detail which showed he *knew*. Whether he did it inadvertently or deliberately, I don't know.'

'Blackmail?'

'In hindsight, I'm inclined to think so.' His hands clenched tight on the tabletop, Markham added, 'One of the team noticed Randall was hyper-watchful . . . "like there was a snake charmer in the room." I felt it myself when we were interviewing him.' The handsome features looked unusually drawn. 'The body language wasn't right. I should've pressed him harder, Ned.'

'Don't beat yourself up, Gil. You made a judgement call.'

'A poor one.'

'You might've pushed and got nothing, mate. Sounds like Randall thought he could handle the situation . . . poor sod.'

The café was starting to fill up with a cheery hum that was markedly at odds with the subject of their conversation. Chester looked wistfully at a shopper who stood at the counter vaping as he ordered breakfast.

Markham grinned. 'Never fancied giving e-cigs a whirl, Ned?'

'Nah, it's hardcore all the way with me, mate.' The journalist whipped his hands behind him in an endearingly juvenile gesture, as though by that means he could banish the urge to have a fag.

'So, what's the plan now, Gil?'

'Back to base to set wheels in motion. Kate's getting an incident room sorted at the gallery, but I have to see the DCI this morning . . . can't stall him forever.' Markham heaved a sigh of pure frustration. 'The thing is, all Sidney ever talks about is PR and damage limitation.' Then, with a touch of compunction, 'Which isn't to say he doesn't care.'

'Perish the thought.'

'But after those murders at the Newman Hospital last year and the police corruption hoo-ha, the last thing he wants is any whiff of civic scandal. To be honest, I think it'd suit him very well if it turns out to be some wacko university student . . . one of that lot jumping up and down and shouting about fascist oppression.'

Chester raised his eyebrows.

'Good luck with that.'

'Well, obviously we'll check them out.' A gleam of humour. 'But even Noakes thinks these murders have to be an inside job . . . and you know how he feels about "long-haired layabouts."'

The other chuckled.

'Better send Little Miss Muffet, then. Otherwise you'll have the vice-chancellor on your back.'

'Him and the rest of Bromgrove,' Markham groaned.

'You said "inside job," Gil.' The journalist's tone was searching. 'Are you linking these deaths to the Carter case?'

'I was wondering when you'd get there.' Markham's expression was rueful.

'Well, it cast a long shadow from what I've heard. Finished a few careers too.' Chester had a faraway look in his eyes. 'I was just a cub reporter then. It was 1997 . . . this time of year.'

'What was the vibe at the *Gazette*?'

'Not a dicky bird.' A disbelieving shake of the head. 'The kid was there one minute and gone the next. No one saw a bloody thing.' There was a wary look in the journalist's eyes. 'Some folk thought your lot got hung up on the mother cos she was a single mum and all that . . . tunnel vision . . .'

'Hmm.' Markham was non-committal.

Chester moved off the subject of police incompetence. 'You said Helen Melville had some sort of thing for child murder, right?'

'According to the facilities manager, she'd unearthed some secret connected to an unsolved crime. And then her ex, Benedict Bramwell, told us she was majorly into the legend of the Princes in the Tower.'

'Oh yeah, the ones killed by the Wicked Uncle . . . leastways he got his henchmen to smother 'em.' Chester's eyes were bright with interest. 'I remember they found a couple of skeletons under some stairs in the Tower of London . . . but Her Maj put her foot down and wouldn't allow DNA testing, so no one knows if it's the two boys or not.'

'Well, the jury's out on who killed them and nothing was ever proved, but it's likely they were finished off and the bodies hidden.'

'Bit of a coincidence, your murder vic suddenly going all Time Team like that.'

'Not necessarily.' Markham explained about the research into *aediculae* while his friend listened intently.

'Creepy,' he said eventually, echoing Olivia's verdict of the previous night. 'Guess that's why I could never stand visits to stately homes with priest holes and such like when I was kid . . . you know, secret rooms and sliding doors . . .'

'I had no idea you were so susceptible, Ned.'

'It's that feeling of something you can't see . . . something *lurking* . . . waiting to jump out at you . . . like there's an evil magician behind the scenes. Hey,' a thought occurred to him, 'wasn't the Wicked Uncle a hunchback. Richard Crookback or something?'

'So the history books say.'

'Well, there you go.' Chester was pleased with himself. 'What if Helen Melville managed to track down the monster in the maze . . . what if this *aediculae* stuff and Princes in the Tower research got her thinking about Alex Carter and then she came across something that fitted — something that solved the case?' He flashed Markham a brilliant smile, his reporter's brain teeming with possibilities. 'Or try this for size . . . maybe she'd come across a secret to do with *another* totally separate crime and it led her to make a connection with the Carter case.' Hooded brown eyes fairly crackled with enthusiasm. 'That whole Princes in the Tower hoojah could've been her way of telling the killer she was on to them!'

'Easy, tiger.' Markham's tone was indulgent. 'Let's not get ahead of ourselves here. She was a bona fide academic, remember. There's an argument for taking the *aediculae* and Princes in the Tower at face value — historical research, plain and simple.'

'You don't really believe that do you, Gil?' Chester enquired slyly.

'No,' the other said heavily. 'No, I don't. Too much of a coincidence and—'

'You don't like coincidences, yes I know.'

At that moment, Markham became aware of a young family at the next table. His gaze rested on the golden-haired toddler.

'I'll be reviewing the Carter file later, Ned. In the meantime, if there's anything you could dig up . . .'

'Always a pleasure, Gil. Provided,' with mock seriousness, 'I get an exclusive in return.'

The other grimaced. 'I'm afraid you might have a long wait. Wheels within wheels on this one.'

'Anything else I can do for you?'

'I appreciated a listening ear, Ned. Though God knows what the DCI would say if he caught me fraternizing with the enemy.'

'Oh, he's not above using us for his own purposes. You wait till the press conference.'

Another grimace.

'Think I'll leave the choreography to Kate Burton. Can't bear the thought of the usual ghastly two-step with Sidney.'

'Too male, pale and stale, eh?'

'Something like that.'

The two men walked through the café towards the escalator which would take them to the ground floor.

'Oh, one other thing, Ned.'

'Name it.'

'See if you can get me anything on a Donald Lestrange.'

'Who's he?'

'Some collector whose papers just went missing from the gallery.'

'Anything to do with . . . the other stuff?'

'Doubt it, but the timing's a bit odd.'

'Wilco, mate.'

With that they shook hands and went their separate ways.

* * *

The interview with DCI Sidney was every bit as tricky as Markham had anticipated, though Markham derived some comfort from the presence of Noakes — stolidly reassuring — at his shoulder.

Miss Peabody, Sidney's PA, was their usual barometer for the DCI's moods, so when she greeted them in an unusually fluttered manner it seemed to augur the worst.

Sidney sat behind acres of polished mahogany, ruminatively stroking his luxuriant beard. While a definite improvement on the wispy goatee, when combined with the macho buzz cut, the overall effect was more Jean Valjean than deep thinker.

Eventually he spoke.

'Art, Inspector, art.'

Oh God, Slimy Sid was in one of his gnomic phases where they were going to have to read the runes.

Something anodyne and non-committal was required before Noakes was tempted to wade in.

'The circumstances are certainly highly unique, sir.'

That should flush it out.

'There's a very dark side to creativity, Inspector. Think of Van Gogh.'

So that was it. Sidney wanted an aberrant arty type — say a deranged student — coughing to two murders in double quick time. Problem being, Markham didn't think there was the remotest chance of this being anything other than an inside job with some as yet unfathomed connection to a long-ago murder.

Glaucous eyes swivelled from Markham to Noakes and back again.

'I understand you've requested the files for the Carter investigation.'

As ever, the DCI's snitches were fully deployed.

Markham shot Noakes a warning look. No way was he going to start on *aediculae*, hidden secrets or the Princes in the Tower with Sidney. That would be asking for trouble.

'Just looking to get a feel for the history of the gallery, sir,' he murmured with well-practised blandness. 'Someone mentioned Carter . . . best to avoid any elephant traps.'

Elephant traps! God, where'd he got that from? He was morphing into one of those droids with their all-purpose phrases who invariably ended up as DCC.

But, wonder of wonders, it appeared to have disarmed Sidney.

'Ah yes, I see. Research. Putting everything in context, quite.' A flash of unnaturally white gnashers. 'Nothing like ancient history for tapping into the vibes.'

Ancient history. As in Case Closed. As in 'Don't even go there.'

Markham knew his cue when he heard it.

'That's right, sir. More idle curiosity than anything else.'

'An' there might be local sensitivities too,' Noakes chipped in with sunny innocence. 'Wouldn't want to upset anyone.'

The DI suppressed a grin. Local sensitivities forsooth. Clearly Kate Burton's PC world view was beginning to rub off on her grizzled colleague.

This transformation of the station's village idiot into a source of Solomonic wisdom left their superior taken aback.

'Important not to cause offence, quite.'

Sidney's expression was baleful, suspicion contracting his features.

'Talking of causing offence, I had James Armitage on the telephone earlier. I gather you didn't bother to interview him or Ms Watson after they took the trouble to attend for that express purpose.'

'Unfortunately, they had left the building before we got around to them,' the DI replied diplomatically. 'Pressing business elsewhere, no doubt.'

Chuffing queue-jumpers. But Noakes didn't say it aloud now that he had a character for preternatural sagacity to maintain.

'No doubt you will wish to remedy the omission as soon as possible, Inspector.' The DCI eyed Markham beadily.

Here it came.

'We all know that famous *flair* of yours.'

Sidney made it sound like a communicable disease.

'But what this case needs is good old-fashioned legwork. No flights of fancy. No *hunches*.'

'No hunches, sir. Absolutely.' Best just to parrot back the garbage and they'd get out all the faster.

Satisfied that he had put Bromgrove CID's wunderkind in his place, Sidney got back to painting.

'Used to dabble a little myself. On the other hand, the lady wife's quite accomplished.'

Markham's gaze flicked to the silver-framed portrait on the DCI's desk of blonde Valkyrie spouse and well-scrubbed offspring.

Of course she would be, he thought savagely.

And no doubt the photo montages of Sidney with the great and good which festooned the walls of his inner sanctum — or Hall of Fame as the station wags had irreverently dubbed it — featured a sprinkling of gallery patrons and artistic celebrities. In the circumstances, there was no way the DCI was going to entertain any suggestion that a psychopath might have somehow polluted the inner circle.

Markham felt a dull ache travel up his spine to his shoulder blades. He'd have to do the usual palaver of running a dummy investigation alongside the real thing. Kate Burton could be head of misinformation and waffle while Doyle drowned the DCI in spreadsheets and spurious statistics.

Meanwhile I can be head of projectile vomiting, he thought wearily as a tidal wave of Sidney-speak washed over him.

' . . . regular updates, Markham, I don't want any surprises.'

He became aware that the DCI had finally ground to a halt and was looking at him expectantly.

'No surprises, sir. Absolutely.'

Christ, he was starting to feel like a ventriloquist's dummy. He needed to get out before his head exploded.

With a testy flick of the wrist, they were dismissed from the presence and Miss Peabody sidled in from the outer office, with her eternal air of one primed to propitiate an angry god.

'Thank fuck that's over,' Noakes grunted, loosening his tie once they were safely out of earshot. 'Don't blame you for not wanting to talk archaeology or whatnot with him, guv. He's not having any.'

'No, as usual he favours the local nutter scenario.'

'D'you think his missus did that picture next to the window?'

'The flower arrangement?'

'I thought they were weeds.'

'That's because you have no soul, Noakesy.' The DI chuckled. 'At least she had the sense to stick to still life — flowers can't complain you haven't done them justice.'

Another grunt, but the DS was pleased to see some animation return to the guvnor's face.

'What now, boss?'

'Can you hold the fort at the gallery?'

'Sure, guv.'

'The incident room should be set up . . . and Kate will've sorted that sweep of the library by now. The SOCOs are going let us have the gallery back by tomorrow, but the building won't reopen until next week. I want all the staff in for interviews covering their movements yesterday afternoon, and we'd better arrange to see those two trustees pronto.' His face expressionless, Markham added, 'The team needs briefing on the DCI's . . . pointers, so if you could take care of that please.'

The DS noticed the other's fists were jammed deep in his pockets, a tell-tale sign indicating that he wanted to punch someone quite badly. No prizes for guessing who.

'You'll be . . .'

'Fitness training, Noakes.'

Which meant Doggie Dickerson's.

Doggie might not know anything about art, but a visit to his den of iniquity, aka Bromgrove Boxing Club, was the best antidote Markham could think of to counteract a dose of DCI Sidney.

* * *

Doggie was looking as villainous as ever, thought Markham later as he towelled off after an invigorating bout. A dead ringer for Fagin, in fact.

On hearing that his 'fav'rite 'spector' was on the premises, the proprietor shambled across to the optimistically entitled 'Sauna' — in reality a mouldering shower room in desperate need of re-grouting — for a friendly catch-up. With his scraggy toupee rammed on back to front, nicotine-stained fangs and rheumy eyes, Doggie was no one's idea of a health guru. But he suited Markham down to the ground. As did the grungy facilities where he felt entirely comfortable, whereas sleeker, slicker outfits left him cold.

To the likes of DCI Sidney, it would no doubt offer further proof of his being a fifth column in the heart of CID — not least as the club was also heavily patronized by Bromgrove's criminal fraternity — but to Markham it was home from home. He refrained from enquiring too closely into the CVs of those sparring alongside him and they, in return, slugged away for all the world as though perfecting that left hook represented the height of their ambition. Everyone a winner.

''Ow was that then, Mr Markham?'

'Not bad thanks, Doggie. Certainly got the blood pumping. Think I'm a bit out of condition, though.'

'I always say a pint of Guinness 'elps with energy.'

'Well I'll certainly bear that in mind, Doggie. Not sure it'd give me the edge over Mr Carstairs,' Markham grimaced, referring to a fellow DI from Vice. 'He was unstoppable today.'

'Try the Guinness, Mr Markham.' Doggie adjusted the skirts of his dingy gabardine-cum-dressing-gown with magisterial gravity. 'You'll see a difference in no time.'

'Will do.'

Having done the honours of his establishment, Doggie moved away, ducking his head to a powerfully-built young man before retreating to his lair in the back office.

'Hail the conquering hero,' Markham observed dryly.

Chris Carstairs flashed the megawatt smile which wreaked havoc amongst young and impressionable female recruits to CID.

'No hard feelings, eh, Gil? I felt lucky tonight.'

'Oh, I'll have my revenge, never fear. Doggie's just been sharing his infallible tips for sporting success.'

Carstairs snorted. 'The old rascal. Something to do with your "fluid intake" by any chance?'

Markham tapped the side of his nose with a grin.

'What gives with that business at the gallery, Gil? I hear there's been another.'

'Early days, Chris, early days.'

It wasn't generally done to talk shop at Doggie's, so he knew he could keep it to a minimum.

'You into art at all, Chris?' he enquired curiously.

'God no, mate. Though the one who did the matchstick men's all right.'

Markham wondered what the hell it was about that painter which made the likes of Noakes and Carstairs brandish his name like a calling card.

'Girlfriend of mine did a student placement there a while back,' Carstairs offered. 'She said it was like a mouse house, with separate burrows . . . poky little corridors and cupboards. A bit creepy, she said.'

* * *

Creepy. That word again, he thought walking back to his car.

Mid-afternoon and the daylight would soon be gone.

The stunted trees in the gym car park stretched their arthritic limbs against a leaden sky as though in supplication.

Or warning.

He had to get back to the — what had Carstairs called it? — burrow and probe those dark corners.

His mobile rang, jolting him out of his reverie.

Kate Burton's voice.

'What is it, Kate?'

'A small fire at the gallery, sir. It's out now, but I just thought you should know.'

'Where did it start?'

'The archives room, sir. No one knows how it started. Accidental most likely.'

No, he thought. This was no accident.

'I'm on my way,' he said.

6. ON THE TRAIL

Bromgrove's Fire Investigation Team was just preparing to leave as Markham arrived. Their chief, Simon McLeish, a sandy-haired man with a strong Northern Irish accent, greeted him amicably.

'Afternoon, Inspector. Don't worry, it's all under control.'

'Are we talking arson, Mr McLeish?'

The other looked genuinely baffled.

'More like a daft prank or mindless vandalism, if you ask me.' He frowned. 'Looks like someone started a little bonfire upstairs in that records room then scarpered when the corridor alarm went off.'

'Mindless vandalism,' Markham repeated.

'Well, they'd chucked files and what have you into the recycling bin and then set it alight. There was no real danger of it spreading.' He shrugged. 'Like I say, no logic to it . . . just a load of mouldy old papers.' He jerked his head towards the front door. 'Noakes was telling me you've had company the last few days.' He grinned. 'Our friends from the university.' A wry chuckle. 'No sign of them today, though.'

'With two murders, they may have decided that discretion is the better part of valour.' Markham sighed. 'I'll send

Kate Burton over to the campus to get to the bottom of this protest or whatever the hell it is. I can't risk Noakes.'

'God no. He's like me . . . thinks they're all Bolsheviks.'

Markham smiled thinly. 'Well, maybe Comrade Burton will winkle out the truth.'

'You sound dubious.' McLeish eyed him narrowly. 'Not convinced it's a prank, then?'

Markham noticed a little knot of people gathered in the café. He moved closer to the chief, keeping his voice low. 'I'd like to play this low-key: give out that we're treating it as vandalism, no connection to the murders.'

Another keen glance.

'Fine by me, Inspector.'

'Okay for me to take a look up there?'

'No problem. Not much to see. Just some smoke and soot damage . . . and a pile of ash in the bin.' The FIO gestured expansively with his clipboard at the baroque foyer. 'Some real treasures here, so just as well it didn't spread.'

The two men walked towards the front door.

'Noakes told me you didn't get far with DCI Sidney.' McLeish's tone was sympathetic. 'Playing your cards close to your chest on this one, eh?'

'Well, no point casting my pearls before' — long pause — 'those who do not want them.'

An appreciative rumble.

'Presumably he wants it all squared away in a couple of days.'

'Something like that,' Markham replied deadpan. 'But even the Almighty took seven, so Sidney'll just have to cut us some slack.'

'I'll email you later, Inspector.' With a laugh and a wave, McLeish was gone.

Kate Burton detached herself from the group in the café and approached the DI.

'So, Kate,' he said loudly enough for his voice to carry, 'looks like we've got ourselves a case of vandalism.'

Burton picked up her cue.

'So it would seem, sir.' She gestured towards the stairs. 'Shall we?'

As before, the route led through the collection.

Even though the rooms all lay wide open, Markham felt the stifling consciousness of something moving stealthily just ahead of him — a phantom with murdering fingers that had caught first Helen Melville and then Charles Randall in its demon-clutch.

So many scriptural pictures, he thought, passing one that he recognized as a depiction of *Jacob's Ladder*, with its column of diaphanous angels stretching far away into the sky.

Then it was on past *Life and Thought Emerging from the Tomb*. Was it his imagination, or did new shadows lie aslant the peacock's garden? Did he detect a new helplessness about the ethereal white-clad figure in the foreground, as though she could tell a story if she chose — as though she shrank from new-hatched plans of evil?

Get a grip, he told himself. But still, for all the bare expanse of polished parquet, there was a sense of suffocating oppression which intensified as they came to the windowless corridor he remembered from before. He felt a momentary mad desire to emulate Jacob and climb out of the warren into the clouds.

Then the feeling passed and he was standing inside the drab stuffy little room, even dingier than before due to the conflagration.

Noakes stood with Rebecca Summerson in the centre of the room, hunching his shoulders and ducking his head like a bull about to charge.

'One of that university lot must've sneaked in somehow,' he greeted his colleagues.

Markham made a non-committal noise that could be taken for assent. Turning to the facilities manager, he asked, 'When did you realize something was wrong?'

'The alarm went off around half past three.' She bit her lip. 'It would have gone off sooner but the sensors on this corridor are a bit dodgy . . . due to be replaced.'

'Who knew about the sensors?'

'Well, everyone really, I suppose.'

The DI examined her closely without appearing to do so.

The woman looked wrung out, ill, blonde hair hanging lank and lustreless. Wearing a black cowl neck shift dress, her pallor was very pronounced and her eyes unfocused.

'I hope you haven't lost anything of great value, Ms Summerson,' Markham said kindly as he examined the recycling bin. 'I don't suppose you were able to salvage much paperwork.'

'Well, there *was* summat,' prompted Noakes.

'Oh yes.' Rebecca Summerson made a visible effort to pull herself together and held out a crumpled piece of paper. 'This must have got stuck behind the photocopier somehow when the intruder was trashing the place.'

It looked like an architect's drawing for a large property. Lots of shapes, squiggles and cross-hatching. At first glance, nothing especially unusual save for an arrow scored so fiercely in biro that the pen had almost torn the paper.

Markham looked closer. The arrow appeared to be pointing to the intervening space between two walls. But there was nothing to show whether the drawing was a ground plan or whether it depicted an upper storey.

Then the DI noticed another odd feature in the way the initials C and H — now plain, now adorned with curlicues — were repeated over and over again along the borders of the page in a sort of tormented graffiti.

Suddenly, his heart stopped.

There it was. A break in the row of initials along the right-hand border.

A name.

Alex Carter.

The question was, had Rebecca Summerson seen it?

If she had, the woman gave no sign.

The DI kept his voice light, casual.

'Some sort of architect's plan from the look of it. Ring any bells, Ms Summerson?'

'Nothing that I recognize, Inspector.' He could have sworn she was genuinely perplexed. 'We just store old monographs and academic articles in here, from before things got digitized. This must have got mixed in with the rest for some reason . . . Can't imagine how. I'm sorry I can't be more helpful.'

'Not to worry.' Markham ushered her towards the door. 'Sergeant Noakes and I will be down shortly to interview staff regarding yesterday's tragic discovery.' It was never the DI's habit to gush or trot out formulaic condolences, but there was no doubting his compassion as he held Rebecca Summerson's eyes. 'Mr Randall's death must have come as an appalling shock to you all.' All of them, perhaps, save one. 'I promise you that we will catch whoever did this.'

The cordial, reassuring tones seemed to come as a relief. She shut her eyes momentarily as though to let them wash over her and then took a deep breath. 'Thank you, Inspector,' she said and quietly left the room.

Once they were alone, Markham handed the crumpled piece of paper to Noakes who then passed it to his colleague. Clearly the significance of the reference to Alex Carter was not lost on them. Thoughts of university hooligans evaporated. The graffiti was a game changer.

'The killer knew that Helen Melville had found something incriminating in here,' Burton said thoughtfully as she handed it back to Markham. 'They wanted shot of all the other junk on the off chance there was anything else which might lead back to them.'

'Yeah,' Noakes agreed. 'Couldn't risk being seen up here poking through the files, so decided to set light to 'em.' He looked round the room speculatively. 'Nearly got away with it an' all.' An idea struck him. 'Hey, d'you remember what the director bloke said about Helen Melville having a thing about doodles? How she rabbited on about Ian Brady being caught out by summat in an exercise book?' The other two nodded. 'Well, what if there's another bit of paper like this floating around . . . from that art collector's file . . . the one that went missing?'

'The Lestrange papers.' Burton was quickly on his wavelength.

Noakes had the bit between his teeth now. 'Randall could've come across whatever she left lying around an' made a connection with someone at the gallery.'

'That's a plausible scenario, Sergeant.' Markham spoke approvingly and Noakes's beefy features mottled with pleasure.

'Alternatively, it's possible that Mr Randall saw or heard something that put him on the killer's trail,' the DI continued. 'Something whose significance he may not even have realized at first.'

Burton's expression was worried. Markham was quick to notice.

'What is it, Kate?'

'The library sweep didn't come up with anything,' she said uncertainly. 'Helen Melville's usual carrel was empty. There isn't a rigid booking system or anything like that, but gallery staff generally stick to the same carrels. They can loan them for up to seven days at a time.'

'How secure are the carrels?' Markham asked. 'Does the library have keys?'

'That's just it, sir. There are some keys kept at the loans desk, but I don't think the library assistants pay much attention to academics and researchers. I mean, they trust them to get on with it really.'

'So, nothing to stop someone having a snoop?' Noakes chipped in.

'It'd be quite easy for someone to wander in if the door was unlocked and Melville was in another part of the library.'

They digested the implications of this for a minute or two.

'Who're we looking for, guv?' Noakes finally burst out in frustration. 'That Summerson one seemed like she was in a daze . . . looked like she'd hit the bottle an' all.'

Markham too had caught the whiff of alcohol, concluding it was more than likely Rebecca Summerson had fortified herself before coming to work.

'We're looking for a risk-taker, Sergeant,' he said slowly. 'Someone who sees a chance and takes it.' Dark eyes surveyed the room. 'If it's one of them downstairs and this is an inside job, then we're dealing with a cool customer. Coming up here was a risk, but still they chanced it.'

'If they did little Alex too, then we've got ourselves a serial,' Noakes said sombrely.

The airless little room seemed to darken at his words. Once again, despite the fug, Markham felt a clammy touch of apprehension, as though he was a dumb animal unable to measure results.

To dispel the impression, he shook himself briskly.

'Right, let's get to it. Noakes and I will take the staff downstairs and see who's alibied for yesterday afternoon when that poor fellow was getting his throat cut.' The DI was still haunted by that disbelieving father waiting patiently for his son who lay stiff and sightless just feet away. Mild and inoffensive, Randall senior had urged, 'Just tell him we're here, will you,' as though unable to comprehend that the silence in his boy's ear was never more to be broken.

'And we need to roust those two trustees from wherever they're lurking,' he added with evident distaste. 'Can't afford to have them running to the DCI with further complaints of *lèse-majesté*.'

He turned to Kate Burton. 'I want you and Doyle to cover the university angle, Kate. Check who's involved in this anti-colonialism protest or whatever it is, have a discreet word with the authorities while you're at it.'

'You don't think—'

'No, I don't reckon we're looking for a student.' The DI's face hardened. 'It's a distraction, though, and one we could do without.'

A thought struck him. 'It may be that one of the protestors noticed something without realizing what it meant.' He exhaled heavily. 'A long shot, but who knows . . .'

'On it, sir.' She looked pleased with the assignment, Noakes noted sourly. Thank Christ he didn't have to waste an afternoon schmoozing a bunch of posers and listening to all their arty-farty bullshit. As for all that abstract stuff, he fancied he could do better himself. Security wasn't that tight in the modern art room. What a joke if someone scribbled a shape on one of those weird pictures with all the squares and rectangles. Probably no one would notice any difference.

'Ready, Sergeant?'

Not for the first time, Noakes had the uncomfortable sensation that the DI could read his mind.

* * *

'Well, we didn't get much out of those two.'

Doyle sounded despondent.

'Spoiled entitled smart-arses the pair of them.'

'You're starting to sound like Noakes,' Burton observed mildly.

That elicited a shaky laugh.

Privately, however, she was inclined to agree.

The two detectives sat in a bland conference room in the Fine Arts Faculty. Though it was now dark outside, Burton was familiar with the tastefully landscaped setting — manicured lawns, Barbara Hepworth style sculptures and Zen cascading bowls. The adjacent corridors were lined with striking examples of modern art and what looked like aboriginal face masks ('like something off Easter Island', muttered Doyle, not at all sotto voce). Although situated just outside the town centre in the predominantly working-class suburb of Medway, the university campus possessed a sheen which could only have come from pots of government and European money. Burton felt quite at ease in the place where she had completed her MA in Gender Studies, but she had sensed her colleague's hackles rise and understood his resentment. With a good brain and a decent set of A levels, Doyle could doubtless look forward to his own career break at some point. The DI had been swift to notice the young detective's interest in criminal law, so it was more than likely he would go on to do a law degree. In the meantime, however, he struggled to control his pique at being patronized by the likes of supercilious students who had clearly dismissed him as 'Plod' and therefore presumably thick as mince.

In their neatly pressed jeans and crisply ironed shirts, the two young men produced by the Dean of the Faculty had been the antithesis of the stereotypical student yobbo so anathematized by Noakes. In fact, after listening to them bore on earnestly — as though their listeners were two exceptionally stupid students — about 'the need to atone' and 'patriarchal hegemonies', she felt reasonably confident that they would soon move on from artistic injustice to the next appropriately 'woke' piece of agitprop.

'One thing's for sure,' the DS said wearily. 'They genuinely knew nothing about the fire.'

Doyle sniggered. 'Their faces were a picture. And then when they went all Mahatma Gandhi on us . . . I mean, all that bollocks about nonviolent resistance. Big yawn to that.' Clearly, he was looking forward to telling Noakes all about it in the pub later.

'Well, they certainly looked convincingly outraged at the mere idea of arson.'

'Yeah, all mouth. Talk the talk but not walk the walk, if you know what I mean.'

'As the guvnor said, we can rule them out for the murders, though we need to take statements so we've got an idea of the demonstrators' movements.'

Doyle groaned.

'Think of it as community relations,' his colleague said ruthlessly.

'Anyway, it wasn't a total waste of time,' she continued more brightly. 'Did you notice how shifty they looked when I asked if they'd been inside the gallery at any point?'

'That's true.' Doyle was thoughtful. 'I mean, it's part of their degree to study paintings and things, isn't it? So no reason for them to look so uncomfortable unless—'

'They'd been up to something illicit.'

'Something involving Melville and Randall, sarge?'

'I don't know.' Burton rumpled her pageboy as though by this means she could fire up the synapses. 'Perhaps them . . . perhaps someone else.' She smiled at the lanky youngster. 'At any rate, it may give us ammo when it comes to the DCI.' As in Operation Misinformation.

'What, you think he wants to pin it on a student?'

'Well, let's just say he doesn't want the boss going anywhere near the gallery bigwigs or the Carter investigation.' She compressed her lips tightly. 'The university Mental Health Advisory Service, on the other hand . . .'

'A bit devious, ain't it, sarge?'

'Don't you go all sanctimonious on me like those two virtue-signallers back there,' she snapped. 'Why should the boss always have to suffer for being an outstanding copper while Sidney gets away with being a perfect shit?'

'All right, all right, keep your hair on.' Doyle was startled by her outburst.

'I'm sorry.' She grimaced apologetically. 'But the guvnor needs space for this one, and if Sidney's all over him it'll just suck the oxygen out of the investigation. You know the score. Remember the Newman case.'

'Point taken. So . . .'

'Check the students' movements and backgrounds . . . any mental health issues . . . links to gallery personnel . . . emotional entanglements, that kind of thing.' She smoothed the lapels of her conservatively cut trouser suit. 'If we blind the DCI with science, there's more chance he'll leave the boss alone.'

'Reading you loud and clear, sarge. I'll swing by Student Administration and make a start.'

'Try the Students' Union as well. I'll square it with the boss . . . call it undercover work.'

'Will do.' The thought of a pint and the company of pretty girls brought a smile to Doyle's face, and he walked off with a spring in his step.

When he had gone, Burton cursed herself for a fool, her face hot.

Why had she flared up like that? What the hell would Doyle think?

She was relieved Noakes hadn't been there. He knew she still carried a torch for Markham and squirmed at the thought of those shrewd piggy eyes taking it all in.

Besides, over the course of the last two investigations, Markham had gradually admitted her to that charmed circle of friendship whose only other members were Noakes and Olivia. It had taken time, but she no longer felt like a gatecrasher confronted by 'No Entry' signs. No way was she going to blow it by letting her feelings get the better of her. In any case, she was engaged to Colin. They were a good team. He had no idea how she felt about her boss, and she intended to keep things that way.

Feeling better now that she had given herself a talking-to, Burton's thoughts turned to the investigation.

None of the gallery staff really made an impression as a likely suspect. There was Bill Hignett, of course . . . If the DCI got a whiff of that, then he'd have the prime suspect all boxed up in no time. As far as Sidney was concerned, if there was an e-fit better than a deranged student, it would be the learning-disabled misfit.

Personally, she didn't see it. The man had struck her as harmless, sweet even. But then there was the mother with those burrowing eyes. Something wary and vigilant about her, but of course it might just be the strain of looking out for her son. Couldn't be easy having to keep tabs on him all the time.

Once out of the building, she drove back to the gallery via St Chad's Parish Church behind the Town Hall. The thermostat in that conference room had been turned up to the max — hotter than Center Parcs — and, with intimations of a migraine throbbing behind her eyes, she needed to clear her head.

A heavy mist shrouded the terraced cemetery, filmy white vapours softening the usual perspective of dank tombs and sodden grass. The air was cold, clean and odourless, as welcome in her overheated condition as a lover's caress.

She sank onto a bench, barely aware of the damp beneath her clothes.

Everything was oddly beautiful, almost weightless. Time seemed suspended.

She looked up at the sky. No stars were out, but street lamps made the darkness mysteriously refulgent like the light from another world.

Burton was not prone to philosophical conjecture, but she suddenly felt a wrenching sadness at the thought that Helen Melville and Charles Randall could no longer enjoy such earthly beauties. All times and seasons were alike to them.

Then she remembered something the local vicar had said at Uncle Phil's funeral. 'When a person dies, their spirit hangs around to watch for a while.'

She shivered.

Were the murdered couple watching and listening at the gallery? Were their souls unable to rest until justice was served? And what of little Alex Carter? Was he there too, a little waif haunting the place for more than twenty years?

Snap out of it, she admonished herself, else Noakes'll decide I'm away with the fairies.

Who were they hunting?

If the three murders were somehow connected, then a killer's hatred had festered underground for years. Like the corrupt watercourse beneath an ancient cemetery, she thought, looking about her with a shudder.

In that moment, the graveyard no longer struck her as beautiful, thoughts of its earth-clogged inhabitants crowding into her mind like ghouls resurrected from their tombs.

Time to leave.

As she walked to her car, the bell tolled six o'clock.

It felt like an omen.

* * *

Back at the gallery, all was quiet.

She found Markham and Noakes in the characterless office next to the exhibition centre which now functioned as their incident room.

'Any joy here, sir?', she enquired after delivering a succinct report on her visit to the university.

'Not to speak of.' Markham sounded discouraged. 'At the time of Mr Randall's murder, all the gallery staff had dispersed. Either headed home for the afternoon or, in the case of senior staff, catching up on work in the library. No alibi worth mentioning in most cases.'

'You missed a bit of a barney, though.' Noakes spoke with lubricious relish.

'How's that?'

'Daniel Westbrook and Rebecca Summerson going at each other hammer and tongs.'

'Westbrook . . . oh yes, the art collector's nephew.' She frowned. 'I recall he didn't seem to like Helen Melville much.'

'Clash of egos, one supposes,' Markham took over. 'Anyway, he made an unfortunate remark about Ms Melville's pushiness—'

'Said she'd have killed her own grandmother to get promotion,' Noakes put in.

'As I say, an unfortunate turn of phrase in the circumstances.'

'And Rebecca Summerson overheard him?'

'Indeed.'

'Ouch.'

'Summerson lit into him.' Noakes was clearly enjoying himself. 'Called him a male chauvinist pig who couldn't bear to see women getting ahead. Then he slagged her off. Said she was a neurotic bitch, a bed-hopper an' a bunny boiler—'

'Amongst other things,' Markham's voice was dry. 'All deeply unedifying, as you can imagine.'

'Took folk's minds off things, though.' Noakes seemed determined to have the last word. 'Their eyes were out on stalks.'

'Miss Crocker and Aubrey Carstone defused it,' the DI concluded, 'before things got really ugly.'

'Christ, tensions are running high.' Burton felt a shamefaced envy at having missed the action.

'Where were the trustees while this was going on?' she asked. 'Don't tell me they got an earful.'

'Oh yeah. Ringside seats.' Noakes was cheerfully unrepentant. 'The snotty one . . . James Armitage looked like he was gonna have a coronary. Must've thought he'd walked into one of them *Carry On* films — all sex and "ooh, er, missus."'

'In the circumstances, I've adjourned our meeting with the trustees until tomorrow.' From his grim expression, this was clearly not how the DI had hoped to start his day. 'Then we're going to have a crack at Westbrook and Summerson separately. If there's a clue somewhere in Summerson's love life, I want to know about it.'

'Do you really think it's about some kind of love triangle?' Burton was sceptical.

'No, Kate, I don't. But we're missing something and the cracks are showing with those two. Time to ramp up the pressure.'

'Did anyone recognize that map you found in the archives room, sir?'

'No. But that's one reason I want another shot at Westbrook. He's our connection to Donald Lestrange.' Markham spoke with careful deliberation. 'I think it's likely that piece of paper we discovered earlier somehow got dislodged from the Lestrange file, either when Helen Melville removed the papers or when our killer trashed the contents of the archives room hoping to obliterate any trace of incriminating material.' He steepled his long slender fingers together in a characteristically meditative gesture. 'We need to know more about Lestrange and his connection with the gallery.'

'You reckon that'll lead us to the house on the drawing, guv?'

'I think it might, Noakes.'

He looked at their tired faces.

'Enough for tonight. Briefing here tomorrow eight a.m. sharp.'

* * *

'*Aedicula. The house within a house.*' It really existed, Markham just knew it.

And when he found it, he would have his murderer.

7. ECHOES FROM THE PAST

Markham passed a restless night.

In his dreams, under the spell of *aediculae*, he fell to castle-building. All night long he was putting wings up, taking wings down, adding a secret chamber and a grated dungeon here, putting in an alcove or cellar there.

He built on and built on, busily, busily all through the night, watching great blocks of stone dangling in the air before being levered into their appointed place. At last, he surveyed the finished work. And there on the battlements was a dark figure like a black stick. He couldn't make out the face, but the phantom's lips seemed to move in an imprecation or chant as though to put a curse on the builder.

Then the figure stretched out his arm and pointed down, down into the bowels of the castle . . . And Markham knew without being told that there was the skeleton of a child interred in a sealed room behind a passageway, left to moulder into dust . . .

He awoke in a cold sweat. The alarm clock said 5 a.m.

Quietly, so as not to disturb Olivia, he slid out of bed and stole into his study where he sat at his desk which faced out into the darkness. Gazing through the window, with the influence of the dream still upon him, he fancied he still saw through the glass that fortified stronghold constructed over the remains of a dead child. It was so real to him, he felt he could reach out and touch it, could hear the voice of the little prisoner pleading with the master builder to uncover his story.

Eventually the sound of Olivia in the kitchen broke the spell.

'It's snowing, Gil,' she said wonderingly as she brought the much-needed coffee.

And so it was, the municipal graveyard next to their apartment block emerged softly-draped as though a pristine counterpane had been tucked tenderly about the sleepers in that quiet earth.

Markham gradually felt the horrors of the night begin to recede as Wednesday morning dawned crisp and bright.

It was the spectre of the Alex Carter investigation getting to him, he told himself. He'd take Noakes with him that afternoon to see Jim McLeod out in Calder Vale. Kate Burton was owed an outing, but Noakes would be a better bet in the circumstances.

'I can't get pictures of castles and ancient buildings and secret stairways out of my head,' he told Olivia ruefully. 'This blasted *aedicula* thing's got a real hold.'

'That and the mystery of the little boy who went missing from the gallery,' she added gently.

Seeing her boyfriend's brows contract, she said in a lighter tone. 'So, which of your suspects is really a belted earl with estates to match? I mean, if that map you found had something to do with the murders — as in X marks the spot — then presumably there's a mansion or manor house somewhere in the mix.'

'That's just it, sweetheart.' Markham burst out in tones of purest exasperation. 'We've got addresses for all of them. Some are well-heeled right enough. Aubrey Carstone's not doing it for the money — private means, I gather. Same goes for Benedict Bramwell, and the other senior staff don't look short of a bob or two. But we're not talking landed gentry.'

He looked out at the cemetery whose serene perfection was testament to the eventual erasure of life's perplexities and mists. 'That drawing with the Alex Carter doodle is the clue to it all, Liv, I'm *sure* of it . . . and those missing documents . . . the Lestrange papers . . .'

'What about the facilities manager? After all, she and your two victims were in some sort of triangle, weren't they?'

'It'd be neat, Liv, no doubt about that. If we can't pin it on a deranged student, then a distraught middle-aged woman would suit the DCI down to a tee. "Emotionally vulnerable . . . difficult time of life . . . balance of mind disturbed . . . "' He had his boss's patronizing nasal tones off to perfection.

Olivia laughed, a full-throated uninhibited peal. 'Just so long as no one at the top of the totem pole's pushed off their pedestal, eh?'

'That's right. Well, you know what Sidney's like.'

'Don't I just!'

'He's not a bad man really.'

There was an eloquent silence.

'It's just that he sees everything in terms of civic image. As though he has to varnish all the surfaces to cover up any ugly cracks . . .'

'He'll need a bloody large pot of varnish for this case, then,' Olivia observed dryly. 'Cracks all over the shop from what you tell me.'

Markham smiled at her. 'Who knows but I'll turn out like the DCI once I've marinated long enough in the higher echelons of CID.'

'Not a chance, my love.' She pulled a face. 'Sidney's a bottom feeder. Always was and always will be. It's in his DNA. Whereas you . . .' She left the sentence unfinished as she slipped an arm about his neck, leaning in as she stood next to his chair.

'What's the plan for today?' she enquired finally after some minutes of companionable silence.

'Another crack at the senior staff,' Markham said heavily. 'After that spat between Rebecca Summerson and Daniel

Westbrook, I want to see if there's anything in the personal dynamics . . . something I'm missing . . .' He shook his head. 'Difficult to see Summerson as a *femme fatale*. She looked almost catatonic yesterday . . . zombie-like . . .'

'Could it be an act?'

'It's possible.' He flexed his long well-shaped hands as though longing to shake the truth out of someone. 'She's not popular with the staff, that's for certain.' He thought for a moment. 'Ageist too. Reading between the lines, she was trying to shuffle off Esmée Crocker towards redundancy.'

'Crocker . . . I forget, Gil, what does she do?'

'She's the assistant curator in Textiles.' He frowned. 'Harmless enough on the surface, but struck me as potentially a good hater. She didn't actually come out and say that Rebecca Summerson was a corrupting influence on Helen Melville and Charles Randall, but you could tell that's what she meant.'

'Ugh. Don't fancy the sound of Miss Crocker one bit.'

'Well, the rest of them like her.'

'Often the way with someone deceitful.'

'True. And I dare say she could tell many a secret. She's the kind of woman people confide in . . .'

'. . . or the sort who listens at doors.'

Markham grinned. 'Nothing gets past her for all she looks a sweet old dear.'

'Maybe she's got sheathed claws.' Olivia thought for a moment. 'What about Westbrook? He's your link to that collector whose papers went missing, isn't he?'

'He's Donald Lestrange's nephew, yes.'

Markham thought of Westbrook's compact, almost simian physique and the impression of repressed energy like a coiled spring.

'Westbrook could have killed Helen Melville and Charles Randall,' he said finally. 'Apparently he was in love with Randall but no dice.'

'"Each man kills the thing he loves,"' Olivia murmured.

'True.' Her boyfriend's expression was bleak. 'It explains Westbrook's outburst about Helen Melville.'

'But you don't think this was a *crime passionnel*?'

'Could be. But . . .' Markham looked up at her. 'When I initially talked to Westbrook, I felt he was holding something back . . . something to do with the archives.' Slowly, he got to his feet, untwining himself from Olivia's embrace. 'But maybe I got that wrong,' he said uncertainly. 'Maybe he was afraid because he had a reason to hate Helen Melville and knew we'd find out.'

'Or maybe he had some inkling of the secret in the archives — the one Helen and Charles Randall were killed for.'

'If so, he's given no hint.'

Olivia placed a detaining hand on her boyfriend's arm. 'Won't he be in danger if he knows who the murderer is?'

'Not if he keeps it to himself.' Markham thought back to Westbrook's demeanour. 'I think he'd be quite capable of that.'

'Even if it means shielding whoever killed the man he loved?'

'If there's one thing I've learned in CID, Liv, it's that love and hate are two sides of the same coin.' He looked at her steadily. 'Charles Randall may have put Westbrook on the rack—'

'You mean deep down Westbrook might actually be grateful to whoever did this? God, that's sick.'

'That's my world, Liv.' Suddenly, Markham's eyes were so full of pain that Olivia could hardly bear to look at him.

'Come on,' she said, hugging him. 'Let's have a big greasy fry up. It'll set you up for the day.'

Given her predilection for muesli ('that birdseed crap', as Noakes referred to it) and healthy eating, this represented a significant concession.

Markham grinned. 'You're on,' he said.

* * *

Two hours later Markham sat in Aubrey Carstone's office which was situated next to the Medieval and Renaissance collection on the first floor, the curator having suggested his quarters as a 'friendlier' environment for interviews than the soulless berth next to the exhibition centre which served as their incident room.

Carstone's office certainly had vastly more character than Rebecca Summerson's impersonal domain. Carpeted with what, to Markham's appreciative gaze, looked like vibrant kilim rugs, the room was decorated with intricate leather hangings, framed tapestries and richly upholstered armchairs in gold and red — the fruits, presumably, of that substantial private income.

When they arrived, Gemma Clarke was standing at Carstone's antique Chippendale desk admiring what appeared to be some sort of vintage map.

'With all the swirling patterns, it's like you can see faces peering out . . . wicked little faces,' she said in wonderment.

'Well, in many of the early maps you'll find gargoyles and costumed figures, my dear.' The curator's voice was kind with no hint of patronage.

It was an amusing study in contrasts — the venerable scholarly septuagenarian and his eager apprentice who glowed with enthusiasm. The frightened snuffling child who had made the dreadful discovery of Helen Melville's corpse was a distant memory.

After she had left the room, Markham remarked on her transformed appearance and air of confidence.

'Oh, there's a lot to Gemma, Inspector. And I think now she'll finally have a chance to blossom.'

Without being cowed by Helen Melville.

The unspoken corollary hung in the air, but Carstone tactfully changed the subject, talking easily about his maps and some of the curios in the room.

'Nice old git,' was Noakes's irreverent comment once he had left the room. 'Thought he'd never stop wittering on.

That chart or whatnot on his desk jus' looks like a load of weird blotches to me.'

'Worth a fortune though, Sergeant,' Markham replied dryly, amused to see scepticism replaced by an expression of almost superstitious respect.

The soothing ambience of the room had failed to relax Daniel Westbrook who was, if anything, even more buttoned up and reserved than before, his eyes skittering round the office as though he expected something to slither out of one of the lacquered cabinets and ambush him. Like one of those ancient gargoyles Carstone mentioned, Markham thought wearily.

Westbrook apologized for his 'intemperate outburst' of the previous day. 'My judgement was clouded by personal feelings,' he told the detectives. Other than that, he wouldn't be drawn. 'Like pulling teeth,' Noakes exclaimed in disgust. There was genuine warmth and respect, however, when he spoke of his uncle, Donald Lestrange. 'My parents were killed in a car accident when I was eight, but thanks to him I had a home and family.'

And yet, Markham thought, there was something, something . . . Westbrook was like an actor who hadn't quite mastered his role. From behind the mask his eyes held a strained watchfulness while an occasional twitch of the lips spoke of anxious efforts at self-control.

'We got nowhere with him,' the DI informed Kate Burton when she joined them, having re-interviewed Rebecca Summerson in the facilities manager's office. 'Any joy with Ms Summerson?'

'Looked like she was cracking up, guv,' was the glum response. 'She and Westbrook clearly can't stand each other, but it's like they've made a mutual pact to keep shtum.'

'Ask me no questions and I'll tell you no lies.'

'I reckon she's hitting the bottle too, sir.'

'Guilty conscience?' grunted Noakes.

'Couldn't say, sarge. She's all over the place, though, no doubt about that. I left her with Miss Crocker. Looks like

Mr Carstone and Miss Crocker will have to manage things between them.'

There was a knock at the door and Cathy Hignett appeared with a tray. Markham jumped up to help her.

'How's morale back there?' he enquired kindly, helping her to distribute drinks and biscuits.

'We're managing.' The tone was ungracious but Markham could see the frightened woman beyond. She stood shifting awkwardly from one foot to the other, greasy hair rumpled into stiff prongs which stuck up all over her head, a dull red colour in her cheeks which was somehow stale rather than fresh. The restless questing eyes roamed around Aubrey Carstone's office as if reluctant to settle anywhere.

She was nervous. But was it simply the result of a double murder or something else? Could she be shielding her son?

She slouched out of the room and shut the door behind her.

Markham placed a finger to his lips and signalled to the others to stay silent. After a few minutes had passed, he went to the door, opened it and looked into the corridor.

'Walls have ears,' he said rejoining them.

'I had some intel from Doyle earlier, sir.' While Noakes made short work of the chocolate digestives ('thought they'd be bound to palm us off with Rich Tea', he said happily, his approval rating for Cathy Hignett going up a notch), Burton checked her notebook.

'Oh yes? I believe you had him recceing the Students' Union.'

Noakes's massive head came up sharply. *Jammy bastard* his expression said.

Burton carefully avoided meeting her colleague's accusing gaze.

'There was this girl who got quite chatty. Said something about having been to "parties" at the gallery.'

'Parties?'

'That's what she said. Told Doyle that "Marky Mark" organized them. Then her friend came over and shut her up.'

'Who the chuffing hell's "Marky Mark" when he's at home?' Noakes grumbled through a mouthful of biscuit. 'I mean, do any of this lot look like a DJ?'

'Marcus Traherne,' the DI said thoughtfully.

'What, the Brylcreemed wonder?' Noakes snorted. 'You're having me on. Looks more like a used car salesman that one!'

'Doyle got the impression there might be something . . . well, something a bit kinky about it,' Burton said awkwardly.

Noakes looked at her slack-jawed, his imagination clearly working overtime, chocolate digestives temporarily forgotten.

'You mean like sex parties . . . *orgies*?'

His fellow DS appeared embarrassed. At moments like this, Markham could see why her father had wanted his only daughter to follow an alternative career path.

'It was the way the girl spoke . . . suggestive . . .'

'Who'd want to . . . have it away with all these creepy statues and things looking at 'em?'

'For some folk, that would heighten the pleasure, Noakes. Like cemetery sex.'

The DS looked as though he might burst a blood vessel. Markham turned to Burton. 'I want you and Doyle to re-interview Marcus Traherne, Kate. If there's some sort of . . . extra-curricular enterprise going on, then it's possible he or one of the students may have seen or heard something.' His tone was grave as he added, 'It could put them in danger.'

The DI walked across to the window which overlooked a narrow alley. Snow was coming down thickly now, the pavement shrouded with a pristine white valance. It had a blinding purity which made his eyes ache. He turned back to face the room.

'D'you think Traherne's our man, guv?'

The mastodon had recovered his self-possession.

'He looks like a smiling assassin,' Burton said unexpectedly before Markham had a chance to answer, blushing furiously as both men looked at her in surprise. 'I just don't like him,' she qualified defensively.

'A killer?'

'I'd say he could be pretty ruthless if he didn't get his own way, sir. I get the impression he bullies the security and admin staff. Ambitious too, so probably felt threatened by this project Helen Melville and Randall were working on . . . afraid they were stealing a march on him.'

'Go in hard as you like then, Kate. I trust your judgement.'

The DS turned even pinker with pleasure.

Silly bint, thought Noakes. But there was no malice in the reflection.

'By the way, James Armitage telephoned to say he and Ms Watson won't be available till this evening, sir.'

'Wants us to dance to their tune, does he?' The DI's lips tightened. 'Well, so be it.' He smiled at Burton. 'Noakes and I will head out to see Jim McLeod.' Observing her face fall, he pointed out, 'McLeod's old school, Kate, and Noakesy was on the original investigation. He'll probably be more forthcoming if we keep this men only. Otherwise you'd be in there with us, never fear.'

'I understand, sir.' Burton snapped her notebook shut. 'Oh, I also had a call from the press office, boss. About Helen Melville's funeral . . . it's tomorrow. She's going to be buried not cremated.'

'What?' Markham was mystified. 'I know the PM didn't throw up any surprises . . . but so soon?'

'Barry Lynch was keeping things close to his chest, sir.'

'That figures,' Noakes harrumphed. 'Conceited little twerp. So far up the DCI's backside—'

'Quite,' the DI interrupted firmly before the other could complete his scatological allusion.

'There was nothing controversial about the PM,' he murmured almost to himself. 'Attempted asphyxiation then bundled into that freezer to finish her off, followed by heart attack resulting from shock . . . If Pathology's got all the samples, the coroner could've authorised release of the body.'

'Friends in high places,' Noakes opined tapping the side of his nose. 'An' Sidney pulling strings.'

'Well, we'll be at the funeral tomorrow. Kate, can you liaise with Lynch about that please.' Markham was notoriously uninterested in CID or civic politics, and there was a finality in his tone which meant he did not care to lift the curtain on whatever wheeling and dealing had taken place behind the scenes. Justice for the dead was all that interested him.

'Leave it with me, sir.' From the faraway look in her boss's eyes, Burton knew he was back at the scene of the first murder, looking down at Helen Melville's corpse curled on its side . . . seeing it lowered into the heathery levels of the municipal cemetery where it would ferment and rot underground while the winter sun rose and cooled overhead.

She felt a prickle of sweat on her forehead. Noakes was giving her a look. The one that meant he suspected her of ESP or some other hippy nonsense.

She cleared her throat. 'Right, sir,' she said. 'I'll be off.'

With the quiet efficiency which characterized all her movements, she glided out of the room.

'C'mon, Noakes. Time to see what Jim McLeod can tell us.' Markham was glad of the chance to escape the gallery's strange airtight atmosphere, almost craving that sharp cold which would feel like plunging into clear crisp water.

There was no one in the corridor outside Aubrey Carstone's room. And yet, Markham could not shake off the uneasy feeling that he and Noakes were under observation.

Walls have ears, he had said half in jest. But something in the eerie stillness made him suspect he had spoken truer than he knew.

* * *

Calder Vale, to which Jim McLeod had retired, was a peaceful rural suburb of Bromgrove.

His picture postcard house was the last in a line of terraced cottages at the end of a street clinging to the side of Calder Hill. A brook flowed down the hillside, passing the squat Saxon church of St Bartholomew in its travels.

Even though the cold sliced his lungs, giving him the sensation of a catch in his breath, Markham savoured the tranquil beauty of the landscape.

A good place to start upon a new existence.

* * *

Jim McLeod had the air of a dissipated cherub. Swarthy and snub-nosed, with springy silver hair, there was something irresistibly merry and puckish about him. A former prop forward with Bromgrove CID Warriors, there were still traces of a robust physique in the commanding figure who greeted them warmly.

Universally popular, McLeod's retirement had come as a surprise. 'I've done my thirty,' was all he said, but Markham knew he wanted to spend more time with gentle fragile Margaret who had never accustomed herself to the demands of his profession. Their childlessness was a source of sadness to both, but for some reason they had never considered adoption. Perhaps, Markham thought, that was why the Alex Carter case had left such an indelible impression.

McLeod was pleased to see them. 'Margaret's at her sister's,' he said, 'but she's just been baking.'

In no time at all they were ensconced in his study at the back of the house with steaming mugs of tea, homemade scones and jam. Noakes, needless to say, did full justice to the spread while Markham merely crumbled his food, breaking off pieces to feed to McLeod's golden Labrador, Clover. A smile hovered at the corners of McLeod's mouth as he sucked his pipe and observed the study in contrasts.

It was a homely but cosy room, with an old-fashioned fire crackling in the hearth, three high-backed chintz armchairs and bookshelves lining one wall. There were lots of titles on history and archaeology, Markham noted.

McLeod followed his glance. 'I was always a bit of an antiquarian,' he offered by way of explanation. 'Old buildings, ruins, stuff like that . . . They held a fascination for me.'

Markham wondered whether this interest post-dated the disappearance of little Alex Carter — whether at the back of McLeod's mind lurked the thought that somewhere out there was a building which might one day be forced to give up its dead.

'I know why you're here, gents.' McLeod's voice broke into Markham's thoughts.

'The Carter case.' He smiled at them grimly and, for the first time, Markham noted the heavy bags under the former DCI's eyes and the gleam of sadness in his expression. 'You'll be wondering if there's a link with these murders at the gallery.'

Markham took McLeod through all the details of their investigation and the older man listened intently.

'I always thought the child had to be out there somewhere,' he said finally, his eyes shimmering with tears.

Markham got up and made a feint of perusing the titles on McLeod's shelves to give him time to recover. Meanwhile, Noakes petted the dog with clumsy affection.

After an interval, Markham returned to his seat.

'There may not be a connection with Alex at all,' he said quietly. 'It's all speculation at this stage, but nevertheless . . .'

'What happened with Alex's mum, sir?' Noakes was uncharacteristically deferential.

'No need for formality, Noakes. I'm not your boss anymore.'

'I'll always think of you as the chief, sir.' It was said with unmistakeable sincerity.

'Thank you.' McLeod's voice was gruff, but Markham could see he was touched.

'She's long dead. Drink and drugs.' A heavy sigh. 'We got it in the neck from the press for focusing on her, but Jesus, there was so little else to go on. And Shelley Carter was the last to see him alive.'

'She was a strange lass,' Noakes said reminiscently. 'A bit fey by all accounts.'

'You're telling me.' McLeod spread his hands in a gesture of appeal. 'Talked a load of hooey about seeing these white hands with fingers waving like serpents, same as one of them conjurors — you know, when they're wearing gloves and doing fancy tricks in the dark. But she was hysterical. None of it made any sense.'

'She saw hands?' Markham was alert.

'And smelled something too, she said.'

'Like what?' Noakes leaned forward, intrigued. 'Chloroform? Summat like that?'

'She just said it was sharp and spicy and then it was gone.'

Aftershave perhaps. Or perfume.

Mentally, Markham was back in the archives corridor. 'Where did she see these hands?'

'The lad went missing from that long corridor leading off the room with the medieval paintings.'

'Yes.' Markham paused. 'I knew from a look at the cold case file where it had happened, but even without that I would have guessed. It just felt that something bad had happened there.' Despite the warmth of the room, he gave a convulsive shiver. 'As though the air had retained an impression . . . almost like a photographic negative.'

'Nasty,' Noakes concurred feelingly.

McLeod looked from one to the other.

'It was barmy really,' he said at last. 'Shelley kept gabbling about hands coming out of a cupboard or a wardrobe.' Rumpling his hair distractedly, he continued, 'There were cabinets and tallboys and what have you . . . but the most likely bet was the private staff staircase.' McLeod was breathing heavily now, caught up in the emotion of that day. 'Shelley was slow raising the alarm and we thought—'

'It was "Here we go Looby Loo,"' interjected Noakes helpfully. 'Like she was out of it or on summat.'

'It was only a few minutes, but that was all it took,' McLeod concluded wretchedly. 'By the time our lot were on the scene, there was no trace.'

There was a long silence, then, 'Whoever it was took one hell of a chance.'

It was an echo of the reporter's verdict on the murder of Charles Randall. The killer took a hell of a chance.

'Nowadays when a child goes missing, after Madeleine McCann, it's amber alerts and all the rest of it. Everything sealed off, no one in, no one out.' McLeod's voice sank to a hoarse whisper. 'But things were different then. It was a Sunday. Just a few visitors, mainly pensioners and the odd student or youngster who'd buggered off before we got the cordon up.'

Markham handed him a list of gallery personnel.

'Lestrange and Carstone, I remember them,' the other said. 'Researchers or something like that. Nice blokes. Couldn't see them mixed up in anything sinister. They helped with the search. One of 'em sat with Shelley . . .'

He ran his eyes down the list. 'Bramwell,' he continued. 'Yes, an academic like the other two . . . younger'n them, though . . . Stuck up. Thought a lot of himself. Got bolshie about giving his contact details.'

Another name caught his attention. 'Crocker. There was a mousy receptionist or secretary.' He chuckled. 'I heard someone call her "the Croc," but she looked the type who wouldn't say boo to a goose.'

McLeod handed back the sheet of paper. 'Hignett rings a bell too. Cloakroom girl, I think.'

His tone thoughtful, he added, 'I don't know about the rest, but they could have been there for all I know. There were a few kids who slipped the net . . . teenagers who'd come in out of the rain most like. So you see . . .'

'I'm really grateful for this, sir.' Markham looked McLeod straight in the eye. 'What happened that day seems more real somehow.'

He meant it.

'Is there anything else you remember, sir? Anything at all?'

'Not that I can think of. Hold on a minute, there was one thing . . . Shelley said she remembered hearing someone humming, a sort of crooning just before Alex disappeared.

How did it go? "I want an old-fashioned house, with an old-fashioned fence. And an old-fashioned millionaire."'

The hair stood up on the back of Markham's neck.

It was as though a killer stood right there in the room mocking them.

* * *

Afterwards, out in the rural winter wonderland, Noakes said uneasily, 'It could've been any of 'em, guv.'

Markham's mobile rang.

'That was Kate. Armitage and Watson await our pleasure.'

The DS sniggered. 'Makes 'em sound like a dodgy comedy act.'

'I doubt this interview will be a laugh a minute, Sergeant.'

They trudged slowly back to the car.

Jim McLeod watched till they had disappeared from sight.

After all this time, he thought, *after all this time.*

8. SECRETS

The art gallery looked as though it was made of spun sugar, Markham thought as they parked next to the entrance. Like the decoration on a bridal cake or something equally superficial.

Yet two innocents had died there, and behind the crystalline facade was a creature with cold eyes that watched the two detectives and knew them for the enemy.

They sat in the car with the heater on, curiously reluctant to make a move, almost somnolent in the cosy fug. Markham sank into a reverie where the titanic subjects gazing and struggling on the walls and ceilings of the gallery broke the spell that lay upon them, stepped out of their gilded portraits and came towards him, whispering a name. Through half-open lids he almost fancied he saw nymphs, goddesses and colossi gesturing to him with excited intention as if to say, 'We hold the clue. There! Look there!'

Then the moment was gone, the prophets and evangelists and angels frozen once more into attitudes of alien remoteness.

Noakes was gently snoring.

The DI gave him a dig in the ribs. 'Wake up, Sergeant. We aren't finished for the day.'

* * *

The gallery felt more sepulchral than ever, as though all the staff had melted away, though Markham had no doubt there were watchers in the wings.

They found Burton and Doyle in the cheerless incident room glumly drinking tea. Doyle looked less than his usual dapper self, with tie undone almost as though he had yanked it loose in an outburst of frustration. Under the DI's coolly appraising gaze, he hastily readjusted it.

'Are we any further forward, Kate?' Markham enquired.

She frowned. Like Doyle, an air of despondency hung about her, but at Markham's entrance she made a visible effort to rouse herself. It was touching the way she always tried to galvanize the team, he thought, watching her straighten up.

'Yes and no, sir.'

'That sounds very enigmatic.'

'Well, the trouble is it looks like they've pretty much *all* got something to hide.'

'How so?'

'It turns out Marcus Traherne's been allowing students into the gallery after hours for . . . recreational purposes.'

Noakes smirked, enjoying her obvious discomfiture.

'You mean shagging?'

'Sex seems to have come into it, yes,' she replied stiffly.

'Was this for money, Kate?'

'He says not, sir.'

Markham turned to Doyle. 'What about the students?'

'They're singing from the same hymn sheet, sir. Just fun and games.' The DC rolled his eyes. 'The way Traherne spun things, he made it sound like he was trying to build bridges with the demonstrators . . . you know, a bit of misguided PR for the gallery that got out of hand.'

Noakes guffawed. 'He must think we were born yesterday. Swinging from the chandeliers and he calls it *PR*!'

Markham's lips curled with distaste and he was wearing what Burton privately thought of as his puritanical look. 'No Sex Markham.' That had been his nickname at Bromgrove CID in the early days. But once his colleagues caught a glimpse of Olivia Mullen — 'a real stunner' being the unanimous verdict — their attitude required recalibration. The DI was now generally regarded as a dark horse and the subject of endless prurient speculation, but he enveloped himself in an air of chilly restraint which repelled the slightest approach to overfamiliarity. 'C'mon, Noakesy, dish the dirt,' was the cry down the canteen. But if Markham's wingman knew, he wasn't telling.

'Gross misconduct.' The DI sat down heavily. 'But without more, it's a disciplinary matter.'

'There was some colourful stuff in Traherne's HR file, sir.' Burton was desperate to give the boss something. Like a kid bringing an apple to their teacher, Noakes thought. It was plain to see she was still holding a candle for the guvnor. And that poor sap of a fiancé didn't have the foggiest.

'What kind of stuff?' Markham's voice was hollow as though he guessed the answer.

'Helen Melville raised a grievance against him a while back for bullying and sexually inappropriate behaviour, but the complaint didn't come to anything. It was put down to "banter" and Benedict Bramwell "had a word." Melville then reported Bramwell to the trustees for not taking her seriously but got nowhere. There was bad blood between them over that.'

'So, bollocks to all that garbage about Bramwell and Melville having an "amicable separation."' Noakes air-quoted gleefully.

'Well yes, it looks as though Bramwell wasn't completely frank, sarge.'

'Did you tackle him about it, Kate?'

'Didn't turn a hair, sir. Said he'd completely forgotten it. Storm in a teacup, hardly worth bothering about, they'd long since put it behind them, etcetera etcetera.'

Benedict Bramwell was clearly a virtuoso in the art of stonewalling.

'Hmm.' Markham impatiently pushed back a lock of hair from his eyes. 'Did the HR files yield any other nuggets about the staff?'

'Miss Crocker "raised concerns" about certain colleagues "bringing their personal lives to work."' Burton was keen to show she could air-quote with the best of them. 'Looks like Rebecca Summerson gave her the bum's rush — basically told her to mind her own business.'

God, what a nest of vipers.

'From Summerson's notes, Crocker came over all gooey and maternal about Charles Randall. Worried that Melville might be compromising him.'

'Did Ms Summerson follow up with Randall?'

Burton's preternaturally solemn expression lightened momentarily.

'He told her, off the record, that Crocker was a nosey old bat.'

The DI laughed. 'There's gratitude for you!'

'Bill Hignett's quite tasty too, sir.' Doyle did not want to be left out.

Markham quirked an eyebrow ironically. '*Tasty*? Come on, Doyle, you know my feelings about sloppy jargon. Let's have the specifics please.'

'Sorry, sir.' The young detective flushed to the roots of his carroty hair. 'There were quite a few complaints about him being touchy-feely. And he had meltdowns too.'

'Is there a medical diagnosis?'

'Autism and ADHD plus sexual disinhibition disorder.' Doyle squinted at his notes. 'The gallery's got some sort of partnership with the Disability Employment team at the council. There's a mentor who comes in now and again. Apart from that, Mum keeps him on the rails most of the time. Aubrey Carstone or Gemma Clarke can usually calm him down when he has a tantrum.'

'Any bullying?'

'Not to speak of. A couple of girls in the café reported him to Rebecca Summerson. Said he gave them the willies — liked coming up behind them and making them jump, that kind of thing. And Helen Melville complained he was always spying on her and Charles Randall—'

'*Spying*?' Markham caught at the word. 'That's pretty strong.'

'Yeah,' Noakes agreed. 'Makes it sound like they were up to summat dodgy and didn't want him snooping.'

'It was all smoothed over in the end.' Doyle resumed his narrative. 'Cathy Hignett's got him on a short leash, so doesn't look as though it went beyond mild perving. She gave staff the rough edge of her tongue if she thought they were too hard on him.'

'Ructions with our two victims?'

'Them and everyone else from the sound of it.'

'Who gave him that nickname . . . "Quasi"?'

'No one knows for sure, sir. Someone said it might've been Randall. But Hignett seems almost proud of it.'

'Like he's some sort of creepy mascot,' Noakes interjected. 'Him and friggin' Mrs Mop are straight out of the Bates Motel.'

'I think we can rule out an Oedipal Complex, Noakes.'

'Eh?'

Seeing that Burton was poised to deliver a mini-lecture on attachment disorders, Markham hastily turned the discussion into another channel.

'Did you turn up anything on Daniel Westbrook? Anything in the HR files?'

'Clean as a whistle, sir.' Burton's tone was resigned. 'A couple of spiky performance management appraisals from Helen Melville, but apparently that was par for the course with her. Aubrey Carstone said she didn't pull her punches but Westbrook took it all in his stride. His own specialist interest is medieval religious shrines and holy places — following in the footsteps of his uncle, Donald Lestrange — so Melville and Randall may have felt threatened . . . like he was encroaching on their territory.'

Could professional jealousy have been the touchstone for something darker, wondered Markham.

His head was beginning to ache.

Idly, he wondered if it was still snowing, already wistful for the tranquil beauty of Calder Vale.

The woods are lovely, dark and deep, But I have promises to keep, And miles to go before I sleep, And miles to go before I sleep . . .

If the DCI had his way, none of them would be getting much sleep for the foreseeable.

He became aware that Burton and Doyle were looking at him expectantly.

'Good work, both of you', he said. 'As you observed, Kate, the field's pretty much wide open.' He thought for a moment. 'What's your take on Rebecca Summerson?'

'She's in bits, sir. Had another rant about Westbrook earlier. Doyle saw a hip flask in her handbag.'

'Would she be capable of a double bluff . . . killing her lover and the man she had taken up with, then setting up Westbrook as the fall guy?'

'According to some of the admin staff, she's a real piece of work. Bit of an actress too by all accounts.'

'If it's acting, then she should get an Oscar,' put in Doyle.

The DI glanced at the ugly wall clock.

Four o'clock.

'What time can we expect the trustees, Kate?'

'Half an hour or so, sir.'

'Right, let's go have a cup of tea — clear our heads.'

'By the way, Ned Chester from the *Gazette* called earlier.'

Markham's head came up.

'Oh. What did he want?'

'He was a bit cloak and dagger. Said he had something you might find interesting. Something to do with Donald Lestrange. Didn't want to go into details over the 'phone.'

'Getting le Carré'd away as usual.' Noakes was pleased with his pun. 'Daft git should stick to arts 'n crafts.'

Burton ignored the interruption.

'I didn't press him, sir. We had all the staff in here at the time — a quick briefing about the gallery reopening next week — and the girl covering reception put him through on speakerphone. Luckily I don't think anyone was really paying attention . . . too busy chatting amongst themselves.'

'Does Ned want me to go across to the *Gazette* offices?'

'He said he'll meet you here tomorrow after work, four-ish.'

Markham wondered if there was time to call his friend.

'He's at some event in Birmingham tonight, sir,' Burton said, anticipating him. 'Heading off straight after he spoke to me.'

Whatever Ned had discovered, it would keep.

'Fine,' he announced. 'I'll catch up with him tomorrow. In the meantime, let's refresh ourselves before we lock horns with Mr Armitage and Ms Watson.'

* * *

The little café at the rear of the entrance lobby was totally deserted.

'I suggest we use the vending machine,' the DI said gesturing to the back of the seating area. 'That way we don't need to be waited on.'

Noakes didn't look particularly enthralled at the prospect but lumbered over with Burton and Doyle to get the drinks sorted.

In the meantime, Markham browsed the shop display. There was a preponderance of glossy overpriced books on the Matchstick Man, he noted with a wry smile. Clearly Noakes was not alone in his admiration for that particular artist.

It was very peaceful in the marble-tiled alcove with, again, a feeling of being in church, so that he half expected to see winking lamps of gold and silver or kneeling figures dotted about in prayer before confessionals, wreathed in the mist and scent of incense. Then, there was that echoey deathlike stillness, as though the gallery was some kind of submarine dwelling, withdrawn from the shores of the upper world, its waves and breakers reduced to the subdued murmur of a lullaby.

It was all somehow disturbingly *unreal*, he mused, his eyes sweeping the dark corners. The weight of centuries seemed to fill the air, paralysing all that was living and warm-blooded.

His attention was caught by the Old Testament tapestry of Jael and Sisera suspended over the front entrance, its colossal figures looming up menacingly in the gloom like the representatives of some sinister ancient priesthood avid for human sacrifice.

Well, they had their human sacrifices, he thought with an involuntary shudder. Two of them. Gone to that undiscovered country from whose bourne no traveller returned . . .

Doyle was about to summon the DI to join them, but Noakes put a hand on his arm.

'Give him a minute, lad,' he said gruffly.

One of the mysteries of the enduring bond between the DI and his uncouth subordinate was the latter's intuitive respect for what he privately called Markham's 'mystical side.' If the guvnor wanted to commune with dead folk, then that was all right by Noakes. To the dispassionate observer, Markham was the blue-eyed boy of Bromgrove CID destined for dizzying heights (DCI Sidney's machinations notwithstanding). But his sergeant knew that this was all dust and ashes to the DI when weighed in the balance against the souls of those whom he had been unable to save. As though there was an eternal ledger in which he would always be found wanting. This only made Noakes respect his boss all the more, though he would rather have died than admit it.

Finally, the DI walked over to his colleagues and for a few minutes they sat companionably sipping their drinks.

'Actually, that's not bad,' Doyle commented, savouring his frothy cappuccino.

'Better'n that stewed sludge we get in CID,' agreed Noakes.

'What are the arrangements for Helen Melville's funeral tomorrow, Kate?'

'Twelve noon at Our Lady of the Angels, sir.' Burton shot a wary glance at Noakes. 'She was RC.'

'Oh yeah,' her colleague put in. 'I remember that church from the Hope Academy case. The one with them spooky statues in the front garden.'

'Representations of the crucifixion aren't generally intended to be all-singing, all-dancing, Sergeant,' Markham pointed out caustically. 'I trust you're not building up to an outburst of "No Popery."'

Nothing abashed, Noakes grinned. 'All a bit OTT for me, boss.' He brightened with remembrance. 'They did a decent spread at The Halfway House once all the caterwauling was over.'

Burton shifted uncomfortably, doubtless recalling her colleague's tendency to treat such occasions as an all-you-can-eat contest. 'Yes, well they're coming back here after the Requiem Mass, sarge. It's just next of kin at the burial . . . her brother's over from Australia.'

'They're having the wake *here*?' Noakes sounded positively affronted.

'Why not? It would seem like the logical choice in the circumstances, Sergeant.'

'In front of all them creepy pictures and things.' The DS waved a meaty paw at the tapestry and other gloomy baroque masterpieces. 'Enough to put me right off my grub.'

Doyle looked at Burton. *That'd be worth seeing.*

'This is a café, Sergeant,' Markham continued patiently. 'Visitors and staff eat here every day of the week.'

'Yeah, but a funeral's . . . well, different,' Noakes persisted stubbornly. 'It ain't decent.'

The DI scrutinized him closely.

'Not going all superstitious on us are you, Noakes?'

'It jus' don't feel right somehow, guv.'

The other two were looking at him curiously. He glared back at them defiantly. 'I'm not being a big girl's blouse, but it ain't . . . fitting.' Groping for the words, he ploughed on,

'Look, Helen Melville and her poor sod of a boyfriend copped it right under their noses.' He gestured balefully at the epic figures looming out of the surrounding canvases. 'It don't seem right to have them peering down an' gloating . . . after seeing what they've seen.' Then he delivered the coup de grâce. 'I'm a verger, so I know what's proper.'

Markham felt a strong inclination to laugh at the bizarre blend of pagan and Christian sentiment. But Noakes's clumsy words struck a chord somewhere deep within him. He too strongly disliked the thought of those frozen forms presiding over the funeral feast.

'Why don't you bring Mrs Noakes with you tomorrow for moral support, Sergeant,' he suggested emolliently. 'Nobody could ever suspect her of being inappropriate.'

The last thing he needed was Muriel Noakes and her ghastly faux gentility, but if it helped keep his wingman on an even keel then he was prepared to grit his teeth. Cunningly he added, 'Olivia will be there too. Between the three of us, we'll pull you through.'

It was a masterstroke. Noakes's florid colour began to subside, his Sancho Panza-like susceptibility to Olivia the clincher.

'Well, if your Olivia's there . . .'

The DI smothered a smile. 'You can swap impressions of Lowry and the Pre-Raphaelites,' he said.

Noting that Burton was looking distinctly po-faced, Markham returned to business.

'Right, anything I need to know before the trustees are upon us?' he enquired briskly. Face darkening, he added, 'First impressions weren't exactly prepossessing.' Armitage had thrown his weight around, while his sidekick had all the allure of a female Kim Jong-un.

'Well actually, there *is* something.'

'I'm all ears, Kate.'

'A few years back, a couple of paintings by minor artists went missing. The art cops investigated but didn't get a result. I did some digging, but looks like the whole thing ended by being hushed up.'

'Any of the staff implicated?'

'It was probably an inside job but CID didn't nab anyone.'

'What about the trustees?'

'In the clear, sir, though they took some flak in the local press.'

Markham felt uneasy. Murder, abduction, and now fraud in the mix.

'D'you think there's a link with Melville and Randall, sir?'

'I don't know, Doyle,' the DI said slowly. 'There *could* be a direct connection with the secret Ms Melville claimed to have discovered in the archives, but it seems unlikely.' He glanced apprehensively around the atrium which suddenly seemed to have become darker. 'On the other hand, we might have a significant clue to our killer's character.'

An inside job. Like the abduction of little Alex Carter.

'What were the paintings, Kate?'

'Nothing all that special, sir.' A quick rustle of the ubiquitous notebook. 'One was a copy of an American painting called *The Secret Room*. The other — oh, that was a copy too — same artist who did that picture Helen Melville was so struck on, *The Soul's Prison House* . . . Not especially valuable, both bequests to the gallery . . . p'raps that's why there wasn't more of a hoo-ha when they went missing.'

Again, Markham felt uneasiness stir.

Room. House. Secret. Prison.

There was a theme emerging. Sequestration, confinement and concealment. Hidden spaces . . . like that eerie Pre-Raphaelite painting of figures emerging from the tomb — the one which held Helen Melville in thrall.

Did this motif hold some special significance for someone at the gallery and, if so, where might it lead? Was someone within these walls consumed by sick fantasies of imprisonment and suffering? Could those missing paintings somehow unlock the mystery?

Maddeningly, with the trustees' arrival imminent, there wasn't time to marshal all the thoughts teeming through his mind.

'I want full details of those two paintings, Kate. And I need you and Doyle to ask around tomorrow. Talk to the staff. See if anyone remembers a colleague being unusually interested.'

'Is it likely we'll get anything after all this time, guv?' Noakes was sceptical.

'You never know. They're on edge, off-balance what with everything that's happened. It might trigger something.'

Something to break open this case.

'*Inspector*!'

The tone was peremptory.

'Mutt and Jeff are here.' Noakes glowered across the foyer.

'Right, here goes.' Markham rose to his feet. 'With luck, we might learn something to flesh out those HR files.'

'Sex, drugs and rock and roll, if Traherne's got anything to do with it, guv.'

Noakes hoisted his belt over his paunch like a grizzled gunslinger.

'Let's see if we can keep things civil, shall we, Sergeant.'

'Oh aye, boss.'

The three detectives walked towards the new arrivals.

And the painted eyes followed where they went.

9. APPOINTMENT WITH DEATH

'Well that was a big fat zero,' Noakes groused an hour later as the team sat in the incident room reviewing progress. 'Them two were like they'd taken a vow of silence or summat.'

It was correct, thought Markham gloomily. The trustees might as well have been Trappists for all the information they volunteered.

'We didn't get anything new.' Burton's biro jabbed viciously at her notebook.

Doyle piped up. 'Armitage had a shifty look about him.' The young DC shuddered. 'And one of those dreadful clammy handshakes. Like haddock on a slab.'

The DI smiled recalling how his colleague had surreptitiously wiped his hands down the trousers of his Hugo Boss suit after being introduced.

'True, Constable. But I don't think Mr Armitage's body language is enough to take him into custody.'

'The dreary sidekick didn't say a word.' Another stab of Burton's pen. 'He'd obviously told her to keep it zipped and leave the talking to him.'

'There *was* something, though, boss.' Doyle's tone was speculative. 'When Armitage was talking about Donald Lestrange having had Alzheimer's or dementia . . . it sounded almost like he was warning us off . . . you know, when he said we shouldn't take too much notice of anything in the old guy's papers . . .'

'Must have heard we were interested in the missing file and that map,' the DI said thoughtfully. 'But why would he want to steer us away from them?'

'Protecting someone, sir? Out of self-interest? Maybe whoever it is has something on him?'

Markham thought back to the fleshy, almost vulpine face with its curiously flat eyes, like black pebbles. 'It's one possibility, Kate.'

'Didn't seem all that bothered about Traherne using the place as a knocking shop,' Noakes pointed out. ''Cept to keep it out of the papers.'

'He and the DCI will be of one mind in that regard, I have no doubt.' There was an edge to Markham's voice.

'What'll you do about Traherne then, guv?'

'I'll let them bury the mess six feet deep, Noakes.' The DI sighed. 'Otherwise it means us going off on a tangent.'

'You don't think Traherne's connected to the murders, guv?'

'He's a sly seedy character who may know something.' Markham began his characteristic restless pacing. 'Or it could be someone is manipulating him.'

'D'you think Armitage's got his snout in the trough, guv?'

'Such felicity of expression, Sergeant! I certainly want to see the gallery's accounts. See to that please, Kate.'

'Will do, sir.'

'There was a flicker when I mentioned the stolen paintings. Yes,' said Markham thoughtfully, 'a definite flicker.' He brought his hands down on the conference table with a resounding thump. 'Let's get their inventories, databases, whatever . . . See if that leads anywhere.'

Burton was scribbling furiously.

'Right.' Markham gestured towards the door. 'Enough for today. We've got Helen Melville's funeral tomorrow at twelve noon sharp. Best bib and tucker for that please.' He looked meaningfully at Noakes who was all airy unconcern. 'And review all your notes.' He leaned in, his voice low but intense. 'We need a break in this case. *Badly*.'

'I'll prepare a briefing note for the DCI, shall I, sir?' Burton enquired with her usual circumspection.

'If you would, Kate.' He tried not to grimace. 'Positive spin if possible.'

'No problem, sir. I'll, er, concentrate on the university angle for now.'

'I think that would be best.'

* * *

Our Lady of the Angels was an unpretentious sandstone church with some claim to architectural merit, boasting features designed by Edward Pugin and John Francis Bentley. Normally its damp-blackened walls had a somewhat lopsided bulging look — as though the building suffered from lumbago — but snow had softened any unevenness and asymmetry, transforming the squat little structure into a confection of crystalline perfection. The minuscule graveyard at the side of the church, reserved for its parish priests, was blanketed in an immaculate white canopy, as though to guarantee that the solemn brotherhood that slept below ground had a sounder and purer sleep than ordinary mortals above it.

Noakes surveyed the scene approvingly, though Markham noted with amusement that he skirted round the Calvary's snow-mantled statues gingerly as though they represented a snare for the unwary.

'The missus is waiting inside with your Olivia,' the DS said with bashful pride as they crunched through the snow.

The DI, who knew exactly how his girlfriend felt about being shanghaied into escorting Noakes's better half, smiled with as much sincerity as he could muster.

'It's very good of Muriel to attend, Sergeant. With her powers of observation, she'll no doubt be quick to notice any undercurrents or tensions amongst the gallery staff.'

Muriel Noakes was a scandal-detector of unparalleled skill. Oh, she was a finely-tuned instrument all right — able to sniff out the potentially scurrilous coefficients of any gathering within minutes of her arrival on the scene.

In a rare instance of conjugal impotence, 'the missus' generally fought a losing battle with Noakes about his wardrobe. When it came to funerals attended as a couple, however, she put her foot down, so that the DS looked almost respectable in his dark suit, replete with Rotary Club tie, albeit with some appearance of straining at the seams.

Unobtrusively, the two detectives slipped into a pew near the back. Burton and Doyle sat three rows in front. There was no sign of the DCI or any of the top brass, but that was presumably in keeping with a desire to keep things under the radar. The strategy appeared to have paid off. Markham couldn't see any stringers from the local press nor any obvious journos. Barry Lynch from the press office was in attendance, but it didn't appear that there was much for him to do.

Markham spotted Olivia and Muriel on the other side of the aisle. Studying his girlfriend's stony profile, it was clear that she had already endured a variety of conversational feints aimed at maintaining the fiction that Markham had fallen victim to Olivia's sexual wiles and under their fatal influence was suffering all kinds of worldly disadvantage. Judging by the complacent expression on Mrs Noakes's face, she was satisfied at having put the younger woman in her place as an artful schemer and now condescended to be gracious. Markham could only imagine how Olivia writhed in the wonderfully mythical role assigned to her, but he guessed her keen sense of the ridiculous found ample compensation in the bobbing feathers of her companion's fussy millinery which was of the type more usually seen at a royal wedding circa the nineteen fifties. As though sensing his presence, Olivia turned around and gave a discreet wave coupled with a roguish wink to Noakes who coloured with pleasure before catching his wife's jaundiced eye. Muriel gave him a meaningful look as though to say his indiscretion was noted in the matrimonial accounts book, before smiling at Markham with the peculiarly arch expression she reserved exclusively for him, patting her stiffly lacquered hair with the air of one whom no social occasion would ever find wanting. Then with regal deliberation, she turned back to face the altar.

The church interior was quite prepossessing, with restrained marble sanctuary, reredos and side chapels. Even the myriad plaster martyrs clutching their respective instruments of torture were somehow rather touching than otherwise. A lapsed Catholic, inhaling the scents of polish and incense, the DI felt as though he had come home. From the stiff-backed posture of Burton and Doyle, he deduced that they felt precisely the opposite and only longed to be out of the place as soon as possible.

Halfway down the church was a contingent from the art gallery, drained of all individuality and somehow swallowed up by their black garb, only Aubrey Carstone with his height and military bearing standing out from the rest. Bill Hignett kept tugging at the older man's sleeve to attract his attention, Carstone responding with untiring forbearance to each fresh appeal. Cathy Hignett stood on her son's other side. Wearing a cheap trouser suit that didn't look anywhere near warm enough, she appeared restless and distracted, fidgeting with hymn books and the order of service.

A gaggle of female staff seemed to be propping each other up, though Esmée Crocker's demeanour suggested she did not much care for the proximity of Rebecca Summerson whose glazed expression hinted strongly at the consumption of a few vodkas beforehand. Benedict Bramwell too regarded the facilities manager with chilly disfavour.

Marcus Traherne managed to look spivvish even in mourning, Markham thought grimly. That brocaded frock coat was hardly appropriate. Made him look like Hugh Grant playing Jeremy Thorpe.

But was Traherne his man, the DI wondered. Venal and sleazy he might be, but was he capable of murder? Not as the principal, perhaps, but Markham could see him as a cat's paw . . . the question being whose?

Markham noted that Daniel Westbrook was not with his colleagues but tucked away behind a pillar in a side aisle. Standoffishness? Dislike? Fear? He certainly appeared reluctant to look their way, the stocky body rigid with tension, muscles tightening beneath the jawline. Traherne shot him the odd furtive look and Carstone's gaze was compassionate, but other than that he appeared curiously isolated from the rest.

A shaft of winter sunlight suddenly streamed through the stained-glass windows above the altar, intensifying the jewel-like splendour of the saints in their emerald, ruby and turquoise robes. The DI caught sight of Gemma Clarke's enraptured face, pinched little features transfigured to something approaching beauty as though she reflected the glory of another world.

A moment, and the glory was no more. The light was all withdrawn and the shining church turned cold and sombre.

Something shifted in the atmosphere and silence fell.

Bearers carried the coffin, heaped with lilies, down the aisle and placed it gently on trestles at the front. Heartbreakingly, a thin spare man with a stoop detached himself from the rest and pressed his lips to the coffin. Presumably this was the deceased's brother, come all the way from Australia to say goodbye to his sister.

Markham felt his guts twist at the thought of the pathetic remains inside, patched and mended after the post-mortem into some sort of presentability — sheeted up to the neck for the viewing room — to conceal the horror and desperation of Helen Melville's final moments.

The organ began to play and the Requiem Mass got underway.

As always on such occasions, Markham felt the funeral pass in a haze of unreality, like an out of body experience where he looked down from above with all the wicked-faced little gargoyles high up on their corbels in the transept.

A survival mechanism, he supposed. It was the same way he coped at the funeral of his younger brother, long since lost to drink and drugs.

There was a short but sincere eulogy by a young priest who was well briefed and appeared to mean what he said, unlike the usual synthetic balderdash and sentimental clichés. Markham felt glad that Helen's brother was there to hear her intellectual and personal gifts acknowledged. Whatever the twists and turns of her life, it was rounded by a dignified and genuine tribute.

Finally, the service was over.

As the coffin departed to an asthmatic recessional from the little organ, Markham felt an uprush of rage at the snuffing out of a life full of promise. It took him by surprise, so that for a moment he felt he could not breathe — as though he was trapped in a bell jar full of poisonous vapours.

And the murderer was *there* inside the church, he knew it. Watching sedately under cover of the congregation while his victim — shut up in a box — was consigned to moulder into dust . . .

Waiting his turn to shuffle out with the rest, the DI's glance fell on the statue of a dark young priest with sorrowful eyes. Its face had a look of Charles Randall. Markham felt a piercing sense of loss as he remembered the young researcher, handsome features alight with enthusiasm, talking about the discovery of St Peter's bones in Rome. Hard on the heels of that memory came the picture of Randall's father waiting patiently for his boy who would never come home.

At least the gallery staff would be spared the ordeal of another funeral any time soon, he reflected. Whatever special courtesies applied to Helen Melville were apparently not being extended to the Randalls. That service would take place at Medway Crematorium, but no date had been set.

Outside the church, Markham and the team paid their respects to Helen Melville's ravaged-looking brother. The DI did not utter a superfluous word, condensing his determination to catch the killer into a strong handclasp and the promise 'She *will* have justice.' The two men locked eyes, then the hearse and funeral cars were pulling out of the car park, headed for Bromgrove North Municipal Cemetery and the private burial service.

Markham's team, various mourners and a gaggle of lesser gallery personnel, amongst whom he recognized Gemma Clarke and several security attendants, clustered irresolutely in the church forecourt as though uncertain what came next.

Olivia hung back, it being part of her delicacy never to obtrude on her boyfriend's professional role.

Muriel Noakes had no such compunction.

'Gilbert, such a *relief* to see you back to your old self,' she gushed in the carefully rounded vowels which he once confided to Olivia affected his nerves like fingernails scraping a chalkboard. 'You were looking so dreadfully *tired* after that business at the Royal Court.' A knowing glance at Noakes. '*Such* a slave to duty, but I told George it was time for you to spread the load . . . let *others* do their share.' The subtext being that her husband's boss was unlikely to receive any such cherishing in the domestic quarter.

God, she was an awful woman. Not least as she appeared to labour under the delusion that Markham had an unspoken tendresse for her, which only misguided loyalty to the flighty Olivia prevented him from disclosing.

Her funeral attire was as dire as the hat, he concluded, trying not to boggle at the faux fur tasselled cape which made her look like a down market extra in *Dr Zhivago*.

But Noakes clearly saw nothing amiss with his wife's couture, beaming with pride at the impression she had produced on the gathering. As far as he was concerned, the cossack-cum-princess-margaret ensemble left the rest of 'em standing. Even Olivia's ethereal beauty could not compete.

The DI reminded himself that there was no accounting for tastes and that the woman doubtless possessed hidden virtues lost on the casual observer. '"A box where sweets compacted lie,"' as Olivia put it. Certainly, to look at Muriel and Noakes, one would never imagine that they were leading lights of Bromgrove's ballroom dancing circuit, where they dazzled like moths emerging from their chrysalis.

Markham was spared from having to having to enter the conversational fray by the arrival of Barry Lynch who murmured conspiratorially, 'Looks like we got away with it, Inspector.' This being the kind of meaningless platitude which was Lynch's stock in trade, the DI merely nodded and turned to the bystanders. 'I believe there are refreshments back at the gallery,' he said. With a smile which managed simultaneously to embrace and dismiss the non-police members of the party — what Olivia called his 'discarding manoeuvre' — he succeeded in dispatching them to their vehicles. Muriel appeared inclined to linger, but Markham personally escorted her to his girlfriend's car, settling her into the front seat with the courtly gallantry to which she was highly susceptible. 'Drive carefully,' he told Olivia and watched sympathetically as she headed out into Chilcot Avenue. It was only a ten-minute drive to the gallery, but he reckoned every minute would feel like an hour to his long-suffering lover.

'Are we going to the eats then?' Noakes lost no time in enquiring.

'Yes, Sergeant.' The DI sighed. 'But can you, for the love of God, show some decorum and try not to scoff everything in sight.'

'Funerals make me hungry, guv.'

'I'm a bit peckish myself,' Doyle chimed in. 'Feels like a long time since breakfast.' Noakes was clearly gratified by the show of solidarity from the lanky DC, though it was obvious that Burton disapproved.

'Well, keep your eyes open while wolfing down the sausage rolls and vol au vents, the pair of you,' Markham said with some acerbity. 'At least I can count on *you* to stay focused, Kate.'

A rosy glow stole into her cheeks that had nothing to do with the falling temperature.

She's still got it bad, Noakes thought to himself, an' the guvnor doesn't have a clue.

With that philosophical reflection, he turned to Doyle. 'Right, lad, you c'n drive me an' Burton. Meet you there, guv,' he said. Instinctively, he knew that Markham needed a few minutes alone in the snow-covered churchyard — to tune into the vibes or undertake whatever personal ritual he needed to perform before adjourning to the gallery.

The DI looked at him gratefully. 'See you down there, Noakesy,' he said, missing the wistful look that flashed across Burton's face.

* * *

In no time at all, the car park was deserted, only Markham remaining in silent contemplation of the powdery mounds where long-dead priests slumbered oblivious.

He felt a sudden sharp sensation of unease and whipped around, looking back towards the darkness of the church porch.

Thinking about it afterwards, he could have sworn he saw a face. An evil, narrow wedge-shaped face looking back at him from the shadows.

A face that was at once strange and yet somehow familiar. A face he had seen before in a different setting.

Come on, get out of it, you fool, he told himself impatiently. His mind was playing tricks on him after the long service. There were probably a few worshipers still in the church — maybe even some of the gallery folk lingering to say their own private goodbyes to Helen Melville. One of them must have looked out at the door. That was all.

* * *

Later that afternoon, the team sat in the gallery café amidst the debris of a buffet, surrounded by plates of sausage rolls, sandwiches, quiche, potato salad, fruit cake of somewhat geological appearance, tea and coffee urns and mountains of industrial white crockery. Markham had packed the staff off home. 'The clearing up can wait till tomorrow,' he told them. 'It's been a stressful day.'

Now it was time to take stock.

'That went okay.' Noakes patted his paunch with satisfaction. 'Thought it'd be jus' cheese on sticks an' Pringles, but they made a bit of an effort.'

'Glad you approved the funeral baked meats, Sergeant,' Markham said drily.

'Well, as my missus always says, there's nothing worse than a stingy wake.'

'Indeed.'

'Helen Melville's brother never showed,' said Doyle.

'No. Barry Lynch told me he had to fly back to Sydney later today.'

'The poor sod prob'ly couldn't stomach it, guv. I mean, let's face it, one of this lot's a murderer . . . he'd have been chowing down with whoever did for his sister an' that poor lad.'

'It was a weird atmosphere.'

'How so, Kate?'

'I don't mean the usual weird . . . I mean, no one's a big fan of funerals,' she replied frowning. 'All that in the church reminded me of my uncle. It was years ago, and I was only a teenager . . . but it was still hard.'

The DI nodded encouragingly.

'And it wasn't just that Helen Melville was murdered,' she went on, looking somewhat embarrassed. 'Oh, there was just something really *off* about it all . . . creepy and artificial . . . like we were on a stage set or something . . .'

'It's all them pictures an' statues an' things,' Noakes said comfortably. 'Watching an' listening — all smug, like they know summat we don't.'

'Maybe that's it, sarge,' Burton conceded. 'When the light falls on them in a particular way, you start to think they're moving, or the expression on their faces seems to change . . . like they've seen something but they're not going to tell you about it.'

Doyle looked from one to the other as though he could scarcely credit this shared flight of fancy.

'Unsettling, I agree.' Markham approved the stirrings of détente. 'Rebecca Summerson's suggestion that people should feel free to explore the gallery was rather out of left field.'

'I showed your Olivia some of them stick figure paintings,' Noakes said shyly. He shot a glance at the remnants of sausage rolls. 'She told me that bloke Lowry said all the art in the world wasn't worth a meat pie if a person was hungry.'

Clearly, as far as Noakes was concerned, no further imprimatur was required.

Mischievously, Markham observed, 'And yet Mr Lowry's favourite painter was Dante Gabriel Rossetti, one of the Pre-Raphaelites.'

'Yeah, we had a look at them too.' Noakes sniffed. 'Not very realistic. An' some of them lasses had too many pies if you ask me.' He caught himself up lest this sweeping dismissal of Victorian art be taken as a criticism of Markham's girlfriend. 'Your Olivia knew all the stories behind the pictures,' he said admiringly. 'She could put any of them tour guides out of a job.'

Just as well Mrs Noakes hadn't come upon her husband listening spellbound to his Scheherazade, Markham thought with amusement.

As though prompted by the pricking of his guilty conscience, Noakes said, 'Jus' before the missus left, she told me something odd happened.'

'What kind of odd?'

'Well, it was by the modern art room.' Noakes cleared his throat. 'She's really into all the abstract stuff, see.'

That figured. Anything pretentiously avant-garde would be right up her street.

'Go on, Noakes.'

'She heard someone in the corridor shout "Get away! I don't want you anywhere near me!"'

'Did she see who it was?'

'Told me afterwards, once she was back downstairs. It was Daniel Westbrook.'

'Who was he shouting at?'

'She left it a minute or so before going into the corridor. Didn't want to look like she was eavesdropping or owt.'

Perish the thought.

'Well?'

'There wasn't anyone else out there, guv. Jus' Westbrook. Gave her a dirty look then legged it.'

'Did she mention this to anyone?'

'She felt a bit awkward . . . didn't know what to do really.' Clearly Noakes was surprised by this rare instance of fallibility. 'Eventually she had a word with Miss Crocker who said she'd ask Mr Carstone to go look for him.'

'Did Mr Carstone have any joy?'

'Nah . . . Westbrook must've buggered off.' Noakes scratched his head. 'Carstone told the missus not to worry . . . summat about the lad needing to work through his feelings an' that. Said it was all a bit complicated.'

'Rather an understatement.' Markham's tone was wry.

'Well, he and the Croc . . . er, sorry, Miss Crocker, were dead nice. Muriel said they were a cut above the rest.' He wrinkled his nose. 'She said that Summerson one smelled like a distillery . . . An' shrieking her head off at Marcus Traherne without caring who heard . . . I mean, there's a time and a place after all.'

'Mrs Noakes heard an argument, Sergeant?'

'She was jus' having a wander round the back of the café . . . overheard this ding-dong in Summerson's office. Summerson shouted summat like "You're a real low life, Marcus. A real piece of shit." Then something about "if they only knew the half of it."' The DS concluded shamefacedly, 'Then Cathy Hignett appeared out of nowhere and told Muriel she wasn't supposed to be there . . . staff only, she said. Told her to push off. I mean,' Noakes waxed indignant, 'how was Mu supposed to know? Summerson more or less said it was access all areas, so she was jus' having a gander. No law against that, is there?'

'Wonder what Summerson meant by saying if they only knew the half of it,' Burton ruminated. 'Sounds like she was threatening Traherne.'

'Maybe it's got something to do with those paintings.' Doyle was eager to contribute. 'The ones that got stolen. Maybe Traherne's some kind of fence.'

'In addition to running a vice ring out of the gallery.' The DI's brows contracted in a manner that boded ill for someone. 'Quite the busy boy our Mr Traherne.'

'I asked around about the stolen pictures, sir,' Burton said brightly.

'Excellent, Kate. How did they take it?'

'Pretty relaxed really . . . no one seemed specially self-conscious. They've got postcards of the paintings in the shop. Helen Melville was keen on both artists apparently.'

She slipped two photocopies out of her jacket pocket and laid them on the table.

The first, *The Soul's Prison House* by Evelyn De Morgan, depicted one of those well-nourished wavy-haired medieval damsels anathematized by Noakes. Sitting on a tomb-like bench beneath a prison grating, she appeared lost in dreamy contemplation of a prayer scroll held in her outstretched hands.

The second was Howard Pyle's *The Secret Room*, which looked like the illustration to a lurid Gothic romance or penny dreadful. Its subject was a haggard-looking woman in crinoline and shawl thrusting what looked like a covered plate at a Charles II lookalike who loomed out at her from a hidden staircase.

'Christ, I wouldn't want either of those on my walls,' Doyle burst out. 'Bloody depressing the pair of them.'

'That one's kinda S&M for Victorians,' Noakes grunted, scrutinizing the Pre-Raphaelite offering. 'An' as for the other one . . . must've been a fan of Sherlock Holmes is all I can say.'

Markham smiled wearily. 'Each to their own,' he countered. 'Evelyn De Morgan was doubtless trying to say something about the soul breaking free of the body in death.'

'Same pack drill as that other creepy picture upstairs, then. The one Helen Melville took such a shine too.'

'Correct, Noakes. As for the other one, I believe Howard Pyle was an illustrator of mysteries and tales of derring-do. So your Sherlock Holmes guess isn't far off the mark.'

The DI's long slender fingers beat an impatient tattoo on the table.

'These pictures held a particular significance for someone in the gallery,' he said.

'Whoever abducted Alex Carter, sir? The kidnapper?'

'Quite possibly, Kate. But they aren't pictures of children . . . so there must be something more.'

'A connection with a house . . . where someone's been locked up . . . maybe even killed . . . an adult . . .'

'I think that's right, Doyle. But,' Markham groaned, 'we're no nearer knowing where it is.'

'It's got to be that house on the plan, sir. The one they dropped in the archives room.'

'What if that drawing was just some imaginary draughtsmanship, Doyle?' Markham decided to play devil's advocate. 'Some practice exercise or other that Donald Lestrange did just to amuse himself? Some "castle in the air"?'

The young DC looked crestfallen. 'But taken together with the Alex Carter doodle, sir . . .'

'Who's to say it couldn't be coincidence,' Markham continued remorselessly. 'Donald Lestrange suffered from mild dementia in his final years. Who can say what tricks his mind might have played on him.'

The DI stretched his arms above his head. Somehow he managed to make even that look elegant, thought Burton.

'Look,' he said finally, glancing at his watch. 'Nearly four. Ned Chester should be along shortly with something for me.' Bracingly, he added, 'Who knows, maybe it'll be a game changer.'

'I can—'

'No, Kate.' The DI was firm. 'I want the three of you to get off. While I wait for Ned, I'll just potter about upstairs.' He grinned at Noakes. 'I'm rather partial to those overfed dames in the Pre-Raphaelites room.'

'Well, some of 'em have a look of your Olivia,' the DS admitted. 'Like they're from another world. But,' he was not to be gainsaid, 'that Proserpine or Persephone or whatever her name is . . . got a neck like a sumo wrestler.'

A case of pot calling the kettle black, thought Markham with the image of statuesque Muriel Noakes indelibly printed on his mind's eye.

But his DS had suffered enough teasing for one day.

'She's certainly an extensive armful,' he said mildly. 'But there's something compelling about her nonetheless.'

Noakes got to his feet.

'Well, if you're sure, boss . . .'

'I am. Do some team bonding or whatever in The Grapes.' He smothered a smile at the expression on Kate Burton's face as she contemplated the prospect of an evening in the pub with the other two. 'Or hunker down with a box set and a nice bottle of wine. Either way, I want you to take tonight off. You deserve it.'

* * *

Fifty highly enjoyable minutes later, Markham found himself in the room devoted to British art. He could see why Noakes, the down-to-earth Yorkshireman, was so taken with Lowry, though after the fluid grace of the Pre-Raphaelites he found the paintings somehow stiff and ugly, the figures too static. Text on the wall beneath the pictures pointed out that in Lowry's paintings the sun never shone, the artist having concluded that were he to include the sun he would not have known where to put the shadows.

No shadows. Perhaps that's why he couldn't relate to the Matchstick Man, Markham concluded — because the darkness was a policeman's element and not the light of day.

Or perhaps it was something about the way those industrial landscapes with their scurrying furtive figures made him think of how, when you lifted a stone, all sorts of creeping things emerged from their hiding place. Like the human vermin he hunted.

Giving himself a little shake, Markham decided he was growing morbid.

He glanced at his watch. Nearly five o'clock and no sign of Ned Chester.

It wasn't like Ned to be late for an appointment. 'Punctuality is the politeness of kings' was ever the reporter's motto.

He wandered across to the window and looked out, pressing his face to the glass, welcoming the icy chill against his forehead.

Rain was coming down hard, punching holes in the snow, as though bent on turning the crisp surface to an oozy sludge. The wind too was getting up, lashing a neighbouring hawthorn into a crazy skeleton dance like a thing possessed.

The DI felt the first stirrings of unease, suddenly conscious of the building's profound silence.

He retraced his footsteps down to the foyer, trying to ignore the hovering presences in their gilded frames which seemed more than ever like a phantom praetorian guard whose surveillance it was impossible to evade.

All was hushed and quiet. Everything just as it was when he made his way upstairs.

Uncertainly, he looked along the vista of the Sculpture Gallery and then back towards Craft and Design, with its Elizabethan suit of armour keeping watch as usual at the entrance.

But then Markham noticed something that made the blood congeal in his veins.

The casque was up.

He forced himself to move closer.

A livid face looked back at him, the eyes filmy and sightless.

Ned Chester had kept his appointment with Markham only to meet death instead.

10. SKELETONS IN THE CLOSET

There was no denying that Noakes really came into his own at times like this, Kate Burton reflected much later on that seemingly interminable night as the team sat slumped, exhausted, in the gallery café. Like a guard dog with its hackles up, Noakes had shielded Markham, protecting him from everyone — SOCOs, paramedics, uniforms, press, bystanders, the lot. Buying him breathing space. 'You get off, guv,' he told him. 'We c'n see to things here. You get off to Station Road.' This being the address where Ned Chester lived with his partner and fellow journalist Carol Anne.

'Chester and the guvnor go way back,' Noakes told the other two. 'Very different from scuzballs like Gavin Conors.' He scowled at the thought of the *Gazette*'s lead gossip columnist with whom there had been some legendary run-ins over the years. 'Chester was a gent. A class act. If you had a deal with him, he never welched. The boss knew he could give him the inside track an' there was no danger of it getting out.' In a voice rough with emotion, he added, 'He was on the boss's wavelength too with all the arty-farty stuff. But there was nothing phoney about him.' Noakes's features passed through some extraordinary contortions as if he was going to cry. Then the moment passed and he glared defiantly at his colleagues, almost daring them to comment on this show of emotion.

Burton and Doyle preserved a respectful silence.

'Didn't disappear up his own backside like your usual posho type.' Noakes's tone was affectionate. 'Liked to take the piss too . . . there was this time at the Town Hall when a waiter asked if he wanted a drink . . . "That's very kind, I'll have a tomato soup," he said. You should've seen the look on that fella's face.'

The defiance was back, tinged with a touch of triumph. 'He liked my Matchstick Man an' all. Said he was a good northerner. When I told him I didn't see the point of them women with too much hair lolling around in baths an' things . . . the ones in the Victorian pictures . . . he jus' laughed and said in the beginning it was a bit like porn . . . folk wanted an excuse to gawp at nudes.'

Burton suspected that Ned Chester had enjoyed winding Noakes up, but she was touched nonetheless.

'Yeah, he had a way with him,' the DS concluded with sorrowful regret. 'Like the guvnor's Olivia . . . Broke the mould when they made those two.'

An unmistakeable softness crept into Noakes's voice as he said this, his trademark pugnaciousness momentarily erased.

Burton felt a needle-sharp stab of pain beneath her ribs before furiously berating herself for being a selfish bitch. Noakes was right. Thank God the boss had Olivia to comfort him in this bleakest extremity. His girlfriend would find the right words.

Doyle cleared his throat.

'What was Chester working on, sarge? I mean, he must've found something out.'

For a moment, Noakes appeared indignant at this interruption of his reminiscences before smiling wryly at his young colleague.

'Aye you're right, lad. Me drivelling on like this won't butter no parsnips.'

He whipped out his dog-eared pocketbook.

'There was a business card in his pocket. From The Anchorage.'

'That's the private psychotherapy centre in town, isn't it, sarge? The one in Crofton Street?' Doyle was suddenly energized.

'Yeah . . . He'd scribbled Donald Lestrange's name on the back, heavily circled . . .'

'So, he was investigating Lestrange's medical history,' Burton murmured, mystified. 'But why?'

Noakes grasped the roots of his salt-and-pepper thatch as an aid to cogitation. It made him look like a startled porcupine. 'We know Lestrange had dementia towards the end. But if there was other stuff wrong with him earlier . . . other mental problems . . . say a breakdown or summat like that, then mebbe the therapist or quack or whoever treated him holds the clue . . .'

'A clue to the Carter case?' Doyle's tone was sceptical.

'You got a better idea?' his colleague demanded belligerently.

'Could be something in that, sarge.' Burton hastened to pour oil on troubled waters.

Doyle remained unconvinced. 'But if Lestrange coughed to something criminal, wouldn't they tell the police?'

'Not if they didn't realize the significance,' Burton leaned forward earnestly. 'Something must have made Ned decide to check out Lestrange's medical history. Then he picked up information at The Anchorage which he thought was worth sharing with the boss.'

'Can't have been that important, though.' Noakes was momentarily downcast. 'Cos he was happy for it to wait till he got back from Birmingham.'

'The killer didn't know that,' said Burton slowly, with a chill stealing over her. 'Ned was on speakerphone when I talked to him, remember . . . said he had something for the boss about Donald Lestrange . . . something he didn't want to say over the 'phone. It was in the incident room and I was in the middle of telling the staff about reopening next week . . . They were all talking amongst themselves when I took the call, so I didn't think anyone noticed.'

But clearly someone had been paying close attention.

'It was my fault,' she whispered, her face ashen. 'All my fault. The killer was listening.'

'No, lass.' Noakes's voice was so kind that it made her want to burst into tears. 'You weren't to blame. Me an' the boss were out in Calder Vale . . . mobiles off till we'd finished with Jim McLeod. So Chester took a chance an' rang the main line here. Didn't say owt about its being confidential or urgent, did he?'

'No . . .' Burton's voice was tremulous. 'But—'

'But nothing.' The curranty eyes held only sympathy. 'That call took you on the hop. An' with Chester being all casual, how were you to know he might be in danger?'

Christ, thought Doyle observing Burton's teary expression, it's like an episode of the frigging *Three Musketeers*. We'll be chanting 'All for one, and one for all' in a minute.

Time to interrupt the unprecedented love-in.

'Hold on a minute,' he said. 'Everything's GDPR and data protection these days. The Anchorage won't just have dished out Lestrange's medical details to any Tom, Dick or Harry.'

Noakes tapped the side of his nose, a favourite gesture with him to denote deviousness far beyond the comprehension of an ordinary copper. 'Ways an' means, Doyle. Ways and means.'

'You mean he went and *bribed* someone?'

'Not necessarily . . .' Noakes was now adrift.

'Ned and Carol Anne had all kinds of contacts.' Burton appeared to have recovered her sangfroid. 'Probably nothing was spelled out as such.'

No names, no pack drill. Deniability all round.

'But *something clicked*,' she said with increasing conviction. 'Something he thought might lead somewhere.'

'And whatever it was, the killer couldn't take the risk.'

'Exactly, Doyle.'

Burton gripped her mug of stewed tea so tightly the knuckles gleamed white. 'Was there anything else on the body, sarge?'

'A bit of paper with contact details for Dr Rod Mengham at the Newman.'

'What, the nuthouse?' Doyle was startled.

Burton frowned but Noakes grinned. 'Yeah, the nut-house,' he said with a degree of truculence that seemed almost expressly designed to counter any notion of him 'going soft.'

Pick your battles, she told herself, pick your battles.

'Was there a name written on the card, sarge?'

'No, but it's a safe bet Chester was checking out gallery staff.'

'Bill Hignett?'

'Could be,' he conceded. 'Or p'raps there was someone else treated in there.'

Doyle whistled, his freckled face wan and wraith-like in the gloom.

'Health secrets,' he said. 'Legally that's a real minefield, isn't it? I mean in terms of getting them to hand over records.'

Burton glanced at Noakes's louring expression which said as clearly as words, *Let them try to stop me.* She strongly suspected he would relish the opportunity to go in mob-handed having conceived an intense mistrust of medical authorities during their investigation at the special hospital eighteen months earlier.

'Ned Chester was bashed over the head,' he said fiercely. 'The psycho who did it meant to kill him or leave him a cabbage. Either way he stood no chance.'

Subdural haematoma caused by blunt force trauma. Burton shuddered.

'No poncey medico's gonna spout legal jargon in my face.'

Burton believed him.

'Had to have been someone strong enough to wedge him upright in that suit of armour.' Doyle's gaze flickered involuntarily to the entrance of Craft and Design, even though the body and its grotesque disguise had long since been removed.

'Or maybe two people,' he continued uneasily.

Burton's nerve ends tingled.

Two killers.

Noakes knuckled his bleary eyes. They looked like a couple of piss-holes in the snow, thought Doyle watching the older man.

'We can't do any more tonight,' the DS said finally.

'What's the plan for tomorrow?' Burton had her own immaculate notebook to hand.

'I'll collect the guvnor in the morning. First stop The Anchorage. See if we can get a handle on Donald Lestrange's mental problems.'

Doyle's mind was busy with ramifications. 'Won't you need a warrant, sarge?'

'Not if we don't freak 'em out.' Noakes never had much truck with formalities. 'We'll keep it nice an' casual . . . make it sound like we're trying to get an angle on Lestrange's missing papers . . . tell 'em we're following up a burglary at the gallery, that kind of thing. You c'n bet Chester won't have gone in shouting the odds, so we play it low-key too.'

'Sensitive background enquiries . . . police not wanting to upset anyone, what with Lestrange being a kind of benefactor and his nephew working at the gallery.' Doyle caught on quickly.

'Exzackly.' Noakes bestowed an approving smile on the DC.

'It's a good cover story,' Burton agreed. 'Provided the media blackout holds and they don't make a connection with Ned's murder.'

'That fuckwit Barry Lynch'll have me to answer to if anything leaks before the evening news tomorrow,' Noakes growled menacingly.

'What d'you want us to do, sarge?' Burton's pen was poised.

'Get over to the Newman. They'll be terrified of another fiasco after the missing patients scandal.' Noakes's face darkened as he recalled the murky goings on at Bromgrove's special hospital which had uncovered medical corruption on an epic scale. 'I reckon Dr Mengham'll be a good little boy scout . . . anything to keep us sweet.'

It sounded reasonable enough, thought Burton, and should hopefully fill in gaps from the point of view of psychological profiles.

'And after that?' she prompted.

'Interviews with all the staff,' came the decree. 'We need to know everyone's movements after the wake . . . from two o'clock onwards.' Noakes swallowed an enormous yawn. 'Especially Westbrook, Summerson and Traherne. Them three were all sounding off an' picking fights as my missus tells it.'

Doyle and Burton exchanged surreptitious looks at the mention of her ladyship. Glumly, Burton concluded that someone would have to take a statement from Muriel Noakes and the task would doubtless fall to her.

'What about the DCI?'

Noakes looked more dyspeptic than ever.

'Me an' the guvnor'll brief him in the morning,' he grunted with a marked lack of enthusiasm.

'He's not going to buy the line about it being some wacko student, is he, sarge? I mean not after all *this* . . .' Doyle gestured helplessly towards the taped off area at the entrance to Craft and Design.

'Let me an' the boss worry about Sidney.' Noakes looked shattered, spider veins and broken capillaries standing out starkly on the florid cheeks as though tracing a route march for endless disappointment and frustration. Burton felt an unwonted twinge of compassion.

'You can play up the psychological profiling stuff, sarge,' she said softly. 'Liaison with mental health professionals and counsellors . . . It's true enough after all, with any luck the DCI'll assume we're still focused on the university.'

Doyle too had noticed his colleague's dejected posture.

'I'll swing by Student Health again,' he said. 'Get some more data.'

Noakes dredged up a smile.

'You're good kids,' was all he said. But it was enough.

Nothing left to do but set the alarm and secure the premises, the three detectives averting their eyes from the cordoned off section where Markham had made his grisly discovery.

Outside it was snowing again, thick flakes driving and drifting against them as they walked, stiffening their clothes and freezing their eyelashes. But they barely noticed the elements, hunched against the blizzard which enveloped the gallery in a white pall.

* * *

When Noakes arrived at the DI's flat the next morning, he found his boss more or less in command of his emotions, though new lines of tension seemed to have sprung up overnight in the handsome face.

'Carol Anne made it easy for me,' Markham had told Olivia who had waited up for him in his study. 'Not a word of reproach. She said Ned was never happier than chasing a lead. It made him feel like an entomologist stalking human insects with a butterfly net.'

Her eyes dimmed with unshed tears, Olivia chuckled. 'Typical Ned!' Gently, she added, 'Hold on to that thought, Gil. Remember he died doing what he loved best.'

With frightening intensity, her lover replied, 'But *he* was the one being stalked. *He* was the one who walked into a trap. God, if you'd *seen* him in that suit of armour, like some horrible metal strait-jacket . . .'

'Try not to think of it.'

'I'll never forget it as long as I live . . . Ned loved those Pre-Raphaelite paintings . . . the medieval romance and the chivalry.' Markham shuddered violently. 'It's like someone *knew* and posed his body out of spite. One last sick joke . . . Sir Galahad and the Holy Grail impersonated by Ned Chester of the *Gazette*.'

Olivia sought to distract him.

'Didn't you say Helen Melville was obsessed with a picture like that?'

'Yes, that's right.' Markham's fists unclenched. '*Life and Thought Emerging from the Tomb*. The painting that shows two figures coming out of a mausoleum — a woman accompanied by a knight in armour.'

'And it's meant to symbolize the body being the soul's prison?'

Markham nodded, piercing dark gaze fixed on her.

'Those pictures that went missing from the gallery — the ones you told me about the other night — they're all about imprisonment as well?'

'Right again.' To Olivia's relief, his exhausted features kindled with renewed animation. 'It felt like maybe there's some paranoid psychosis bubbling away beneath this case. Someone seriously disturbed . . . endlessly revisiting a crime from the past but never achieving closure.'

'And Donald Lestrange holds the clue?'

'Ned died after he called the gallery to say he had some information about Lestrange. So he must be the key to it all, Liv.' Markham saw this conviction reflected in his lover's face.

'But there's someone standing behind Lestrange,' he continued. 'The puppet-master . . . the one who pulled the strings. The manipulator. The controller.'

Olivia suddenly felt herself go cold, as though a shadowy, ghostly figure had sidled into the room to stand behind her. As though the killer was breathing softly down her neck.

'You'll get him, my love,' she repeated over and over. 'You'll get him.'

Arriving in a damp flurry, Noakes echoed her mantra. 'We're getting close, guv, I c'n feel it,' he declared. 'It's jus' a matter of time.'

Markham looked wordlessly out at the snow-clad cemetery, seeing Evil burrowing like a mole underground, staking its claim to another mound of earth . . . a dank cell to house the remains of Ned Chester. Impossible to credit that their goodbye in Waterstones was for all time . . .

'George, I think you and Gil need something more substantial than a cup of coffee inside you today,' Olivia said lightly. 'It goes against my principles,' she sighed theatrically, 'but what would you say to a "coronary on a plate"?'

Noakes's beatific expression indicating that this arrangement was eminently acceptable, she ushered him out of the room towards the well-appointed galley kitchen at the back of the apartment, leaving Markham to follow when he was ready.

* * *

Dr Christina Skelthorne, chartered clinical psychologist at The Anchorage, was a petite kewpie doll of a woman whose immaculate maquillage, raven chignon and what Noakes called 'droopy clothes' gave her a geisha-girl quality that Markham found disconcerting. Even more so the irritating sing-song neatness of her speech and head-on-one-side posture suggestive of talking someone down from a ledge. Which, the DI supposed, was commensurate with her calling.

In the event, it was surprisingly easy to extract the required information, Dr Skelthorne accepting at face value his justification for their visit, namely that they were looking for anything in Donald Lestrange's personal background which might identify a motive for the theft of his papers. Left hanging in the air — albeit not in so many words — was the suggestion that they were there at the trustees' behest, to ascertain whether embarrassment was likely to be caused should personal details about the collector enter the public domain. To Markham's ears it sounded somewhat thin and unconvincing, but by some miracle the psychologist didn't call their bluff.

'Your civilian investigator, Mr Chester, explained the position,' she informed them blandly.

The DI didn't dare look at his colleague, but felt an inward glow at his friend's ingenuity.

Well done, Ned. Well done.

'Obviously, I merely summarized the general therapeutic outcome,' Dr Skelthorne intoned. 'As I told Mr Chester, client confidentiality is paramount.' Her voice held a question.

'Mr Chester hasn't had an opportunity of briefing us in full, Doctor.' And never would, Markham reflected with a gnawing at his guts. 'He suggested it was worth our coming to see you in person.'

'Indeed.' She looked gratified at the implied compliment.

Blindside them with flattery. Worked like a charm every time, Markham reflected wryly.

Dr Skelthorne padded across the shag pile carpet to a filing cabinet which was the only functional item in a room as impersonally furnished as a Trusthouse Forte Hotel guest suite.

Her movements calm and deliberate, she removed a slim manila folder before reseating herself in the comfortable overstuffed armchair and scanning its contents. Perched side by side on a slouchy lilac sofa, the two men waited expectantly.

Finally, she closed the folder.

'Some years before he died, Mr Lestrange had experienced persistent nightmares.' She paused, giving the impression that she sought to reduce complex processes to layman's terms. With a sphinx-like smile, she elaborated. 'To put it at its simplest, he was troubled by recurring flashbacks related to a chronic anxiety disorder.'

'What kind of nightmares?'

Dr Skelthorne blinked. Clearly having intended to lead up to the subject in stages, she hadn't reckoned on Noakes's preference for the full-frontal approach.

She looked towards Markham as though expecting him to intervene, but the DI merely watched her with brooding, unfathomable eyes.

'Mr Lestrange believed that he had been complicit in a criminal enterprise,' she said finally.

'Eh?'

'Could you perhaps be more explicit, Doctor.'

'He was troubled by dreams in which he watched a child being buried alive.' The professional smile firmly in place, she added, 'Of course this was a case of symbolic displacement . . . suppression of early-life trauma leading to dissociative re-enactment.'

Before Noakes could butt in requesting a translation, Markham enquired easily, 'Was therapy successful in locating the relevant childhood episode?'

The professional mask slipped a little, but the Colgate smile was swiftly back in place.

'We concluded there was unlikely to have been any *specific* trigger. It was more a question of authoritarian parenting leading to sexual confusion and gender ambivalence.'

Bollocks to that. Noakes's mutinous expression said it all.

Heading off any Freudian or Jungian exegesis, Markham interposed, 'Did Mr Lestrange identify any particular setting for this burial . . . or say who was involved?'

'Well obviously, one must distinguish reality from illusion.'

'Oh, naturally.' The DI's manner was smoothly insinuating, his expression that of the fascinated amateur. 'But allowing that this was fantasy . . .'

The psychologist was disarmed.

Smarmy bugger, thought Noakes watching admiringly. Always has poncey types eating out of his hand. Pound to a penny, she'd love to get him on the couch . . .

The DS was brought sharply back to reality when Dr Skelthorne said, 'Mr Lestrange was convinced that a child had been walled up in front of him.'

Markham's mouth was dry, but somehow he forced the words out.

'Did the child have a name?'

She shook her head. 'He called him the Lost Boy.'

Despite the warmth of the room, Markham felt goosebumps.

'Did he say where this happened?'

'He described features of a typical country house, most likely a National Trust property he remembered from childhood . . . Gawthorpe Hall perhaps . . . or Knebworth House.' She patted the manila file complacently. 'A fixation with hidden rooms and recesses is not uncommon in such cases, as a signifier for the divided self.'

No, thought Markham. Donald Lestrange didn't conjure up some imaginary topography. He was reliving something he had *witnessed*. Something which rose up uncontrollably in his dreams to haunt him. Something he desperately wanted to expunge from his memory.

'And the perpetrator? Man or woman?' The DI's tone was casual, giving no clue to the thoughts that raced through his mind.

'He would never say. But,' another smug tap of the file, 'clinically speaking, this presented as a textbook case of patricidal impulse. Killing the father,' she added benignly for Noakes's benefit. 'Of course, with the rapid onset of dementia, Mr Lestrange's day-to-day care became a matter for the local health authority and his treatment here was unfortunately discontinued.'

'Would you say he experienced any relief from his symptoms after psychotherapy? Did the nightmares stop?'

Dr Skelthorne pursed her lips as though Markham had made a gaffe.

'By articulating his fears in a *safe* environment, he acquired a measure of control over them.'

That would be a *no*, then.

'What about doodles?'

'I'm sorry . . .' The psychologist looked blankly at Noakes.

'Scribbles, drawings, stick men . . . did he ever do owt like that in any of the, er . . . sessions? I mean,' he jerked a thumb towards a tasteful still life on the far wall, 'art was his thing . . . so stands to reason he might jot summat down.' The DS looked wildly about him for inspiration and finding none, concluded lamely, 'He might've tried to get the bad thoughts out of his head by putting 'em on paper.'

'Ah, I see what you mean.' Regarding Noakes warily as though he belonged to some primitive species not previously encountered, the psychologist enunciated her words carefully. 'No, we didn't adopt that approach in his past life regression therapy. It was thought best to keep the personal and professional halves of his experience distinct.'

More's the bleeding pity.

'Mr Lestrange wasn't a suitable subject for hypnosis and, as I say, his therapy was interrupted by the onset of dementia.'

They had circled as near as they dared to Alex Carter and the possibility of Lestrange's connection to a serial killer. Time to beat a tactical retreat before Dr Skelthorne became suspicious and raised the drawbridge.

Markham gave her a charming smile. The one he reserved specially for dippy women, as Noakes thought of it.

'Thank you for making time to see us, Doctor. In cases of . . . personal delicacy, it's invaluable to hear directly from health professionals.'

Blah blah blah. The standard BS.

Cordial handshakes all round and a few minutes later they were standing outside the clinic.

'What now, guv?'

It felt raw and damp, the short perspective of Crofton Street with its elegant Georgian houses obscured by mist which, in Markham's current mood, seemed to hang over everything like a filthy curtain.

'"The longer the beard, the shorter the art."'

'Eh?'

'That's what your Matchstick Man said about artists. It's why Lowry shaved with a cut-throat razor until the day he died.' A harsh bitter laugh. 'Ned loved stories like that. Loved debunking all the academic claptrap.'

The DS looked anxiously at his boss.

'Don't worry, Noakesy, I'm not going to lose it. Not now.'

'Wonder what put Chester on to The Anchorage, guv.'

'Someone must've let something slip and then Ned was on it.'

'Like a rat up a drain,' Noakes said admiringly. 'That was dead crafty passing hisself off as an investigator.'

'Wasn't it just,' echoed Markham, forcing the words past an enormous lump in his throat.

'What now, guv?'

'Well, at least we're getting somewhere. It's looking very much as though little Alex Carter *was* abducted and murdered.'

'An' Lestrange knew who did it . . . that's what sent him doolally.'

'More than likely.' Markham sighed heavily, watching his breath spiral into the cold air. 'But Ned never got anything concrete. Presumably that's why he thought his news could wait.'

'The killer wasn't to know that. So he decided to fix him good an' proper.' Lugubriously, Noakes mimed bashing someone over the head before self-consciously recollecting himself.

'I want to pay the Land Registry a visit,' Markham said. 'Lestrange lived in a big stone semi the other side of Calder Vale. Nothing on the scale of a country house, but that architect's plan in his papers—'

'The one with the doodle . . . the one the killer dropped . . . with Alex Carter's name on it?'

'The very same. We need to see if it rings a bell with property services. Could be a long shot, but worth trying the recognition factor . . . local knowledge.' His mouth twisted. 'I'm willing to bet it's not sodding Gawthorpe Hall—'

'Nor Knob House, neither.'

'Knebworth House, Sergeant.'

'Are we going now?'

'We need to see the DCI first obviously.'

Noakes's face fell.

'Come on, let's get it over with.'

At that moment, Markham's mobile sang out.

The exchange was short and to the point.

Turning back to Noakes, the DI said, 'Kate has some interesting news for us from the Newman. It appears Donald Lestrange was not the only one with medical secrets in his past.'

11. A BEND IN THE ROAD

'Well, that was a turn up for the books,' the DS observed to Markham later on Friday morning, sounding as though his world had tilted on its axis.

The two men were sitting in the canteen at Bromgrove Police Station. Largely deserted, they had the place pretty much to themselves, save for a few young traffic cops who kept a respectful distance.

Notwithstanding his earlier cholesterol-laden breakfast, Noakes was tucking into the 'station special' — a sausage, bacon and scrambled egg muffin with extra ketchup on the side. From the wink bestowed on him by the motherly supervisor, it was clear his reputation had gone before him. 'Gotta keep our strength up,' he told the DI, chomping happily. 'Can't do owt on an empty stomach.'

No danger of that in your case, the DI thought wryly.

Aloud, he merely said, 'The DCI certainly showed his best side today.'

And it was true. Sidney had appeared genuinely shaken by Ned Chester's murder, the trademark bombast and braggadocio totally absent in his tribute to the dead reporter. 'I always found him upfront and honest,' the DCI told Markham. 'Which is more than can be said for the rest of that shower down at the *Gazette*.' His gaze reflective, he added, 'Chester's coverage of those murders at the Royal Court last year did CID no harm at all . . . could've been a real hatchet job, but in the event it was a remarkably fair and objective piece of journalism.'

It would have been expecting too much of Sidney to imagine that he could have laid the credit for Ned Chester's sympathetic analysis at Markham's door, but his condolences at least were sincere. 'I know you and Chester were friends,' he said with unwonted kindness. 'If you need to take any time, Inspector . . .'

On the DI readily assuring him that his top priority was to apprehend a triple-killer, Sidney, with evident relief, got back to business. 'Why would Chester have been a target?' he enquired, gimlet gaze raking the DI. 'Please don't tell me you'd been sharing details of the investigation with him, Inspector.'

Markham duly delivered a suitably expurgated account of the conversation in Waterstones. 'Ned was a mad enthusiast for art, sir.' Again, he had to force the words past a golf ball sized lump in his throat. 'And of course, he immediately made the connection with Alex Carter.' It felt like a betrayal, but he didn't want Sidney learning anything about Ned's unauthorised enquiries at The Anchorage. 'I think,' he said carefully, 'Ned may have decided to do some background digging on his own account and in the process inadvertently stumbled across something that threatened the murderer.'

'What kind of something?' Sidney's darkening expression suggested a cold weather front was on its way.

'That's what we need to find out, sir,' Markham temporized. 'Of course, we'll be checking his movements and contacts over the last few days.'

The DCI smoothed his beard magisterially. 'I want you and your team available this afternoon at four sharp to record a slot for the evening news bulletin.' The glance Sidney shot at Noakes, whose combination of flecked tweed jacket and shiny polka dot shirt was strongly suggestive of his having got dressed in the dark, expressed the conviction that the latter was unlikely to add much lustre to the occasion. 'Best bib and tucker of course, sir,' Markham said reassuringly.

'I'll be needing a statement of progress to date,' the DCI concluded, 'though of course the priority is to avoid causing unnecessary alarm — nothing melodramatic and,' he said pointedly, 'no reference to Carter. The last thing we want is to muddy the waters at this stage.'

'What if the journos ask about Carter?' Noakes asked stubbornly.

Sidney's long-lived wondering frown suggested he expected them to come up with the necessary fancy footwork. Markham duly obliged. 'We can say there's no reason at this stage to believe the two cases are connected,' he murmured deferentially.

Thus appeased, Sidney waved them towards the outer office where Miss Peabody hovered. 'Sergeant, I think you've got something there on your tie.' She made little dabbing gestures in the direction of the offending article.

'Don't you worry, luv.' The DS brushed ineffectually at the congealing detritus. 'It's jus' a bit of brekkie from earlier.' He beamed at her confusion. 'That's what comes of eating on the hoof.' The PA shuddered fastidiously as Markham, with an apologetic grimace, whisked his colleague away before she could make any further discoveries.

'We *know* there's a connection with Carter, guv,' Noakes mumbled through a mouthful of station special. 'You've got Melville suddenly getting all aerated about secret cubbyholes an' buried kiddies . . . the Princes in the Tower stuff . . . plus the missing papers an' that map with the doodle . . . then Donald Lestrange telling the trick cyclists he saw a child being walled up.'

'It's all circumstantial, Sergeant.' Intimations of nausea circulated round Markham's digestive system as he watched Noakes finish off his 'snack' with Falstaffian relish. 'Any half-way decent lawyer would demolish it like a pack of cards.'

A snort from across the table offered eloquent testimony to Noakes's opinion of legal eagles.

'Besides,' the DI gloomily opined. 'No way can we get on to Lestrange's medical history. The ethical standards mob would have a field day. I mean, think about it — casting aspersions on this respected local figure who died after a tragic battle with dementia. I don't see Daniel Westbrook or the trustees taking that on the chin, do you?'

'S'pose not,' the DS grumbled.

'And the DCI would go ballistic.'

'That figures.'

Markham gulped down his coffee. 'Let's check what Kate has for us,' he said. 'From the sound of it, she may have uncovered something useful at the Newman.'

* * *

It was a cold, dank day. Snow was no longer falling, but the curtain of mist persisted so that the gallery seemed to hang in the air as though suspended from angry skies.

Inside was warm and quiet, however.

No sign of Kate and Doyle in the incident room, so Noakes padded off to look for them.

Markham, meanwhile, betook himself to the room allocated to British art — the place where he had loitered just before the terrible discovery of Ned Chester's body.

Somehow he felt close to Ned as he contemplated the Matchstick Man's dark scurrying figures set against a plain flake-white background which gave the pictures their eerie dream-like quality. Scrutinizing the fly-like congregations of busy people, Markham remembered Carol Anne's poignant description of Ned tracking human insects with his butterfly net.

None of the figures in the Lowry paintings communicated with the rest, he noticed. Not even in the smaller groups. Unsmiling and aloof, they might as well all have been strangers to each other.

Was that how their murderer felt, he wondered. Robotic. An outsider. Detached from humanity. Never touching or being touched.

He moved slowly around the room, pausing before a collection of Lowry grotesques — misfits, down-and-outs, solitaries, the physically deformed — on loan from Manchester. Their strange and ghastly beauty had a queer effect on him. Again, he gazed searchingly at all the examples of human degradation before him as though, if he looked hard enough, they might eventually yield a clue to the conscienceless killer who lurked just outside his field of vision.

'That one's a crazy.' Noakes's rumble interrupted his thoughts. 'Talk about mad eyes.'

'It's a self-portrait, sarge. Lowry's mother was dying when he painted it.' Burton spoke diffidently, looking uncertainly from Noakes to Doyle as though she suspected them of forming a conspiracy against her.

'Looks like he oughta be in an asylum, if you ask me.'

'Talking of which, how did you and Doyle get on at the Newman, Kate?' the DI enquired as they stood huddled in front of the *Man with Red Eyes*.

'Well, it turned up some interesting intel, sir.'

She handed the DI a sheet of paper which he swiftly scanned.

'So,' he declared softly. 'Esmée Crocker was an inpatient for a time after postpartum psychosis. What was the outcome?'

'She made a complete recovery after treatment, sir.'

'And the child?'

'Put up for adoption. Husband walked out and she went home to Mum and Dad. Young enough to make a fresh start, so looks like the family sorted things. It wasn't that unusual back then.'

'Child snatcher?' wondered Noakes.

'There's something twisted about her all right,' Burton replied slowly. 'One of those female cats, I'd say . . . but abduction's a stretch.'

'Not if she was desperate to replace the kid she lost,' put in Doyle. 'Her big thing's arranging exhibitions of children's fashions.'

'Hardly an indictable offence, Doyle.' Markham spoke with some asperity. 'She works in Textiles, after all.'

Interestingly, Doyle stuck to his guns. 'Something, oh I dunno . . . something *sneaky* about her,' he said. 'All fluffy on the outside, but then you catch a look in her eyes . . .' He jabbed two fingers expressively at his own.

'Easily manipulated do you think, Constable?'

'Hard to say. Gushes over Bramwell and the other blokes . . . doesn't have any time for the women.'

'Hmm.' The DI turned to Burton. 'Anything else, Kate?'

'Bill Hignett's a long-term outpatient, boss. There's learning difficulties, obviously, but he's being treated for sexual impulsivity connected with the autism.' She screwed up her face in concentration. 'Though Dr Mengham said the prospect of actual sex would scare him to death and he wouldn't be able to handle an intimate relationship.' Ignoring Noakes's sceptical expression, she ploughed on. 'Partly a developmental disorder, partly something to do with the relationship with his mother . . . very clingy and immature.'

Oh for fuck's sake, not all that again. Noakes might as well have said it out loud. He'd clearly had enough transactional analysis for one day.

'So, he'd be curious about sex,' Burton continued. 'But it wouldn't go much further than that. He'd more likely be drawn to immaturity or innocence in others . . . maybe to the point of getting himself into situations he couldn't handle.'

'You mean kids.' Her colleague could contain himself no longer.

'But not necessarily in a . . . well, a deviant way, sarge. Dr Mengham said it's more about patients like Bill relating to someone at the same emotional age . . . someone who doesn't threaten them . . . who doesn't make them frightened.'

'Someone like little Alex Carter,' Noakes said flatly.

Burton looked doubtful. 'Was Bill even around when Alex went missing?'

The DI looked up at the disturbing self-portrait in front of them as though for inspiration. 'Jim McLeod mentioned the name Hignett rang a bell.'

'Yeah, that's right, guv. Told us he remembered the "cloakroom girl."'

'But from what he said when he looked at the list of gallery staff, it sounded as though most of them were in the vicinity at the time Alex went missing.'

Noakes ticked the names off on pudgy fingers. 'Lestrange, Carstone an' Bramwell were all around . . . academic research or what have you. Crocker was a receptionist—' He broke off and turned to Doyle. 'Big Jim said he heard someone call her "the Croc," so you might be right about her being a tough nut.' Doyle tried not to preen. 'Then there'd be the cloakroom an' security people, Cathy Hignett for one . . .'

'Did Mr McLeod mention Bill, though?' Burton enquired, terrier-like.

'Nah,' Noakes admitted. 'But he said there were folk drifting in and out, with it being Sunday — most likely getting out of the rain an' killing time . . . teenagers, pensioners, students . . .'

Burton looked thoughtful. 'Bill's thirty-nine. Back then he would have been—'

'Nineteen.' There was a glint in Noakes's eye. 'If he was there an' the doc's right about him wanting to hang round with kids, then that puts him in the frame.'

'But we don't know for sure he was there, sarge. I suppose we could try asking Cathy.'

'Like *she'll* tell us owt,' the other grouched. 'She'll put two an' two together an' we'll get bloody zilch.' He scowled. 'But I bet he *was* around that day. Mum takes him everywhere, so stands to reason.'

Markham shook his head slowly. 'It won't fly, Sergeant. Not unless we've got witnesses to place him at the gallery . . . and after all this time, it's unlikely.'

'Plus, the staff'll close ranks if they think we're making him a scapegoat,' Doyle added sagaciously. 'One of their own and all that . . .' He trailed off uncertainly at the ferocious expression on the older man's face.

'We're talking about a little lad being kidnapped . . . most likely *murdered*, for Christ's sake. He was only *six*.' Noakes looked, as Doyle later put it, as though he was about to burst a blood vessel. 'An' that poor cow of a mother ended up being suspected of it.'

In some cranny of Noakes's constitution, Markham reflected as he watched the little scene unfold before him, up a great many steps and in a corner easily overlooked, there was a secret door with 'Compassion' written on the spring. At a touch from the past, it had flown wide open.

'Look, here's the thing.' The DS took a deep breath, wiped his sweat-bedabbled face with a none too clean handkerchief and told the other two about what he and Markham had learned at The Anchorage. They listened attentively, Burton drinking it all in, wide-eyed with consternation, and Doyle too, somewhat paler by the time Noakes concluded his recital. '*Walled up*,' the young DC repeated shakily in disbelief. 'That's like a horror story. *The Canterville Ghost* or something.'

Burton raised her eyebrows interrogatively.

'It's the one where this bloke's locked up and starved to death in a castle cos of past crimes. He starts haunting the place . . . The family that live there can't get rid of the ghost till they exorcize it so he can rest in peace.'

'Well, little Alex Carter and his mum chuffing well ain't resting in peace,' Noakes said grimly. 'An' someone here knows what happened.'

'I agree, Hignett's the obvious suspect,' Markham addressed them quietly. 'But we have nothing to place him in the gallery at the relevant time, Sergeant. And remember, Mr McLeod couldn't say with certainty who was there and who wasn't. Things are different now,' he added soberly. 'Madeleine McCann has seen to that. But back then it was another story. The gallery wasn't computerized and it was all fairly relaxed . . . pretty much easy come, easy go. As you said, Noakes, people just drifted in and out.'

'True.' Noakes's face was downcast. 'An' Jim admitted folk could've slipped out before they got the cordon up.'

He sighed gustily. 'Alex's mum was no help neither . . . all that cobblers about white hands waving in the dark . . .'

'White hands?' Doyle was mystified.

'Sorry, yeah. What with everything that's gone on, we must've forgotten to tell you that bit.'

It was true, Markham realized with compunction as he observed a shadow pass across Kate Burton's face.

He dredged up a smile.

'Alex's mother spoke of having seen white hands with fingers waving in the dark like serpents . . . or a conjuror wearing gloves.'

'Very poetical,' Noakes sniffed. 'But she could've been tripping . . . thought she smelled summat too . . . Then there was the song.'

'Song?' Doyle looked as if he'd had as much Gothic detail as he could take.

'Some creepy lullaby or nursery rhyme.'

'"I want an old-fashioned house, with an old-fashioned fence. And an old-fashioned millionaire."' Markham recited.

There was dead silence for some moments before Burton cleared her throat.

'That's fairly childlike behaviour, sir . . . Could maybe fit Hignett given his immaturity.'

'The song's from the fifties or sixties, though, isn't it?' Doyle mused. 'Odd choice, though I suppose he could've heard it on the radio or somewhere . . . maybe his mother . . .'

Markham was clearly uneasy. 'There's something fetishistic . . . ritualistic about this scenario. I can't seem to square it with Bill Hignett.'

'Was Rebecca Summerson around when Alex disappeared?' Doyle's mind was running on other suspects.

'Could've been,' Noakes replied glumly. 'Same goes for Traherne and Westbrook, for that matter. Twenty years ago . . . They'd likely be in their teens then.'

'D'you see a *kid* doing something like this?' Burton's tone suggested they were clutching at straws.

'You've obviously never heard of Mary Bell or the Bulger case.' Noakes sounded huffy.

'It's not that, sarge.' Burton was emollient. 'It's just whoever did this was pretty resourceful . . . cunning . . . They'd have to have had their wits about them and been pretty strong into the bargain.'

'Maybe there were two in it together.'

'That's an interesting suggestion, Sergeant.' Markham revolved the idea. 'Our last murder—' he couldn't bring himself to say Ned's name, 'would certainly have required some muscle and maybe a lookout . . .'

The DI fell silent, the faraway look in his eyes telling his subordinates he was reliving Ned Chester's final desperate minutes alive.

Surreptitiously, Burton ran her tongue over her bottom lip and loosened her collar as though the room suddenly felt stuffy and close. Noakes and Doyle, meanwhile, pretended deep interest in a composition on the other side of the room. Children dancing splay-legged on a pavement in some industrial city, pinched little nutcracker faces ugly and blank like puppets at a carnival with bleeding gashes for mouths. 'God, they're *horrible*,' whispered the DS feelingly.

'It's your Matchstick Man painted 'em,' Doyle pointed out with a touch of malice.

'Well I s'pose everyone has their off days,' the other replied with a final long, hard look. 'But them kids look like they're *possessed*.'

The DS shook himself. This flaming case was getting to him, he reflected sourly. Couldn't look at a perfectly ordinary painting without freaking himself out. Out of the corner of his eye, he noticed Burton affecting to examine an industrial landscape.

'Right, team.' The DI wore a quizzical expression as though perfectly aware of their little subterfuge. But there was affection in the look too, thought Noakes with satisfaction.

'We've got a press conference at four,' Markham announced. 'I plan to take a back seat and leave the talking to you.'

Doyle looked dismayed. 'What're we going to say?' he asked bluntly.

'The usual platitudes from CID's playbook, Constable. You can divvy them up between you.' The DI tried not to sound cynical but failed. '"Pursuing various lines of enquiry . . . several promising leads . . . marvellous response from the public . . . important not to compromise ongoing enquiries . . . consideration for the bereaved . . . investigation at a delicate stage . . ." yadda yadda yadda.'

'The journos won't let us off the hook that easy, sir.'

'Barry Lynch can schmooze a few of them beforehand,' Markham said crisply. 'Soften them up, make them feel they're being invited into the tent. That should help.'

'We can talk about the gallery reopening next week,' Burton ventured.

'Right, Kate. If in doubt, deflect.'

'Sidney should be good for that,' Noakes grunted.

'They're bound to ask how a *Gazette* reporter wound up dead in the gallery?' Doyle blurted it out, attracting a scowl from Noakes.

But Markham remained calm.

'"Wrong place at the wrong time . . . no reason to suppose any connection other than professional interest . . . tragic misfortune . . . "' He had it off pat. 'Depend upon it, Sidney'll head them off at the pass.' The DI's voice hardened. 'He'll spout some guff about a reporter's instincts and Ned's dedication to his readers . . . Nothing to suggest the *Gazette's* finest were ever in bed with CID, of course.'

Noakes cracked a grin. Attaboy, he thought.

'If all else fails, you can talk about liaising with everyone in the academic community,' Markham continued. 'The DCI wants us to steer clear of the art world.' His mouth twisted. 'I don't think he'll be averse to our throwing the university into the mix.'

'Deranged student an' all that,' Noakes said in disgust.

'Exactly.'

'Talking of students, sir, I had a call from the vice-principal earlier.'

'Indeed? What did he have to say, Doyle?'

'Apparently, there's some sort of demonstration planned for the weekend. He was a bit vague about the details.'

He would be, thought Markham.

'What, pray, is the point of this demonstration?' he enquired with weary sarcasm. 'A protest against colonial oppression or have they moved on to something else . . . Affronts to the LGBT community perhaps?'

Noakes sniggered appreciatively.

'Just cuts to higher education funding, I think, sir.'

'Oh well, we can probably cope with whatever they spring on us.' He thought for a minute. 'If the gallery staff think our attention is focused elsewhere, it might even prove useful.'

'As in people might lower their guard?'

'Precisely, Noakes.'

'Where are we up to with interview statements, Kate?'

'Doyle and I are just going through them, sir . . . nothing jumps out, though.'

'Get that wrapped up and try tapping junior staff about the bosses . . . somewhere in there we'll find a clue that will blow this case wide open.'

Please, God.

'In the meantime, Noakes and I will head out to the Land Registry.'

'D'you think someone will be able to make a match with that drawing, boss?'

'It's a long shot, Doyle. But it may start a ripple . . . you never know.'

Quietly, they dispersed to their various jobs.

Silence fell once more on the wizened changelings, eccentrics and grotesques. And the man with the red eyes brooded inscrutably over all.

* * *

The Land Registry was some way out of town on the far side of Calder Vale.

Noakes drove with elaborate care and attention, casting the occasional furtive look at his boss.

'It's all right, Noakesy,' the DI said eventually, 'I'm not an invalid. No need to tiptoe around me.'

'Never dreamed of it, guv.'

'Hmm.'

They drove in companionable silence for a time, Markham watching the picturesque snowscape slip by.

'Would I be right in thinking you're somewhat disenchanted with your Matchstick Man after seeing those pictures of down-and-outs back there?'

The DS looked sheepish. 'Well it's real life, ain't it, guv . . . but kind of ugly too.' He paused and then, 'I remember Ned Chester saying even Lowry's family found 'em a bit weird. His mum used to turn all the paintings towards the wall whenever they had visitors.'

'And yet now those same pictures fetch millions of pounds.'

'Yeah.' Unexpectedly, Noakes chuckled. 'Chester told me he used to get £5 per signature whenever he did signed prints. One time there was this dealer came in and he jus' signed a shortened version of his name. The dealer asked why an' he said L. S. Low was a small signature cos it was a small fee.'

The DS gripped the steering wheel as though for dear life.

'I guess it was jus' that some of them oddballs he painted gave me the heebie-jeebies . . . like he was obsessed with folk who had nothing . . . whose life was a big hole . . . a big fat zero.' A pause and then, 'D'you think our murderer's like that, guv? Someone who's got a great empty hole where his heart should be . . . like he's maimed or crippled or summat?'

Markham reminded himself that it never did to underestimate Noakes. Many in CID dismissed the uncouth shambling DS as a Neanderthal — a throwback to some primitive era before policing had fully evolved. But the DI hoped he knew better. He kept a special place for his colleague in his heart. A place of which he had never taken the measure, either by rule or compass, but which seemed to magnify and expand with the passing of the years through some mysterious alchemy which could never be put into words.

'Maimed or crippled,' he now repeated thoughtfully. 'Yes, Noakes. I reckon you're right. Someone with a terrible sense of inner isolation reduced to simulating human emotions without being able to empathize . . . A hollow man.'

Not a complete person at all. Rather, some sort of subtly constructed reflex machine which mimicked others.

'What d'you think made him like that, guv?'

'Perhaps something happened. He was overtaken by some sort of catastrophe and it flipped a switch.' Reading his colleague's mind, he added, 'And no, it doesn't mean I'm going all "bleeding-heart liberal" on you.' A vein pulsed near the DI's temple. 'Nothing . . . *nothing* can excuse the deaths of three innocent victims. It's just that I have a feeling about this.'

'You know what the DCI says about your hunches, guv.'

'By heart.' Markham's brows knitted. 'But nonetheless . . .'

'Where do we go after the press conference, boss?'

'I want you and Kate to do some research in Central Library.'

'Oh aye.' Noakes sounded less than thrilled at the prospect. 'What're we meant to be looking for?'

'Local records. Anything and everything on the gallery.' The DI's voice was hoarse, urgent. 'I want to know what flipped the switch, Noakes. What it was that turned our murderer's world upside down?'

'Well there's nowt Burton likes better than nosing through microfilms an' local whatnot, boss.' He couldn't resist the dig. 'What with her university educashon an' all.' Which made it sound like a communicable disease, reflected Markham.

'Think of it as an opportunity for team bonding.' The DI was inexorable. 'Or some mentoring,' he added slyly. It was worth stretching a point.

Noakes looked pleased. 'Well, you can't put a price on experience.'

'Quite.'

The DI's expression was opaque, shuttered.

'Time's running out, Noakesy. With the gallery reopening next week, we need a way into this case.'

And how.

'My missus thinks it's gotta be someone with a thing about being a painter.'

'Oh?' Polite neutrality was always the best bet when Muriel Noakes had a Quincey moment.

'Yeah. She says if you look at history, lots of creative types had a screw loose . . . Van Gogh . . . Beethoven . . . Vivien Leigh . . . the Sherlock Holmes guy . . . all sorts . . .'

'Well, it's definitely something to bear in mind.'

'Someone happy in their own little world . . . prefers their own company . . . Like them people with Asperger's — the ones who live in their own head a lot of the time.'

Markham was genuinely curious, 'Did Mrs Noakes identify anyone who fitted the bill?'

'Not exzackly,' the other admitted. 'But then, they'd be putting on an act . . . covering up.'

'Hmm. I'm not sure someone afflicted with Asperger's would necessarily be able to conceal it.'

Noakes was momentarily deflated, but then he rallied.

'Mebbe it's not the worst kind, guv . . . like they're on top of it most of the time an' folk jus' think they're odd rather than freaky.'

'You could be right. In many ways, the artistic world's a one-person world whereas we live in a two-person world. We talk to people, have relationships with people. But art's focused on what's inside . . .'

'Yeah, stuff that happens inside the head.' Noakes was gratified the guvnor appeared to be coming round to Muriel's way of thinking.

'"Call no man an island."'

'You what?'

'It's something the poet John Donne said.'

'Oh aye.' The DS awaited enlightenment.

'But our man — or woman — *is* an island. *In* the world but not *of* it. Much like one of those wrecks of humanity you were studying back there in the gallery.'

'Must get a bit stressful . . . like having shell shock or summat.'

'That's why we need information. *Fast*.'

'Muriel didn't mind most of that crowd at the gallery.' Noakes became expansive. ''Cept the drinky one an' that Cathy Hignett. The rest were okay. She prob'ly surprised 'em,' he added complacently.

'How so?'

'Well, they'd be thinking she was only interested in pretty pictures. The kind on biscuit tins. But she's up to all sorts . . . all the modern stuff.'

Having spent what felt like a lifetime battling the Noakes's inverted cultural snobbery, Markham preserved a discreet silence on the subject of taste in art.

'Mrs Noakes wasn't too impressed by Daniel Westbrook, as I recall.'

'Oh yeah. But,' with magnificent condescension, 'she said arty folk are bound to be a bit neurotic . . . specially after what had happened.'

'True.'

'An' galleries are spooky places to start with . . .' Another of those sidelong furtive glances.

'What's bothering you, Noakes? Come on, spit it out.'

The other kept his eyes riveted on the winding road.

'I keep having dreams about doors,' he said gruffly, sounding distinctly embarrassed.

'*Doors?*'

'Yeah.' The DS gnawed his nether lip and then resumed. 'Well, the same door really . . .'

It was evident Noakes would require some prompting.

'Whereabouts is this door?'

'In the dream, I'm standing in that corridor in the gallery.'

'The one with the archives room?'

Noakes nodded.

'Well, there's this door, see. An' I know there's a dreadful secret . . . something dangerous behind it.'

'What happens?'

'Benedict Bramwell an' Mr Carstone come along . . . there are a couple of other folk too, but I can't make out their faces . . . like they keep melting into each other.'

'Then what?'

'They've got all these planks and nails an' things to make the door secure . . . everyone gets stuck in, hammering away.'

'So they make it safe?'

With one hand, the DS tugged at his collar as though he suddenly found it too tight.

'The nails keep breaking an' the wood keeps crumbling an' splintering . . . like worms between their fingers . . . they hold up their hands to show me.'

'Ah.'

'There's a creature on the other side . . .' Noakes's embarrassment was palpable, but he had clearly decided in for a penny, in for a pound. 'Dunno if it's a man or an animal. But I've got to keep it closed up.' Another vicious yank of the collar. 'Then one of 'em standing there asks if I want to know its name an' says he'll whisper it.' The DS's voice sank to a mere thread. 'I c'n see his lips forming the letter "A" an' then someone screams that the secret's discovered. That's when I wake up,' he concluded lamely.

'It's all perfectly explicable, Noakes,' the DI said, though as his colleague spoke he felt a prickle of apprehension. 'The murder investigation and Alex Carter case are preying on your mind, so your subconscious takes over at night . . . translating your anxiety into physical symbols.'

'I ain't got a split personality or owt like that, mind.' Typically belligerent at having exposed his vulnerable underbelly, thought Markham.

'Not at all,' he answered repressing a smile. 'I've had a few bad nights myself as it happens.'

His colleague was mollified. 'D'you think we'll get anywhere with this lot at the Registry, guv?'

'Well, we know it's not Donald Lestrange's place. And none of the gallery staff have aristocratic pretensions, so, far as I'm aware.' Markham's lips quirked at the memory of Olivia enquiring which of his suspects was a 'belted earl.' 'But maybe there's a connection with a heritage property or public building . . . the National Trust . . . something that leads back to the gallery or someone connected with it . . .'

'Good to get out of town at any rate.'

The DI couldn't deny it. Already he was dreading their return and the press conference.

'Right, guv, we're here.'

The brutalist architecture of the office block which housed the Land Registry was softened by its mantle of white, not yet turned to slush.

Markham looked up at the building, feeling an anticipatory quiver in the pit of his stomach.

Hardly daring to hope, he suddenly had the oddest feeling that their luck was about to turn.

12. OUT OF THE SHADOWS

'Let's have a look. Hmm, I think that might be part of Greygarth House.'

Veronica Yately, statuesque and plummy-voiced, squinted at the drawing the DI produced from his breast pocket. Blessedly incurious — or, more likely, possessed of such perfect breeding as to inhibit any vulgar inquiry into the purpose of their visit — she whipped out her spectacles for a closer look.

'Yes,' she said straightening up with an impressive creaking of corsetry, 'definitely Greygarth.'

'I believe I've heard of it, Mrs Yately. 'The artists' colony out towards Troutbeck?'

'Colony?' Noakes frowned. 'What's one of them, then? D'you mean a commune . . . some sort of hippy house . . . like them kibbutzes?'

Unfazed, the administratve officer beamed at him.

'That's certainly one way of describing it, Sergeant.' She gestured to the office breakout area. 'Sit yourselves down. How about some refreshment too — I normally have elevenses round about now.'

The production of tea and biscuits certainly rendered Noakes more amenable to Mrs Yately's local history lesson.

'The idea for Greygarth came from Red House,' she told them.

'Ah.' Markham's interest was piqued. 'The place the Pre-Raphaelites designed. It's on my "bucket list" of places to visit . . . a riot of medieval murals and Gothic flourishes, isn't it?'

'That's right, Inspector. The likes of Burne-Jones, Rossetti and William Morris all lived there together for a time . . . in line with their ideals of artistic brotherhood,' she cast a mischievous glance at Noakes, 'and free love.'

Clearly the DS had decided chocolate Hobnobs were worth a certain amount of aggravation, appearing almost resigned to learning that Greygarth was a similar hotbed of sexual iniquity.

'So a crowd of potheads an' squatters set up camp, did they?' he enquired beadily. 'All bongo drums, spliffs an' gardening in the nude.'

Mrs Yately chuckled. 'Sorry to disappoint you, Sergeant. The Pre-Raphaelites might have whooped it up, but Greygarth was a *much* staider affair. More like a group of middle-aged academics and art historians seeking to recreate their university days than anything "alternative."'

'Oh.' Noakes blinked, recalibrating his mental impressions. 'So it was sort of . . . seminars an' workshops an' stuff . . .'

'That's right. Plus exhibitions of local artists and the occasional grander event when they could persuade galleries to stump up sponsorship.'

'Who owned the place?' The DS was puzzled. 'We're talking stately home, right? You're not telling me a bunch of lefty lecturers an' dropouts could afford anything like that.'

'It was in the hands of a junior branch of the Stanley family for many years, but then I think the line ran out and the house became quite derelict. In the end, I believe the artists' cooperative, or whatever they called themselves, got it for a song.'

'How many of 'em were there?'

'Around a dozen or so, all well-heeled. Not too many Citizen Smiths among them. A couple of universities pitched in with grants too, and parts of the building were rented out to schools and colleges for different events, so it ticked over quite nicely for several years.'

'Is it still going?'

'Eventually they transferred it to Bromgrove University, Inspector.'

For a fat profit no doubt. Amazing how these arty-farty unworldly types were never backward when it came to sniffing out a good deal.

'What does the university use it for . . . accommodation?'

'It's a conference and hospitality centre now, Sergeant . . . Still got the heritage feel, but all mod cons inside.'

'Did you know the place in its heyday, Mrs Yately?'

'I visited a few times with my late husband.' Her eyes were misty with recollection. 'He was an amateur artist and enjoyed the painting weekends.' There was something attractively girlish about her giggle, and for a moment the years fell away. 'My daubs were dreadful, but the tutor said Peter showed real promise.'

'How come you recognized the architect's drawing so quickly?' It felt like rank ingratitude to put the question after being spoiled with tea and biscuits, but Noakes couldn't help feeling suspicious.

'Oh, I've got a photographic memory, Sergeant. Once seen, never forgotten. That's the library and interconnecting snug on the ground floor.' Her eyes crinkled with amusement. 'Members of the cooperative stuck floor plans and diagrams outside each room when they were doing "refurbishments" . That soon fizzled out once financial reality hit home, but I think in the beginning they had grand plans for renovation and wanted to stress their respect for history and continuity . . . quite sweet really.'

Less sweet if it turned out the remains of Alex Carter were concealed somewhere within the walls.

Markham repressed a shudder and handed Mrs Yately the same list of gallery personnel he had shown to Jim McCleod.

'Can I ask you to run your eyes down that list and see if you recognize any of those names.'

'Certainly, Inspector.' She studied the paper with careful deliberation.

'I remember Mr Carstone. As I recall, he would have been in his late forties, early fifties.' She shook her head slowly. 'I really can't be sure about the others.'

Noakes's shoulders sagged.

She sensed they were deflated at her response.

'I'm sorry, gentlemen,' she said quietly. 'I can see this is important to you. My husband and I joined the *Friends of Greygarth*, helping to drum up support for various conservation projects. Mr Carstone was an energetic fundraiser and always very appreciative of local help.'

'Does the name Donald Lestrange mean anything to you?'

'Yes,' she replied with a wry smile. 'He was the nearest Greygarth got to its own resident celebrity . . . making a bit of a reputation as an art critic.'

'You said Greygarth was an artists' cooperative, Mrs Yately. Does that mean there was a community in residence there?'

She made a little moue.

'Perhaps not in the accepted sense of the word, Inspector. More of a floating population, you might say.'

Noakes perked up. 'So it was all fairly relaxed, then . . . no one monitoring comings and goings . . .'

'Well, I remember there was a visitors' book and a roster of student types who manned the gatehouse and helped out with the grounds but no one bothered much about security. There was always quite a lot of traffic through the house and nowhere was out of bounds.'

'Did people actually live in the property, as in stay overnight?'

'Yes, I believe so, Inspector. Renovations were very much a work in progress — fitted in round people's day jobs — but the bedrooms were habitable and outsiders could book a room provided they didn't mind having to "slum it."

Peter stayed over once or twice, but I wasn't up for roughing it.' She grinned. 'Too fond of my creature comforts.'

A short time later, back in the car, Markham quickly googled Greygarth House on his smartphone, the DS looking over his shoulder.

'Hmm.' The DI contemplated the elegant double-fronted Queen Anne property before scrolling through tasteful shots of banqueting and bedroom suites.

'All very *Pride and Prejudice*,' Noakes grunted. 'Can't see the DCI letting us spoil the party with cadaver dogs an' the like.'

Markham flexed his hands in front of him like a trapeze artist balancing on a wire, desperately looking for some object to steady himself.

'No,' he said bitterly. 'There's no likelihood of our being allowed to pollute the shades of Greygarth based on what we've got. Christ, I can almost hear Sidney going off on one now, "*Don't let flair lead you by the nose, Markham*!" It doesn't bear thinking about.'

Although it was only early afternoon, masses of cloud shone in the murky sky with a lurid light, like heaps of copper that had been heated in a furnace and was growing cold. There was something demonic about it, Markham reflected in his despondency.

Dark satanic mills, he told himself, his thoughts wandering to those grim industrial scenes back in the gallery.

'Pity Mrs Yately didn't recognize anyone, guv . . . I mean, apart from the old git.' He rolled his eyes. 'I mean, I don't see our Aubrey making human sacrifices down in the cellar or what have you.'

Markham grimaced.

'Hardly.' He stared moodily out of the window, remembering the relentless castle-building of his dreams. Now it seemed as though he was confronted by precipitous new heights, forced to scale them with ladders that were too short or ropes that swung and swayed as he clung to them . . . and all the time a figure moved inexorably away into the distance, its face livid and deadly . . . a figure that eluded his grasp.

'But we know there's a link with Greygarth House,' he said defiantly. 'That drawing of Donald Lestrange's with Alex Carter's name gave it away. That's why the killer went back to the archives room. In case there was anything else that was incriminating.'

Noakes's mind was running on suspects. 'Any of 'em could've been around Greygarth back then, guv,' he said thoughtfully. 'The place was like Piccadilly bleeding Circus. Mrs Yately said so herself. We jus' need another piece of the jigsaw.'

But in the meantime, the enemy's hiding place eluded them.

Down the road from the Land Registry stood the little squat church of St Mary the Virgin, its old grey spire surmounted by a cross standing out starkly against the horizon. Markham could almost fancy it looked down sorrowfully on the afternoon prospect as though lamenting the existence of those who cared nothing for the lesson which those emblems conveyed.

* * *

'Was it as bad as you expected, then?'

Olivia asked the question curled up next to her lover on the chesterfield in their living room at The Sweepstakes.

By mutual consent they had avoided the topic of the investigation during their evening meal, but now, with curtains drawn tight against the darkness, she felt able to broach the subject of the press conference.

'Sidney kept us moving like a brigade of skaters. You could see the press were fed up. It was one sodding platitude after another.'

'Nobody got bolshie?'

'No.' Markham sighed. 'I don't know what it was . . . respect for Ned, perhaps . . . but no one cut up rough, though there was quite a bit of muttering in corners.'

'Sounds like Barry Lynch earned his salary, then.' Olivia was no great admirer of the media officer who she felt availed himself rather too enthusiastically of the PR man's traditional licence to 'press the flesh.'

'Well, as he told me afterwards in that ghastly shopworn phrase of his, it "looks like we got away with it."'

Olivia giggled. 'Master of the cliché.'

'Well, he certainly gave the DCI a run for his money. They were both pretty nauseating, but it did the trick.' Unexpectedly, he laughed. 'I caught sight of Sidney's notes. He planned to finish off with "the darkest hour is just before the dawn" but must have baulked at the last minute . . . too pukeworthy even for him. As it was, Noakes wore that expression of his . . . you know, the one where he looks as though something's gone down the wrong way.'

Another giggle then Olivia turned serious.

'So, you've kept the Hydra at bay for now?'

'Well, there's no doubt we're in the last chance saloon. Afterwards, Sidney was making noises about the Yard taking over the case if we don't get results . . . like he couldn't keep a lid on it for much longer.'

'The papers haven't said all that much really,' Olivia said thoughtfully. 'Nothing about there being a serial killer on the loose or anything like that. The *Daily Post* made it sound like some sort of love triangle and there was no mention of Alex Carter. From what the *Sentinel* implied, it was a vendetta against the university . . . politically motivated.'

'Sidney's been calling in favours. Mission "Throwing Dust in the Public's Eyes." The last thing he wants is a repetition of last year's scandal at the Newman.'

'But now with Ned . . .'

'Yes. The awkward squad isn't going to be fobbed off with that "in-the-wrong-place-at-the-wrong-time" gambit for long.'

'On the news, Sidney almost made it sound like Ned had interrupted a burglary or something . . . without coming right out and saying it.'

'Not particularly convincing, was it?'

'To be honest, no. And the fact that he looked like a shifty snake oil salesman didn't help either.'

'In fairness, he's stalling for time. But he can't keep up the damage limitation for much longer.'

A bell tolled mournfully somewhere in the distance, recalling Markham's thoughts to the little church he had passed earlier on the road.

An hour nearer to death, an hour nearer to heaven or hell.

Olivia snuggled up with the fluid elegance of a Siamese cat.

'What's the plan for tomorrow, Gil?'

'A student demonstration at the gallery needs to be contained.'

'Should help with Mission Disinformation — playing up the political angle.'

'True.' Markham stretched luxuriously, savouring the cosy complicity. 'Plus, it gives us an opportunity to watch our gallery suspects while they believe we're looking elsewhere.'

'D'you think the killer's going to let something slip?'

'Makes me sound fey, Liv, but I can't help feeling we're very close now.' He cast a fond look at the delicate hopeful face turned towards his. 'The way Ned was killed suggests deep fear and paranoia.'

'You mean putting him in the suit of armour?'

'Yes . . . almost as if after the murder he wasn't really seeing Ned at all, but *himself* . . . as though he wanted to hide from the world behind that helmet . . . just the eyes peering out . . .'

'Someone at war with the world . . . always "on guard."'

'I knew you'd understand,' Markham said comfortably. Drawing her closer, he added, 'I've got Kate and Noakes lined up for library research duties tomorrow afternoon.'

'Can't imagine George being ecstatic about that.'

'He wasn't, but it was the library checks they did that cracked the Hope Academy case, remember.'

There was a smile in Olivia's voice as she said, 'In addition to cementing their *entente cordiale*.'

'Well, I think that's when they began to develop an appreciation of each other's . . . er, special qualities.'

'And George was really shaken when Kate was abducted last year. Suddenly looked like he'd aged ten years.'

Markham still had nightmares over the Newman investigation, unable to believe how close the team had come to losing Kate Burton.

'Let's just say normal service has been resumed and they're back to the love-hate relationship,' he said. A sudden impish grin lit up the sombre features. 'Noakesy's never at his best in academic settings, but Kate's learned how to handle him. So long as she keeps off the Pre-Raphaelites, they'll be all right.'

'I take it Kate's interested in the Skinny Lizzies.'

'Very much so.' Another grin. 'Though from a feminist perspective, you understand. Formed part of a module on *Sexual Stereotypes* in her MA.'

'Not much meeting of minds there, then . . .'

'Well, Noakes isn't totally anti-art. He volunteered some surprisingly perceptive comments on Lowry.'

'Ah, the working man's painter . . . all those gritty industrial scenes.'

'It was more Lowry's paintings of down-and-outs and grotesques which seemed to fascinate him actually.'

'Oh yes . . . vagrants with hunched backs, missing limbs and facial deformities . . . the tragic outsiders.'

'I overheard him telling Doyle it made him think . . . about how bad luck could happen to anyone and we're all just one step away from disaster.'

'"There but for the grace of God . . ."' she murmured. Then more lightly, 'How did Doyle receive this dose of philosophy from CID's resident philistine?'

'Oh, you know the youngster . . . didn't bat an eyelid . . . Lowry was a cricket and football fan — painted a crowd scene at Man City's Main Road Ground — so that makes him okay in Doyle's book.' Markham paused. 'To be honest, though, I think he felt the same way as Noakes did about the pictures of misfits and the people who'd lost their minds . .

. that there was something sordid and soulless in them . . . like the murderer . . .'

'Is that why you want to search the local records?' Olivia asked softly. 'To find the life event that produced a killer?'

'Sounds a bit desperate when you put it like that . . .'

'Not at all.' She squeezed his arm. 'I just hope there's a clue waiting there.'

Anxious to banish her lover's despondency, she turned the conversation into lighter channels.

'I'm quite partial to Lowry myself.'

'Really, Liv?'

'Yes. There was something endearingly . . . well, subversive about him . . . never became an establishment figure for all his eventual fame.'

'As I recall, he didn't really win success till quite late in life.'

'That's right. Worked as a rent collector till he was sixty-five.'

'Noakesy'd definitely approve of that. Real man of the people.'

'Oh yes. The story goes that when a posh lady arrived at his house asking to buy "a good painting," he told her "I only paint bad ones" and slammed the door in her face.'

'Better and better,' Markham chuckled. 'I'm rather warming to him myself.'

'I imagine Muriel's not a Lowry aficionado.'

'God no. Apparently abstract art's her thing.'

'In which case, she'll have *adored* how George came across on the telly. He looked like a walking example of pointillism gone wrong.'

'Don't remind me.' Markham groaned in mock horror. 'Sidney was simply furious about it. I meant to get Noakes into a different outfit, but . . .' he shrugged helplessly, 'he wasn't exactly cooperative. I thought he was going to punch the make-up artist when he suggested some pan stick.'

'Priceless. I bet Sidney loved all the fuss and salaaming, though.' She slipped into a cruel imitation of the DCI's supercilious honk. '"Which is my best side, Inspector?" Not a problem given the fact he's got two faces.'

'It comes with the territory, sweetheart,' Markham observed pacifically. 'I'm just grateful to be spared all of that.'

'Oh, there was no question of letting the number two steal his thunder, Gil. Strictly the support act, that's you.'

'And more than happy for it to stay that way.'

She shot him a contrite look. 'I know, dearest, I know.' Then lovingly, she suggested, 'What about a nightcap and then something lowbrow on the box . . . I think we've had enough high-minded conversation for one night.'

The lovers settled down together while across the city Bromgrove Art Gallery slumbered uneasily under the eye of night.

And meanwhile a murderer awaited, wakeful and watchful, the advent of morning.

* * *

'Who tipped off *Bromgrove News*?'

Noakes scowled at Burton and Doyle as though he held them personally responsible.

'Not guilty, sarge,' came the laconic reply from Doyle. Yawning, he observed the motley group of bobble-hatted students as they marched slowly up and down the pavement outside the gallery doing their best to look unconscious of the television crew on the other side of the road.

'For fuck's sake, this is all we bloody well need . . . long-haired layabouts prancing around like they're on some flaming reality TV show.' Blowing on icy fingers the colour of chopped liver, the DS stamped his feet to restore circulation while casting baleful glances in the direction of the youthful protestors.

'Actually, sarge, with that duffle coat and Doctor Who scarf, you could go over and blend right in.'

Shooting the DC a dirty look, Noakes gestured towards the gallery where faces clustered curiously at windows.

'Like we're gonna get anywhere with this three-ring circus caterwauling out here . . .'

Kate Burton, sensibly but smartly clad in a beige blanket coat, tailored black trousers and suede ankle boots, remained composed.

'It'll likely work in our favour, sarge,' she said equably. 'I mean, draws the heat away from the gallery . . . gets everyone focusing on the university.'

'It's a frigging distraction, that's what it is.'

'But a useful diversionary tactic,' commented a calm voice.

The DI had come up unobserved behind them.

Eyes narrowed against the wintry sunshine, he appraised the television unit.

'Just three of them,' he murmured. 'Nice and unobtrusive. Perfect.'

'Whaddya mean *perfect*?' In Noakes's eyes, the media were enemy Numero Uno.

'Perfect for having them do some background shots and so forth inside the gallery . . . keeping eyes on our suspects without them realizing.'

'You think the killer might break cover, sir?'

'I think there's a chance, Kate . . . especially if they're lulled into a false sense of security by seeing us taken up with the students.'

'What if we got something on camera . . . I mean, like *hard evidence* . . .' Doyle was enthused.

The DI was determinedly objective. 'I'm not optimistic about our chances of that,' he said quietly. 'But the crew might capture something we've missed.'

'What do we tell the gallery crowd, then?'

'We stay low-key, Noakes. Give them some spiel about letting local news place the student demonstrations *in context* . . . a chance for some sympathetic journalism . . . redressing the balance, that kind of thing.'

Ned would have known how to play it, he thought sadly.

'I want them distracted . . . off-kilter,' he said with increasing conviction.

Off guard.

'Sometimes when you're too close to the action, you miss things,' the DI continued. 'Think of the camera crew as a fresh pair of eyes.'

The sound of some muted chanting floated over to them. '*Hands off our culture!*' Half-frozen hands waved placards which read: No More Cuts.

'Up the revolution!' mocked Noakes. 'Power to the people!'

Doyle smirked. 'We shall overcome!' he carolled before subsiding beneath a withering glance from the DI.

'That's enough,' Markham rapped. 'Noakes, you and Kate can set things up with the TV crew.' He turned to Doyle. 'Constable, I'd like you to speak to Cathy Hignett and whoever else you can find and see if they can organize some hot drinks and snacks for the students.' He glanced at his watch. 'Only ten o'clock, so maybe we'll have more along in due course.'

'You must be joking,' Noakes retorted. 'They'll all be sleeping off last night's ale like as not.'

'In which case, it'll be a very orderly and well-mannered demonstration.' The DI was firm. 'The crew can do some filming out here . . . perhaps an interview with whoever's in charge.' He pointed to a bespectacled beanpole of a lad who, red-nosed and listlessly brandishing a megaphone, was hardly anyone's idea of Che Guevara. 'That one looks good for a few soundbites. Then they can quietly disperse.'

'And once it's fizzled out, we move the TV unit into the gallery, sir?' Burton clearly chafed at wasting time on a damp squib demonstration.

'That's right . . . but we need to dress it up as some kind of PR exercise.'

'We can make out it's a community initiative, sir . . . You know, people getting behind the gallery before it reopens next week.'

'Good, Kate.' Markham rubbed his eyes which were suddenly stinging in a sharp wind that had whipped up from nowhere. 'You can talk about TV doing some tracking shots and talking heads stuff for *Bromgrove Roundup* . . . nothing to do with the murder investigation, just a local news feature . . . cuts in arts funding . . . preserve our heritage for future generations . . . foster appreciation of cultural diversity . . .'

'You'd be a natural at politics, guv,' Noakes said admiringly. 'Got it all off pat.'

'Must be the DCI's lessons paying off,' his boss replied glumly.

'Folk love getting their faces on telly.' Doyle jerked a thumb towards the gallery. 'They'll all want a piece of the action, you can bank on it.'

'All the better for us. With their defences lowered, something might slip out.'

'We can ask to see the camera footage too, sir,' Burton said brightly. 'Check out the body language.' She was evidently keen to try out some insights from her Psychology degree, thought Markham, suppressing a smile. He noticed the other two exchange wary glances. The prospect of a session exploring human behavioural traits with their colleague was clearly not one they relished. In fact, judging by the expression on Noakes's face, it was probable he considered root canal work without anaesthetic preferable to hearing Kate Burton bang on about the neurobiology of crime suspects. Wisely, however, the DS held his peace.

'Excellent idea, Kate. You can be responsible for reviewing whatever they shoot today.' The DI's glance fell on the Central Library. 'But before that, I want you and Noakes to check out local records in their archives department . . . like you did in the Hope Academy investigation.'

Noakes's resemblance to a dyspeptic bulldog was more than usually pronounced, but Markham affected not to notice.

'Go back a few decades before the Carter abduction.' Markham gulped down cold damp air as though it was medicinal. 'Human interest stories . . . anything connected with the gallery . . . local colour, scandal, gossip about the staff . . . it's got to be in there . . . Here's the thing,' he looked at them squarely, 'Doyle and I will go over all the statements again with a fine toothcomb, but I don't think we can nail the killer that way . . . they've been too careful.'

A creeping numbness was making its way up from his feet. Time to wrap this up.

Succinctly, he updated Burton and Doyle on the outcome of the visit to the Land Registry.

'*Jesus*.' The young DC's face had a greenish tinge. 'D'you think Alex Carter's buried in this Greygarth place then, sir?' He looked sick. 'Shoved behind a wall like a pile of rubble.'

'I'm keeping an open mind, Constable.'

Which is more than DCI bloody Sidney would be doing, he thought viciously. Any hint that Markham was circling civic institutions as opposed to student riff-raff would send his boss batshit, but looking at the ragtag assembly of dispirited undergraduates the DI was more than ever convinced the answer to the gallery murders lay elsewhere.

'Hey up.' Noakes's voice broke into his thoughts. 'Bandits at six o'clock.'

Rebecca Summerson came pitapatting across the snow towards them.

The facilities manager certainly looked a great deal healthier than of late, as though some haze had dissolved and her surroundings had at last swum into focus. The DI suspected her relationship with Helen Melville had involved a certain amount of emotional abuse, while the complicated triangle with Charles Randall only compounded her confusion.

Were those deaths rooted in an unhealthy sexual dynamic that had nothing to do with the mystery of Alex Carter's disappearance, he wondered in a sudden spasm of self-mistrust.

Had he been so beguiled by all the talk of *aediculae* and secrets, that he had somehow blundered off the straight path into a succession of anterooms and passages which led nowhere?

No, he told himself. *No*. Whatever unwholesome currents eddied around the gallery, the long-ago disappearance of that little boy was somehow at the root of it all. Donald Lestrange. The Anchorage. Greygarth. Everything led to that diminutive figure at the heart of the maze . . .

'Mr Westbrook called in sick this morning, Inspector, but otherwise there's a full complement.' The facilities manager frowned slightly. 'And Bill Hignett seems to have gone walkabout—'

'When was that?' Markham's voice was sharp, all his senses alert.

'I'll have to check with Cathy,' was the vague reply. 'It's the sort of thing he does from time to time.'

But not in the middle of a serial murder investigation.

Markham gritted his teeth.

Easy, he told himself, *easy*.

He turned to Doyle, eyes flicking an urgent signal.

'Constable, I'd like you to check with Bill's mum right away please.'

The tall gangling figure moved smartly towards the gallery.

'I'm sure you're right, Ms Summerson, and there's no cause for alarm,' he said levelly. 'But with Bill being a vulnerable adult, in the current circumstances I think it would be wise to have him accounted for.'

'Of course, Inspector.' She looked across at Noakes's 'barmy army' and the television crew. 'Are you expecting some sort of trouble?' she asked uncertainly.

Markham forced a laugh.

'Oh, I don't think anyone needs to man the barricades just yet.' A weaselly-looking member of the crew was growing visibly impatient. '*Bromgrove News* are just going to do a short feature on student concerns about cuts to the arts, and then they want to do some filming inside,' he nodded significantly at Burton and Noakes. 'Maybe get a few quotes from staff on funding and your plans for the future.' Avuncularly, he added, 'Nothing about recent events, naturally . . . Call it a vote of confidence in the gallery before you reopen next week.'

Burton gave him a discreet thumbs up. Looked like he'd blagged his way out of it.

'Right, officers . . . if you would,' he said, gesturing to the small crowd which seemed to be waiting for something to happen. 'Perhaps we should leave them to it, Ms Summerson, before frostbite sets in.'

* * *

As they walked towards the gallery, Markham thought he saw something shift at one of the upper windows. Something bat-like that for a moment seemed to blot out the winter sun.

Then it was gone and all he saw was the glassy reflection of clouds scudding across the cold, grey sky. Like dream shapes racing to some appointed end.

Dies irae, dies illa . . . . . .

13. DEADLY PERIL

The library's local records section was adjacent to its impressive Round Reading Room.

Recalling, from the Hope Academy investigation, that this was one feature of the building which met with Noakes's approval, Kate Burton lingered for some minutes, contemplating its ornate Edwardian grandeur.

'S'like an aquarium,' her colleague whispered as they surveyed the circular interior with its domed ceiling and wrought iron spiral staircases leading to rows and rows of old oak shelves. 'All still and echoey . . . An underwater paradise.' Smiling bashfully, he added, 'You half expect dolphins an' exotic fish are gonna come swimming past.'

Trying not to laugh at the analogy, Burton nodded agreement.

'That's how I used to feel whenever I came in here to work for my A levels, sarge,' she said. 'Like I was on the ocean floor . . . far away from everything, and nothing could disturb me.'

'Yeah, dead peaceful.'

Noakes couldn't help wondering how his daughter, Natalie, had somehow managed to escape the spell of the Reading Room despite apparently spending vast swathes of time immured in scholastic seclusion. All's well that ends well, he told himself. A levels weren't everything. Nat had a good steady job as an apprentice beauty therapist at Bromgrove's *Lifestyle Collective*, and no need of further education. But looking around at the regiments of books lined up behind gilt balustrades and all the silent students hunched over leather-tooled tomes under a huge ormolu clock, he felt an obscure sense of loss.

Their own destination was a small office within an airless linoleum-floored modern complex which had about as much character as a Holiday Inn, he reflected crossly.

To makes matters worse, that hideous crone from last time was bearing down on them with a determined look in her eye.

'Sarge, you remember Miss Todd who gave us so much help on the Hope Academy investigation.'

Don't I just. His heart sank at the sight of the librarian in 'good citizen' mode.

Why'd they always look like frigging prison warders? he asked himself, taking in the severely cropped hair and dreary beige two-piece. God, he needed a double strength latte before he could face the old witch . . .

'Tell you what, sarge,' Burton said, registering the look of almost terminal gloom on her colleague's face, 'why don't you pop downstairs to Costa and have a quick drink before getting started. In the meantime, I'll explain what we need so Miss Todd can set us up on the microfilm readers.' She flashed the older woman a propitiatory smile. 'Sergeant Noakes noticed the *Book Art Fair* exhibition on the way up . . . he's just looking for an excuse to check it out.' Wickedly, she added, 'He's got a real interest in the Pre-Raphaelites.'

Noakes assumed what he fondly imagined was an intellectual air. Unfortunately, the resulting effect made him look cross-eyed.

'Uh-huh,' he muttered, desperately trying to recall the contents of the Victorian room in the gallery next door. 'All them, er, myths an' legends . . . amazing . . .'

'The Arthurian connection,' Burton interposed helpfully.

'Exzackly.' He swallowed gratefully. 'Knights of the Round Table an' that.'

Miss Todd was more frightening when she smiled, he decided, doing his best not to look at the vast expanse of gum.

'Oh, in that case you'll really enjoy the display on Rossetti's illustrations for *The Lady of Shalott*, Sergeant.'

God. It meant he'd have to look at this cruddy woman, whoever she was. No doubt some droopy creature lying around half-dressed with everything hanging out so decent folk didn't know where to look . . .

He could swear bloody Kate Burton was *enjoying* this. But at least she was playing along. Probably looking forward to some highbrow chit-chat with the old battle-axe. Well sod that for a game of soldiers. 'Right then,' he said heartily, engaging in some dumb show calculated to express eager enthusiasm for the building's cultural — as opposed to comestible — goodies before sidling towards the exit.

His colleague grinned as she watched him depart. No doubt she would be required to ad-lib again when he reappeared. Though on reflection, it might be fun to watch him squirm under Miss Todd's crossfire.

Unlike Noakes, she found the desiccated librarian a congenial reminder of carefree times as a student, so that for a moment she wished herself back in the safety of the academic bubble, far removed from the squalid reality of man's inhumanity to man.

Nostalgia ain't what it used to be, she told herself with a barely perceptible shrug, consigning thoughts of buoyant college days to the back-burner . . .

Once settled at the microfilm reader, her thoughts turned to the DI.

Ned Chester, she sensed, had been a member of what she privately termed Markham's Magic Circle — the vanishingly small group of intimates her tall aloof boss allowed into the inner sanctum of his emotional world . . . a world to which she knew instinctively Noakes belonged but to which she herself as yet possessed no pass key.

No Admittance. No Admittance.

The soundtrack to her story with Markham.

To her horror she found her cheeks were wet, and angrily scrubbed them with the back of her sleeve. Mercifully Miss Todd, behind her desk on the other side of the room, was busy answering the telephone.

C'mon, she told herself fiercely, this is no time to be so fucking *selfish*. Ned going like that . . . it's ripped the boss's insides out . . .

By no means normally inclined to flights of the imagination, she found herself desperately hoping that the reporter with his languid smile and heartbreaker's charm never saw the end coming — that he was somehow still there with them on the case. If she half closed her eyes, she could almost fancy she saw him leaning against the door urging her on . . .

The librarian had finished her telephone conversation and was looking at her curiously.

Time to get a grip. She mimed a vigorous thumbs up before turning her attention to the newspaper records.

Noakes had compared the Round Reading Room to an aquarium, she recalled. Well, she and the team formed a shoal of an entirely different kind . . . as if they were swimming around the souls of Helen Melville, Charles Randall and Ned Chester, trying to protect them from all the terrors of the deep . . . trying to avenge their slaughter by the dead-eyed shark masquerading as a member of the human race.

Resolutely, she squared her shoulders and set to work.

* * *

Forty minutes later, some instinct made her look up.

Noakes was hovering shiftily in the doorway.

'It's all right,' she grinned. 'Miss Todd got called away to Reprographics. And then she's got a meeting in Rare Books.'

'Thank Christ for that.' Her colleague shambled over and sank into a chair. 'I thought she'd be waiting to give me the third degree on that Lady of the Lake bollocks.'

'*The Lady of Shalott*,' Burton replied patiently. 'There was a curse put on her and . . . never mind,' she said watching Noakes's eyes glaze over at the prospect of a mini-lecture.

'Whatever,' he sighed. 'I jus' knew it was bound to be some load of hocus pocus like that. Beats me why folk are so hung up on all them poxy fairy stories.'

'I suppose because it offers an escape from everyday reality, sarge,' she said mildly.

'Yeah, well that's half the trouble these days . . . people living in cloud cuckoo land instead of making do with what they've got.'

To her surprise, Burton experienced something close to affection listening to George Noakes's prescription for happiness. There was something blessedly normal about his world view, which felt like an ever-fixed bulwark in the face of encroaching evil. Perhaps that was the secret of his seeming unshakeable bond with the DI.

'Anyway,' he said, shelving further philosophical nostrums for the time being. 'Any joy with the local rags?'

Burton knuckled her eyes. Fortunately, since she favoured a make-up free look, there was no risk of mascara running. Her usually bouncy bob looked dry and tired.

'Not as yet, sarge.'

'No sexual shenanigans? Thought our mate Traherne might be good for summat in that line . . .'

She shook her head.

'One of the catering staff brought a race discrimination claim against the trustees in 2005 . . . that's the only negative story I've come across . . . And even then, the employee lost at tribunal, so the gallery came out of it smelling of roses . . .'

'Fingers in the till . . . financial scandals?' Noakes enquired hopefully.

'Not a dicky bird.' Her voice was dispirited. 'And we never got anything from the gallery accounts, so if there *was* anything of that sort, they covered their tracks well.'

'Nothing new on the weirdy paintings that went missing . . . the ones CID never traced, 'bout folk being locked up?'

Another disconsolate shake of the head.

'Nowt about any of the gallery staff?' Stubbornly, he persisted. 'Shagging on the job . . . Managers banging the help . . . Bullying . . . Bust-ups with visitors . . . ?'

'If there *was* anything, sarge, then it didn't find its way into the papers.'

'How far back have you reached?' After two latte macchiatos and a danish, Noakes was disposed to be magnanimous.

'2000.'

'An' the boss wants us to go back as far as the 1970s . . . let's say the 1960s to be on the safe side.' His face fell. 'That's a tall order all right.'

Burton fished around in her capacious bag and came up with a pair of horn-rimmed glasses that she jammed firmly on her nose, as though digging in for the long haul. They made her eyes look enormous.

Noakes recoiled slightly as though encountering Miss Todd's twin.

'What's with the spooky specs?' he asked faintly.

'I only have to wear them occasionally.' Her voice was defensive. 'If I'm at the screen for a long time.'

'Well, looks like you'll be needing them today, then.'

'Any news of Bill Hignett, sarge?'

'The guvnor's really antsy, but they're still checking out Hignett's usual hidey-holes. Mum's not the sharpest tool in the box, so it's like pulling teeth.' Mixed metaphors with Noakes were a sure sign of frustration. 'Missing Persons is on it.' The DS's tone didn't suggest he held this department in overly high esteem. And given what they had learned during the Newman Hospital investigation about huge gaping cracks in the care system, Burton couldn't find it in her heart to blame him.

'Right.' He tugged off the horribly discordant tweed jacket and tie and rolled up his sleeves. 'I'm on this one, am I?' He gestured at the microfilm reader next to Burton's. 'You're sure the Todd creature ain't coming back any time soon?' he enquired with a shudder.

'Relax, sarge. I reckon you're safe for the day.' A chuckle escaped Burton. 'Though I'm sure she'll want to catch up with you about those engravings.'

Noakes's scowl suggested he regarded a lingering death in boiling oil as being infinitely preferable to any such prospect.

'Jus' show me the hang of it an' I'll get cracking.'

'That one's got the *Sentinel* and the *Recorder*. So if you'll check what's on there while I go on with the others . . .'

'Righto.'

'We can do printouts of anything that looks promising.' Burton was soon in her element demonstrating the wonders of modern technology. Her demonstration concluded, there was no sound for some time afterwards but the subdued hum of machinery, the rhythmic click of reels turning over and an occasional spluttered curse from Noakes as he inadvertently skipped several pages at once.

* * *

After two hours of fruitless endeavour, by mutual consent the two detectives decided to take a break, Burton happily acquiescing to the suggestion that they should adjourn to Costa on the ground floor while inwardly lamenting the fact that vegan smoothies were unlikely to feature on the menu. Miss Todd having entrusted her with a laminated key fob, they were able to lock the office behind them, leaving everything as it was.

Burton could see Noakes enjoyed riding the escalators, gazing about in childlike wonder at the acres of gleaming chrome, pine and tinted glass, no doubt a far cry from the fusty library interiors of his youth. She noted with amusement that he averted his eyes hastily from the *Book Art Fair* banners as though half expecting his nemesis Miss Todd might jump out from behind them.

Despite it being a Saturday, Costa was peaceful and practically deserted. Of course, the weather would doubtless have put paid to the usual influx of visitors, she concluded. To say nothing of the murders next door.

She made no demur when Noakes took charge of ordering the refreshments. On the rare occasions that he was not bugging the hell out of her, his company could be rather soothing. In a cosy corner, with lattes and chocolate muffins arrayed before them, he looked as though life could hold no higher bliss. Even in a triple homicide where their enquiries were going nowhere fast.

Maybe that's what I need to do, she told herself. Live in the moment. 'Do a Noakes.'

It was getting dark outside, blue-black twilight stealing across the library forecourt towards the atrium where the coffee shop was situated. She gave a start at her own image reflected spectrally back at her in the floor-to-ceiling plate-glass window.

'Evening all.'

DC Doyle appeared at their table and flopped heavily into one of the trendy tub chairs.

''Lo mate,' said Noakes through a mouthful of double chocolate chip. 'Any news of Bill Hignett?'

'Nada.' The young detective looked weary, the energy in his face dimmed to about three-quarter strength.

Burton frowned. 'Who saw him last?'

'That's just it, no one seems to know.' He grimaced. 'The DCI's cock-a-hoop . . . wants Hignett named prime suspect.'

'Fuck-a-doodle-do. You're telling me Sidney seriously thinks that poor sod could've pulled off those three murders.'

'I know, sarge, I know, but you have to admit there's something iffy about him doing a disappearing act.'

'Maybe he got spooked . . . afraid they'd pin this on him,' Burton ventured.

'Well, he got that bit right.' Noakes sounded disgusted. 'Typical bleeding Sidney. Plumps for Nutters 'R' Us an' hey presto it's case closed.'

'The boss is in a Gold Group meeting now.'

'Fat lot of good that'll do . . . shovelling shit from on high.' The other pushed away his plate as though he had suddenly lost his appetite. Burton too felt sick at the thought of Markham stuck in a room with the top brass, politicking and bargaining to save the investigation. She could imagine how he would look . . . chiselled features, rigid as those of an effigy on some medieval crusader's tomb, masking his disdain for a 'quick fix.'

Her head hurt trying to absorb it all, and she felt a sudden irrational urge to lie down in the crisp cold snow outside and go to sleep . . .

Dammit, she couldn't check out now. Discreetly, she fumbled in her shoulder bag for some Nurofen. She'd slug a few when Noakes and Doyle were looking the other way.

'What's the boss want us to do?'

Doyle pushed a jiffy bag across the table to Burton.

'That's the film from this morning. You've got footage of the students doing their thing outside and material shot inside the gallery.'

Her headache was intensifying by the minute.

'Thanks,' she said listlessly. 'I'll check it out once we've finished going through the newspaper stuff.'

Looking at her white strained face, Noakes expressed his sympathy in the only way he knew how.

'Lemme get you a top-up,' he said with clumsy bonhomie. 'Don't want you conking out on us.' And with that, he shuffled off to the counter and a spot of banter with the peroxide blonde examining her fingernails, who promptly brightened up at the attention.

'I c'n have a look first if it'd help, sarge.' Doyle too was doing his best to muster some esprit de corps.

Burton dredged up a smile.

'No, you're all right,' she said. 'Appreciate the offer, though.' She stifled a yawn. 'Can't imagine there's anything useful on there.' Her earlier idea of checking out the body language had lost its shine. 'You didn't notice anything unusual, I suppose?'

'Nah. Just boffin talk really . . . Bramwell giving it the great "I Am" while the rest jockeyed for position in the background.' He smiled slyly. 'I was right about them wanting to be on the telly. Even the catering lot had fresh pinnies all round. And a couple of the security guards were prancing about like they thought it was a remake of *The Thomas Crown Affair*.'

His colleague chuckled, her mood lifting.

'Well, you never know,' she said with a shrug. 'Once I'm bored of the newspaper cuttings, I'll give it a whirl. What'll you be up to in the meantime?'

'I'd better get back next door. Someone from Family Liaison's with Cathy Hignett.' He pulled a face. 'I'm not looking forward to her reaction when she finds out that Bill's in the frame for three murders.'

'And maybe Alex Carter too.'

'God.' He looked at her disbelievingly. 'It won't come to that, will it? I mean Hignett's not all there and couldn't organize his way out of a paper bag.'

Their colleague was back at the table with drinks for the three of them. Burton winced when she took a mouthful of hers. There was so much sugar, she could almost feel cavities forming on the spot. Observing, however, that the DS was watching her shyly out of the corner of his eye, she feigned delight. 'Perfect!' she exclaimed, 'I really needed that.' She could tell Noakes was pleased, though as usual he took resort in gruffness.

'Have you two geniuses decided who dunnit, then?'

Disconsolate shakes of the head.

Throwing caution to the winds, Burton knocked back the Nurofen. Her colleagues looked very much as though they wished they could do the same.

'If Sidney's dead set on Hignett, then we have to come up with something fast,' Noakes ruminated. 'Trouble being, we've got sweet FA.'

'What if Hignett's been helping someone?' Burton said slowly.

The other two stared at her. 'Like who?' Noakes asked flatly.

She gulped down more too-sweet macchiato.

'Someone who's stayed well back in the shadows . . . Someone who had a hold on Donald Lestrange . . .'

Doyle sat up straighter. 'You mean as an accomplice in the Carter abduction?'

'Accomplice . . . accessory after the fact . . . reluctant bystander . . . God knows. But one thing's for sure. Our man — or woman — held Lestrange fast. Trapped. Who's to say Hignett wasn't caught in the spider's web too?'

Noakes rumpled his hair savagely so that it stood on end in stiff little spikes. Not a good look, thought Burton idly. More Ben Gunn than *Miami Vice*. She repressed a rising urge to giggle.

'D'you remember Hignett being specially matey with anyone?' her fellow DS asked.

'Nobody in particular,' she admitted, her tone defeated. 'There're a few people he's good with.'

'But not to really talk to, as in proper buddies like,' Noakes pressed.

'No, that's true. But he may have been instructed by the killer to keep his distance at work, especially once we came on the scene.'

'Would he be bright enough to stick to a plan?' Doyle was doubtful.

'Or keep it from his mum?' Noakes put in.

'I think he might,' Burton replied, absently stirring her gloopy drink. 'Low-functioning autism doesn't rule out basic cunning . . . or self-preservation. If he's highly suggestible, the killer might have hit pay dirt.'

The other two looked unconvinced, but Noakes looked at the hollowed-out, peaky girl in front of him and spoke kindly. 'Might be summat in it,' he said. 'Hignett's got the brawn all right, an' if someone else was the brains . . .' Turning to Doyle, he added, 'Dig around a bit more.'

The DC looked put-upon but nodded.

Noakes scratched his bristly chin. 'Didn't you say something a while back about folk making complaints cos Hignett was perving?'

'Yeah,' agreed the DC warily. 'Didn't come to anything, though. Something and nothing . . .'

'See if there's paperwork, anything in HR. Find out: did anyone speak up for him, volunteer to help with mentoring or whatever they call it.'

'There's the Disability Employment lot down at the council.' Doyle's expression said he was clutching at straws but prepared to suffer for the cause. 'If I don't get anywhere with Rebecca Summerson, they might stump up.'

'Give it your best shot, lad,' Noakes urged with Olympian condescension. He wheeled round to Burton. 'Right, luv, reckon it's time for round two.'

Doyle watched as his colleagues wended their way towards the escalators.

The old devil was making a real effort with Kate Burton, he concluded as he observed Noakes's arm shoot out to steady the younger woman. Despite her highfalutin claptrap, she wasn't so bad when you came to think of it. Prepared to sweat blood if it meant finding a killer.

Their figures disappeared out of sight. He felt curiously unwilling to see them go.

No time to get sentimental, he admonished himself before heading for the exit.

* * *

The wall clock in Miss Todd's office said 5.30 p.m.

'Don't time jus' fly when you're having fun,' Noakes commented grumpily as they settled themselves back down at the microfilm readers.

Burton turned to face him.

'Will they blame the boss for this, sarge . . . the fact that we haven't got anyone yet?'

Her heart was on her lips.

Instead of feeling exasperated or contemptuous, Noakes was surprised by a certain reluctant tenderness which stole over him.

Wonder if that boring fiancé of hers knows she's carrying a torch for the boss, he thought.

Well-accustomed to women falling like ninepins for Markham, he sensed that Burton's devotion was somehow different . . . purer . . . like they were on some sort of quest together.

He blinked at himself in surprise for coming over all poetical. Must be all that baloney about King Arthur rubbing off on him. God, much more of it and he'd be able to give the old bat Miss Todd a run for her money after all.

He cleared his throat. 'The boss knows what he's doing, luv. We're only a week in, an' this ain't your run-of-the-mill enquiry, what with Carter an' all the other stuff.'

'They're all so jealous of him, sarge, the higher-ups . . . just waiting to see him get his comeuppance.' Her face was very red now. 'Like crocodiles in one of those David Attenborough documentaries.'

'Well he's got you, me and Doyle in his corner, luv. The A-Team.' His voice surprisingly gentle, he added, 'He's weathered worse than this — an',' a note of pride crept into his voice, 'his clearance rate's better'n anyone else at his rank.' An awkward pat on the arm. ''Sides, Sidney owes him big style.' And loves him none the better for it. But Noakes kept that reflection to himself. 'C'mon,' he said, 'let's give this another crack an' if we haven't got anywhere in an hour or so we'll call it a day.'

'Deal.'

Diligently, they ploughed on, looking for all the world like a couple of ill-assorted amateur folklorists digging back into the past.

An hour and a half later, backs and eyes aching, they were forced to admit defeat. Noakes had clearly reached saturation point when it came to the North West cultural scene. 'Pretentious old farts the lot of them,' he said, then looked round guiltily as though one of the anathematized species might be lying in wait to ambush him.

Burton grinned weakly. For once they were 'on the same page.'

'It's heavy going, that's for sure,' she agreed.

They looked at each other, savouring the rare moment of uncomplicated amity.

'You look knackered, sarge. And we can't sit here all night. Besides,' she smiled tremulously, 'the boss'll be needing you back at base.'

It was a generous admission borne of the fact that Burton felt she had mysteriously arrived at some understanding of their respective places in Markham's heart.

Noakes looked at her wan, vulnerable little face.

Christ, he thought, she looks about twelve. He knew it wasn't 'feminist' or 'woke' or whatever they called it these days, but at times like this he couldn't help wishing she was safely tucked away in some department where they didn't have to deal with sick bastards and wackjobs.

'What about you?' he asked. 'Won't your fella be expecting you? Reckon you've earned a chippy tea with your feet up in front of the telly.'

'He's on a course in Hendon this weekend.' Her voice was dull, inflection-less. 'Corporate crime and market abuse. So, it's baked beans out of a tin for me, and only the cat for company.'

'The missus does spag bol Saturdays.' Noakes looked suddenly embarrassed at this culinary one-upmanship. 'You'd be welcome . . . I mean she makes loads . . . always room for one more . . .'

Burton was touched. 'That's really kind,' she said sincerely. 'But it's family time and Mrs Noakes will want you to herself for a bit.' She gestured to the microfilm reader. 'I'll hang on a while longer, skim some more. If I print stuff off, I won't have to do it all here.' She tapped the jiffy bag Doyle had given her. 'I can have a popcorn moment later, see what the TV people got in the can.'

'Rather you than me, luv.' Noakes eyed the package with disfavour. 'Bramwell an' the rest of 'em showing off . . . Ugh!'

'It won't be a barrel of laughs,' she conceded. 'You'll think I'm mad, sarge. Call it superstition, but I can't help feeling there must be some way of telling who it is . . . some tell-tale sign . . . Maybe they caught it on camera . . . Guilt . . . fear . . . hatred . . . *Something*.'

'Whoever it is, they're a dab hand at hiding what they feel.' Noakes's face was grave. 'And that makes 'em dangerous.'

'D'you think Bill Hignett's come to harm, sarge?'

'If you're right about him being part of this . . . then he could be a threat . . . a risk . . .'

'But Bill's a poor soul. Harmless.'

'Maybe not to the killer.'

Kate was aware of a screaming noise in her throat. She felt an underwater blur of terror.

'We've got to find him.' Her speech seemed to have thickened.

Noakes looked at her with something approaching concern.

'We're on it,' he said firmly. 'You finish up here an' get off home, otherwise you'll be fit for nowt tomorrow.'

He lumbered towards the door and peeped into the corridor.

'Coast's clear.'

He was about to make his getaway when something prompted him to look back.

'Sure you'll be okay?' He didn't like leaving Burton in the sterile little office. Around them the rest of the library was eerily quiet, like a slumbering leviathan of the deep.

'I'll be fine.' His colleague plastered on a bright smile. 'You get back to HQ.' She made a show of looking at her watch. 'I'll make tracks in another hour or so.' She forced a laugh. 'Anyway, you know me and libraries, sarge . . . home from home.'

Reassured, he winked and vanished with a cheery wave.

Relieved of the need to put on a front, Burton slumped in her chair. The headache was back along with a nagging conviction that she couldn't go just yet . . . *had* to give it one last push. She just couldn't believe that their killer had covered the trail so completely as to leave no trace.

'First rule of forensics,' she muttered to herself. 'Locard's Principle. The perpetrator always leaves something behind. *Always.*'

Head down, shoulders hunched, she pored over the microfilm records with renewed intensity.

* * *

Forty minutes later. 'Oh my God.'

Just three words. The merest thread of a whisper.

Burton shook her head as though her vision was indistinct.

Then she craned forward avidly, drinking in the contents of the screen for dear life.

When she had finished, she got to her feet and began to pace the office restlessly in a manner reminiscent of her boss.

After the initial elation, self-doubt assailed her.

It was a story all right. A secret that hadn't come to light until now.

But one that didn't necessarily mean anything. Didn't automatically make a killer.

Unless . . . unless . . .

No. It just didn't make sense. And where did Bill Hignett fit in?

It might be a lead of sorts, but the DCI wouldn't entertain it for a moment.

Her brain was fragmented, unable to join pieces of the puzzle.

The office felt oxygenless. Like that underwater world Noakes had described when they were in the Round Reading Room.

Atlantis, she thought on a rising wave of hysteria.

For a moment, she wished fervently that she really was floating on the ocean floor, with only the sound of breathing and bubbles, fish gliding sleekly by, beautiful and peaceful — electric blue, bright yellow, stripy, spotty, silver — and not another human in sight.

Sweat broke out on her forehead. Am I coming down with something, she wondered. Of all the times for it to happen . . .

Suddenly giddy, she groped her way back to the microfilm reader and sat down once more.

What to do?

She reached for the mobile in her bag and then slowly withdrew her hand.

Noakes and Doyle were busy about their own tasks. Suddenly, she was transported back to police training college, listening to the instructor. Time to 'take ownership.' Think for herself.

The gallery was right next door. She'd nip back to the incident room and check the witness statements with a toothcomb. One person's in particular. Her gaze fell on the jiffy bag. She'd play back the TV footage while she was at it, looking for some betraying slip that might help nail a killer.

With shaking hands, she pressed 'Print' and scooped up copies of a grainy article. Then she scribbled a note of thanks for Miss Todd and left it on her desk along with the librarian's key fob.

Outside the building, the freezing air cut through her like a knife. But the clean sharp pain was almost welcome, her mind suddenly clearer.

Her discovery was something the DI really ought to know about.

She reached once more for the mobile and this time dialled Markham's number. It went straight to answerphone.

'Sir, it's Kate. Er . . . Don't know if you're still in meetings . . . er . . .' She began to stutter. God, why hadn't she planned what to say beforehand. She tried again. 'I've come across something in the newspaper records . . . a piece about one of the gallery staff . . . something they hadn't told us . . .' Feeling foolish at her disjointed rambling, she endeavoured to sound cool and collected. 'Probably best if we speak in person, sir. I'm just going to finish up in the incident room and I'll check in again after that.'

That was better. Didn't want him thinking her a total moron.

The gallery loomed up before her, stark and crystalline. A real ghostly galleon.

For a moment, she hesitated. Should she wait for Noakes or Doyle before going in?

Then, impatiently, she chastised herself. She had her passkey and the DI had arranged two night patrol officers, so there was nothing to fear. Plus, no one knew what she'd found out. She'd type a quick précis for Markham and then whiz through the videotape. In and out in under an hour tops. After that, back to the station. For all she knew, they'd located Bill Hignett or made a breakthrough. Now her racing thoughts were calmer, it seemed increasingly unlikely that what *she* had discovered would blow the case wide open. Too incredible, frankly. But you never could tell . . . At least it might breathe some new energy into the investigation. If they lifted a few more stones, who knew what else might be uncovered. And it showed everyone had their secrets.

Her ungloved hands were starting to tingle with cold. Better get in there.

* * *

Stolid PC Dave Elson, completing his *Gazette* crossword at the gallery shop counter-cum-reception desk, glanced up as she came into the lobby.

'Evening, sarge. Thought you lot would've finished for the day,' he greeted her.

Looking round the shadowy interior, she remembered the DI's warning. *Walls have ears.*

'Just one or two things to finish off, Dave,' she replied with assumed nonchalance. 'You know, dotting the i's and crossing the t's. A slave to duty, that's me.'

'Right you are. Well, don't overdo it.' Like Noakes, he thought she appeared a bit peaky.

'I won't.' She was about to go then turned back to him. 'Anyone else on patrol with you?'

'Bob Cunningham's doing the rounds upstairs.' He gestured to a clipboard. 'All the staff signed out a while back.' He chuckled. 'Probably worn out from the excitement. It was quite a circus what with the students' demo and then those telly people doing interviews.' Another rumble. 'Amazing how a bit of fame goes to some folk's heads.'

She rolled her eyes. 'I'll bet!'

Reassured, she made her way past the exhibition centre to the incident room.

Again, that strange sense that she was moving underwater, the statues and sculptures along her route seeming to advance and then recede like the bleached guardians of some tropical coral reef.

Arriving in the incident room, she felt curiously lethargic, the stuffy warmth neutralizing her bracing exposure to the weather outside. Her head felt full of cotton wool too. Damn and blast, she *was* coming down with something. How long since the last dose of Nurofen? No, better not risk taking any more otherwise she'd end up sparko.

What was that?

She stiffened, listening intently before relaxing her alert posture.

For God's sake. The night patrol was on site and everything secure. It was just the strain of the last few days getting to her.

For a wistful moment, she contemplated the long evening ahead, half-wishing she'd accepted Noakes's invitation. Muriel Noakes might be an overbearing bossy-boots, but her heart was in the right place. And heaven knew she deserved some sympathy what with that spoiled daughter leading them a merry dance . . .

It occurred to her suddenly that she hadn't yet taken a statement about the altercations Muriel witnessed on the afternoon of Helen Melville's funeral. That redoubtable lady was positive she had heard Daniel Westbrook shouting at someone to get away from him.

Burton looked down at her grainy printouts.

Was it possible?

She shook herself and put the kettle on. Black coffee and lots of it.

Having made herself a drink, she logged on to the computer and methodically began to type up a report for the DI. Then she scanned one of the printouts and attached it to her covering email.

Done!

Might as well take a shufti at the film footage. After all, there was nothing waiting for her at home apart from *Strictly* and a scratch supper.

After a few false starts, she got the DVD up and running. With a pen and Post-It to hand, she settled down to watch.

Dave Elson was right, she reflected with a grimace as she watched the gallery staff pose to best advantage. Benedict Bramwell sounded a real pompous twat, while the rest of the senior staff came across as awkward and stilted. Mind you, they *were* dealing with three murders so you had to cut them some slack.

Hold on a moment. Hold on. There it was . . . that bit there!

Galvanized into action, she jabbed 'Stop' and frantically rewound.

Desperately, she scrabbled for her glasses, ramming then on with a force that brought tears to her eyes.

Then she replayed the five second clip over and over.

Freeze, rewind, play. Freeze, rewind, play. Freeze, rewind, play.

She couldn't be sure precisely what she'd seen, but she *thought* she could pinpoint the words 'What have you done?'

Just a scrap of conversation in the background.

But the camera had caught it before, maddeningly, the two figures moved out of shot.

She leaned back and closed her eyes.

Was she imagining it? Getting carried away? Seeing what she *wanted* to see, manipulating the facts to fit a particular scenario?

She'd need a forensic lip-reader to be sure.

Burton felt her heart slow as she replayed the image repeatedly in her mind. It was succeeded by other images. Images of throttling and throat-cutting . . .

But still somehow, she couldn't make sense of it all.

With a great intake of breath, her heart steadied and her mind cleared.

Long-forgotten words from a school play came to her: *One may smile, and smile, and be a villain.*

The more she thought, the more she could see how it all might have come about.

The DI needed to know about this. She'd try his number again.

No joy.

Right, she'd give Noakes a call.

At that moment, finger poised above the keypad, she was startled by the intermittent sound of an alarm going off.

Probably just a blip, she decided recalling frequent references to false call-outs and defective sensors. No doubt Dave and Bob were on it.

God, she was tired, her lids heavy. She felt herself drifting off . . .

A sudden noise brought her bolt upright.

The door handle of the incident room slowly turned.

She had expected to see Dave or Bob standing in the doorway.

But it was neither of them.

It was the person she least expected to see.

The one above all others she needed to avoid.

She opened her mouth to speak, to act causal and unafraid. But in an instant of pure terror, she realized that her face had given her away and pretence was useless.

He knew.

* * *

A short time later, PC Dave Elson put his head round the door of the incident room.

'Sorry, sarge, false ala—'

But there was no sign of DS Kate Burton.

14. RECALLED TO LIFE

Sunday morning was cold and crisp, but the sky was clear and the sun rose bright and beautiful.

After a tense meeting with the Gold Group on Saturday evening, which finished with DCI Sidney hissing, 'You've got forty-eight hours, Markham, *forty-eight hours*', the DI had headed to Doggie Dickerson's to clear his head with a cathartic bout of shadow-boxing. A cursory check of his emails disclosing nothing urgent, he then returned to The Sweepstakes for supper with Olivia, followed by mindless oblivion in front of the box. But however hard he tried, the night shadows of the investigation pressed upon his mind. Somewhere in Bromgrove was a heart which enclosed a deadly secret, like water locked in an eternal frost. He had to break through that icy carapace to find what lay submerged beneath the surface. The force was on full alert to find Bill Hignett, but so far there had been no sightings nor any helpful information from his mother.

Noakes and Doyle were already in the incident room when Markham arrived, the former shaking himself out of a tangle of parka and long shaggy scarf and looking rather like a larger sort of dog.

'No Kate?' the DI said in a tone of surprise.

He noticed that the DS seemed vaguely troubled.

'I checked in with the night patrol yesterday evening around ten-ish, guv.'

'And?'

'Well, Burton had been in earlier. Told Dave Elson she'd got a couple of things to finish off. He thought she was doing a report for you or summat like that, guv.'

Markham frowned. 'I didn't get anything from her.'

'Mebbe she changed her mind an' decided to call it a day.' Now Noakes too was frowning. 'Dave said they had a bit of a problem with the alarms—'

'What kind of problem?' Markham was no longer relaxed but whipcord taut.

'Jus' the usual. It only lasted a few minutes. This was around half nine. He an' Bob Cunningham sorted it out, then he swung by to check on Burton but she was already gone . . . He assumed she'd had a bellyful an' gone home.'

'Did Elson actually *see* her go?'

'Now you come to mention it, no. But he said she'd looked knackered . . . completely done in . . . like she was coming down with summat.' Noakes was fidgety now, alternately scratching his head and chin. 'I wanted her to come home with me for her tea, like . . . but she was dead set on checking them newspaper records, so I left her doing that in the library for a bit. Afterwards, she was gonna check out the TV footage.' He shrugged helplessly. 'You know what Burton's like when she gets a bee in her bonnet.'

Doyle had moved across to the computer terminal and was scanning the screen.

'Boss,' he said urgently. 'She sent you an email yesterday.'

'What time was this?' Staccato like the rattle of hail.

'Eight forty-five. Hold on . . .' Doyle squinted at the screen. 'There's a failure notice in her inbox timed eight fifty. Looks like she mistyped the address, sir . . . must've been seeing double or something.'

'She was sick and in a hurry to get finished up,' Markham muttered, feeling increasingly anxious.

'In her email it says she left a message on your mobile, sir.'

'I got the start of an answerphone message, but it was very crackly and indistinct. Something about an item in the newspaper records, but then her mobile cut out,' he said. 'I presumed she had a bad signal and would call again later.' Markham's hands balled into fists. 'I didn't realize the significance and she didn't ring back.'

Noakes took a step towards the DI before recollecting Doyle's presence. 'Don't beat yourself up, guv,' he said with low-voiced earnestness. 'If anyone's to blame, it's me. I should've stayed with the lass. Anyone could see she was off colour an' that fiancé of hers is away on some course.' He shuffled from one foot to the other. 'But that library fair did my head in. All I could think about was getting home to the missus an' some decent grub.'

'There's an attachment with her email, sir.'

'Print it off will you, Doyle.' Markham's face was set.

Swiftly and efficiently, the DC proceeded to print off three copies, one for each of them.

Standing, the three men read in silence.

The short piece was from the *Gazette*, dated 29 November 1996.

> Vice-Principal George Courbold said Bromgrove University was greatly saddened to learn of the death of Sir Arthur St John-Crawley, aged 82, after a brief illness.
>
> A vivid and dynamic personality, as well as a tireless fundraiser for the arts, Sir Arthur was a scion of the Stanley family. In 1990 he generously transferred Greygarth House to the Bromgrove artists' cooperative at a knockdown price.
>
> Remembered by contemporaries for his upright character and strong adherence to traditional country values, Sir Arthur was educated at Eton and Sandhurst before going to Magdalen College, Cambridge, to read History. He was subsequently

commissioned into the Blues and Royals and held a series of regimental and staff appointments, including tours of duty in Northern Ireland. On the death of his father, he inherited the title and took over the running of the family home where, a keen gardener, he was happiest of all with a spade in his hand and golden retriever, Jimmy, at his side. Always active in the charitable sphere, when managing the estate became too much of a challenge he chose the artists' cooperative to continue his legacy of promoting regional talent and fostering a love of art in all its forms. In retirement at Calder-under-Medway, he participated enthusiastically in the life of the community and was a patron of various local organizations.

Sir Arthur's own life was touched by tragedy when in 1953 he and his wife suffered the loss of one of their twin boys. Charles Henry was just six years old when he disappeared while he and his brother were in the care of housekeeper, Mary Knollys, during his parents' absence on a visit to family in Ireland. After an extensive search, the little boy's body was finally discovered in a long disused mausoleum on the outskirts of the estate next to Greygarth Parish Church. It appeared that while exploring he had somehow slipped through a narrow space into one of the coffin shelves before becoming stuck and unable to extricate himself despite frantic attempts to do so. Charles Henry was asthmatic and death supervened through acute respiratory distress. The coroner delivered a verdict of accidental death and the building was subsequently deconsecrated, coffins being reinterred in the church graveyard where Charles Henry is also buried.

Sir Arthur married Venetia Carstone, daughter of a former Lord Mayor of Bromgrove, in 1943.

> She never fully recovered from her loss and died in 1964 of alcohol-related cirrhosis.
>
> These family tragedies were undoubtedly a factor in Sir Arthur's untiring work on behalf of Child Bereavement UK, and he was always ready to share recollections of Charles Henry, whom he described as an exceptional child. In 1975, he dedicated an impressive rose window on the north side of Greygarth Parish Church to his son's memory.

'Jesus,' breathed Doyle. '*Carstone.*'

'Carstone,' echoed Noakes. 'He used his mother's maiden name, nothing to show who he was . . . That artists' outfit an' the university prob'ly had no clue about his background or any connection with Greygarth.'

Markham looked stunned, his lips very pale.

'Veronica Yately certainly didn't make the connection,' he said. 'As far as she was concerned, he was just a visiting lecturer and fundraiser.'

'A six-year-old brother . . .' By turns rubbing his chin and rumpling his hair, Noakes pursued his argument. 'That article doesn't say what Aubrey was up to when the little lad died. What if it was him who did for the kid—'

'And Alex Carter too,' put in Doyle excitedly. 'The boys were the same age.'

'An' don't forget them initials on Donald Lestrange's drawing,' Noakes resumed. '"CH." CH for Charles Henry. Smack next to the doodle of Alex Carter's name.' He looked steadfastly at the DI. 'Gotta be more than coincidence, guv.'

'No wonder Burton was spooked.' Doyle shivered. 'She must've got the shock of her life coming across that.'

'And now there's no sign of her,' Markham said tersely.

Something of his alarm communicated itself to the other two.

'But she went home, didn't she?' Doyle began uncertainly. 'Couple of Night Nurse then off to bed . . .'

The DI had his mobile out.

'No answer from her landline,' he said before keying in another number and waiting grimly. 'And her mobile's ringing out.' He turned to Doyle.

'Constable.' The DC snapped to attention. 'Take a uniform with you and get round to Kate's flat. Break in if you have to.' His expression was withdrawn. 'If there's no sign of her at home, check with her parents and friends . . . if she's not well, it's just possible she stayed the night somewhere else.'

'I'm on it, boss.' And with that, their colleague was through the door and heading at speed for his car.

Keen eyes raked the incident room and fell on the empty jiffy bag. 'She was checking the TV footage when someone interrupted her, Noakes.'

'It's in the DVD drive, guv,' the DS confirmed. 'Right, let's see where she'd got to . . . Hold on a minute, there's a Post-It here.' Triumphantly, Noakes brandished a scrappy bit of paper. 'It's got 35.11 written on it. Must mean she was just over thirty-five minutes in.'

They seated themselves in front of the screen and watched intently.

Like Kate Burton the previous night, they paused and rewound, paused and rewound . . . over and over.

'S'that bit where you can jus' see Cathy Hignett an' Carstone standing behind Esmée Crocker,' Noakes said finally. 'The bit where Crocker's boring on about Queen Victoria's knickers or some such . . . Looks like Hignett says summat to him dead quickly before they move out of shot . . .'

'Agreed.' Markham's face was dark with concentration. 'Tell me what you think she's saying.'

'Difficult to say, guv . . . on account of she looks like she's talking out the corner of her mouth.'

'Oblige me.'

When the DI spoke in that tone, it meant he wanted answers fast.

'Don't hold me to this, boss . . . but mebbe "What did you do?" or p'raps "What have you done?"'

'Good. We're of one mind, then.'

Even at such a moment of critical extremity, Noakes felt ridiculously proud. Then reality kicked in.

'What did she mean by asking him that, guv . . . unless . . . unless she's guessed he's behind it all? But why would she . . . ?'

'There must be something between them, Noakes. Something we missed.' His voice harsher than a steel trap, the DI rapped out the order. 'I want Cathy Hignett and Daniel Westbrook located right away, Sergeant. And we need to find out where Aubrey Carstone is.' He fought down a sick lurch of fear. 'Kate Burton's safety might depend on it.'

* * *

Thirty minutes later, having received news from DC Doyle that Kate Burton did not appear to have returned home the previous night, Markham confronted Cathy Hignett across the conference table of the incident room. The fine straight lines in the almost transparent pallor of his face had never looked more implacable.

'I believe you are in a position to help us find the person responsible for four murders,' he said quietly. 'It appears that the abduction of a police officer can also be laid at this person's door.'

No one was better than the guvnor when it came to being angry in a low voice, Noakes thought admiringly. Much scarier than if he'd screamed and raged and burst a blood vessel.

Cathy Hignett looked utterly wretched, looking at Markham like some dumb animal, hands shredding a soggy tissue to pieces.

'Aubrey Carstone,' the DI said.

Two words, but they released the red-eyed lumpen woman from the spell that held her tongue-tied.

'I never knew for certain,' she said desperately. 'You've got to believe me.'

The cast in her right eye made it difficult to see where she was looking, giving Markham the unnerving impression that there was someone at his shoulder. In a sense, perhaps there was. Aubrey Carstone, now their prime suspect.

'What's the connection between you?' he continued inexorably, determined to leave pity out of the equation.

'My mum was Aubrey's, Mr Carstone's nanny . . .'

'Mary Knollys.' This was Noakes.

'That's right. Knollys was Mum's maiden name.' She contemplated the remnants of her mutilated tissue as if unsure who had shredded it. Markham produced an immaculate snow-white handkerchief and handed it across the table. Something in the grave courtesy of his manner seemed to steady her.

'There was a terrible accident when Mum was looking after the twins — Charles Henry and Aubrey. She didn't say much about it, but you could tell it preyed on her mind. She was never the same afterwards . . . blamed herself for what happened.'

'Did the family . . . ?'

'Oh no. They were very kind. She stayed on as housekeeper and looked after Aubrey till he went away to school. Later she met my dad and had me.' A pause, then, 'It was only after she retired, towards the end of her life, that she opened up a bit.'

'When was this?'

'She went into the hospice in 1994 and died the year after.'

'What did she tell you?'

'Just that it had been one of those scorching summer days . . . very hot, with the threat of thunder.' Cathy Hignett's voice was remote, as if she was recounting a dream. 'Mum had one of her migraines — they only happened once in a blue moon — and needed a lie-down. She asked the girl who did the cleaning — Maggie her name was — to keep an eye on the boys, just for half an hour or so. But there was a delivery to the house and Maggie got distracted . . . when she turned round to see where they were, the boys had gone.' Suddenly the woman looked distraught. 'Mum nearly went off her head, she was so frantic to find them . . .'

It was obvious this piece of family history had haunted Cathy Hignett for years.

Patiently, compassion for her obvious distress welling up despite himself, Markham waited.

'They found Aubrey wandering in the woodland garden on the far side of the estate. He said his brother wanted to play hide and seek. When it was his turn to look, he couldn't find Charles Henry . . .'

Her face mottled with agitation, she gulped and gasped. It was a horrible sound. Like a fish hooked out of water and floundering on dry land, thought Noakes fascinated.

'It took a while before the search party found Charles Henry in that creepy little house where they kept the coffins piled up inside . . . and by then it was too late.' Her lips were working convulsively. 'Mum always wondered . . . she was never sure . . .'

'She thought Aubrey might have killed his brother.' The DI was very gentle.

Cathy Hignett wiped her sweat-streaked forehead with the handkerchief.

'He was only six. It didn't seem possible. But Aubrey was quite jealous. They were non-identical twins . . . Charles Henry was the special one even at that age . . .'

An exceptional child.

And the less-favoured brother . . . the bad seed?

'There were things . . . Once, Mum caught him with his hands round Charles Henry's throat, and another time he pushed Charlie's head under in the bath, but she didn't think then that he was going to hurt him, not really. I mean, children play games, don't they? It was only later she wondered . . .'

'Did Aubrey ever say anything about what happened the day his brother went missing?'

'Not really . . . in those days, you weren't encouraged to dwell. No counsellors or anything like that.'

'But Aubrey's explanation didn't sit easy with your mother?'

'It was just . . . there was this one time he mentioned it. He said something like wasn't it strange to think of Charles Henry being shut up in that funny little house all the time — "the Hansel and Gretel house" he called it — locked in with the coffins on their shelves . . . maybe trying to scratch a message into the wood.' Her face was running with perspiration. 'Mum told him not to be morbid, but she remembered how he looked . . . said his eyes were all glittery and strange . . . It bothered her.'

'And your mother was in the hospice when she told you this?'

'Yes, she was drugged up with morphine and all sorts by then of course . . . wandering in her mind quite a lot.'

Markham regarded her thoughtfully.

'See here, Inspector.' The discordant sing-song voice held a pleading note. 'Mr Carstone always kept in touch with Mum and the family. Then later, when I had Bill and . . . there were problems . . . he looked out for us . . .'

'Looked out for you? How was that, luv?' Noakes was non-judgemental, almost affable.

'My husband walked out on us when Bill was eight. Couldn't cope with having a son who wasn't, well, normal.' Her eyes were suddenly bitter, hard. Clearly it hadn't been an easy life. 'Mr Carstone helped me get a job at the gallery. Then later, he did the same for Bill.' A poignant note of pride crept into her voice. 'He was a sort of mentor . . . kept Bill on track . . . made sure any . . . well, any misunderstandings were smoothed out.'

'Misunderstandings, Mrs Hignett?'

'Some people had it in for Bill, Inspector.' Her voice was angry now. 'Never willing to give him a fair chance. But Mr Carstone wasn't like that.'

Noakes recalled his instruction to Doyle the previous evening. See if you can find out who spoke up for Hignett when he was accused of perving. It must have been Carstone who pulled strings so that Cathy Hignett's troublesome off-spring kept his job.

'Jus' your everyday superhero then,' said the DS, wearing his blandest expression.

'I s'pose it was a case of hero worship,' Cathy Hignett said. 'Bill really looked up to Mr Carstone, would have done anything for him.'

Anything.

The word hung in the air between them.

Face aflame with ugly red blotches, she tried to backtrack.

'I don't mean Bill would have done wrong,' she stammered. 'He wouldn't have hurt anyone. Couldn't have.'

'What if he thought someone was a threat to Mr Carstone, luv?' Noakes moved in for the kill. 'What then?' He looked sideways at her with a stronger compound of keenness and suspicion than was compatible with his previous assumption of relaxed indifference.

'Had it ever occurred to you that Mr Carstone might in some way have been grooming Bill with a view to making use of him?'

'Grooming?' Her voice was shrill now. 'What the hell do you mean, Inspector?'

'Oh, I think you know, Mrs Hignett.' Markham's voice was hypnotically soft, subduing her like some enchanted incantation. As if the boss was one of them Eastern dervishes or summat, Noakes thought with increased admiration.

Cathy Hignett couldn't tear her eyes away from the DI.

'When Helen Melville began shooting her mouth off about a secret in the Lestrange papers . . . when she suddenly became obsessed with past crimes and the Princes in the Tower . . . it got you thinking, didn't it?'

Still her eyes remained riveted on the clear chiselled whiteness of his face.

'You knew Aubrey Carstone was in the gallery that day when little Alex Carter vanished from the face of the earth . . . just as Charles Henry was never seen alive after he went off with his brother for a game of hide and seek.' Markham spoke quietly, but each word, each syllable was brutally distinct. 'You remembered what your mother had said, and the past came flooding back, didn't it? Even though you'd done your best to keep troublesome thoughts buried fathoms deep.'

Stricken, the woman nodded dumbly as though she didn't trust herself to speak.

'You knew Aubrey Carstone and Donald Lestrange were friends. They were even together the day Alex Carter went missing.' Markham's gaze drilled into her. 'What if Lestrange knew something incriminating about Carstone? What if he'd left a clue behind when he died?' The DI brought a hand down on the table with frightening suddenness. 'That's what you began to ask yourself, isn't it?'

The silence was so absolute, it felt as though the building held its breath.

'And then the murders started.'

She flinched as if this was death by a thousand cuts.

'You couldn't face the truth could you, Mrs Hignett?' The DI continued, wielding his scalpel with remorseless skill. 'Didn't want to face the truth.'

Noakes couldn't recall when he'd last seen so much abject misery concentrated in one face. Poor cow, he thought. Then he thought of Kate Burton and his expression hardened.

'You began watching your son and Aubrey Carstone . . . thought you saw signs of an understanding between them.' Markham's voice was insinuating now, almost caressing in a shocking parody of intimacy. 'Up till then you'd been able to deceive yourself. No doubt Aubrey was able to lull your suspicions. There was no shortage of other suspects, after all, and anyway, how could a man of that age have pulled off three murders all by himself?'

'See, here's the thing, luv.' At an imperceptible nod from the DI, Noakes took over. 'Carstone wasn't doing it all by himself, was he? He had back up.' The DS wagged his head sagely. 'Had your lad to do the heavy lifting.' Looking at her levelly, he added, 'Mebbe that's how it was even as far back as 1997.'

'That's a lie.' Cathy Hignett looked close to collapsing. 'That's a lie,' she repeated, her voice cracking.

'Is it?' Markham took up the reins to deliver the coup de grâce. 'If you thought it was a lie, why did you confront Aubrey Carstone?'

'Confront him?' Her voice sank to a hoarse whisper.

'Yes, Mrs Hignett. We've just been replaying footage shot by the TV crew yesterday and there's a moment when the camera catches you speaking to Aubrey Carstone.'

'We're pretty sure you said summat like "What have you done?" Now that's an odd thing to be asking old Aubrey out of the blue, ain't it?' Noakes jabbed his forefinger at her. 'What's he supposed to have gone and done, then?' The DS thrust his shaggy head towards her. 'An' it's a bit of a coincidence you asking him a question like that the same time as Bill does a disappearing act.'

'My Bill's done nothing.' Her voice had risen an octave higher, the words jerked out of her in spasms. 'Absolutely bloody nothing.'

'I don't believe it. And deep down, nor do you.'

She stared back at the DI as though turned to stone.

'Where did they go, Mrs Hignett? What was their special place?'

The silence stretched for an eternity.

'Greygarth,' she breathed. 'Greygarth.'

Noakes was puzzled. 'But doesn't the university own it now—'

Markham raised a hand, his eyes never leaving Cathy Hignett's, and the DS fell silent.

'You said Aubrey Carstone talked about the "Hansel and Gretel" house.'

'Mum said he and Charles Henry loved Grimm's Fairy Tales.' Her voice was mechanical now, as though the fight had gone out of her. '*Hansel and Gretel* was Aubrey's favourite, he was pretty much obsessed with it.'

The story of a cannibalistic witch luring children into her cottage in the woods. An early indicator of pathological impulses?

'That's partly why Mum wondered . . .'

'About how Charles Henry really died?'

'Yes. It was the fact of Charlie being found in that mausoleum place and Aubrey having a bit of a thing about it. The building was out of bounds to the boys, but he was always fascinated by it . . . said it was like Greygarth had another house inside it . . .'

The house within a house.

Aediculae. Houses of the dead. Hidden spaces. Shelves, niches, burials.

How he must have resented any encroachment on his preserve by colleagues looking to make a name for themselves.

Markham brought his attention back to the woman sitting opposite.

'So, Aubrey Carstone had continued access to Greygarth.'

A statement not a question.

'It was his family home when all's said and done. If anyone had a right to be there, he did.' Defiance flared briefly in the red-rimmed eyes.

She quailed slightly under Markham's gaze.

'When Sir Arthur sold the place, he made it a condition that there was a flat for the family so they could come and go as they pleased. Mr Carstone said the university continued the arrangement. All legal and above board. Plus, he did lectures and talks and things, which meant he was still involved with the place. Helped with events for local primaries too. He was good with kids.'

Good with kids. Despite the heat of the room, Markham felt cold. From the grim look on Noakes's face, the significance of those words was not lost on him either.

Was it possible that they would uncover more than just Alex Carter's jumbled bones at Greygarth? Were there other cries unheard echoing down the arches of the years?

Though seriously unnerved, the DI gave no sign.

'Presumably your son was also a visitor to Greygarth, given his attachment to Mr Carstone.'

'Mr Carstone was good about taking Bill sometimes . . . to help me out . . . give me a bit of a break. Bill wasn't always easy to manage.' The admission appeared wrung from her. 'Don't get me wrong,' she went on hastily, 'I don't mean he did anything criminal. He was just fractious occasionally, but Aubrey . . . Mr Carstone . . . well, he had a way with Bill — calmed him down if folk wound him up.'

'People like Helen Melville an' Charles Randall,' put in Noakes.

'Well, not just them.' For all the dull vacancy, the implications were not lost on her. 'There was teasing and folk could be unkind . . . nicknames, stuff like that.'

'Oh yeah,' Noakes smote his forehead theatrically. '"Quasi"! That was Charles Randall, wasn't it? Not very nice.'

Her tone suddenly viperish, she positively spat at him. 'He was an arrogant stuck-up piece of work, picking on someone like Bill to get cheap laughs. Strutting and preening like he thought he was God's gift to women. Him and that Helen Melville made me sick the way they threw their weight around.'

'And now they're both dead.' Markham's voice was toneless.

'So, what if I *did* hate them?' Saliva pooled in the corners of her mouth and her features were distorted. 'There's no law against it.'

'But there *is* such a thing as perverting the course of justice, Mrs Hignett.' Markham's face seemed carved out of granite.

'You've got to understand.' She was whining now. 'He's my son. And Aubrey Carstone's family . . . all the family I've got.'

And there it was, Markham realized. The psychological blocking mechanism which had enabled Cathy Hignett to protect her mind from unbearable truths. If the housekeeper-nanny, Mary Knollys, had dissociated herself from reality — deliberately and with quite remarkable dexterity — what cause was there for wonder in the fact that her daughter had done likewise.

He pressed again.

'So, your son comes and goes at Greygarth?'

'He may have done, yes.'

A strange look of dislike and distrust crossed her face when he mentioned the name of the house. Clearly it filled her with some unconquerable dread.

You knew, Markham said to himself. All that time, you knew and said nothing.

Suddenly the figure of Ned Chester swam before him as he was in life, brim-full of intelligence and energy, and he experienced a wave of revulsion for the woman in front of him so strong that he felt he must pass out.

'Guv,' Noakes said quietly, his expression concerned.

The light-headed sensation receded.

'We'll interview Daniel Westbrook on the way over to Greygarth, Sergeant.' It was the familiar decisive tone. 'I want everything low-key. No sirens, no cordon, no tactical support. Nothing.'

'Hearing you loud and clear, boss.'

'Carstone knows by now this is the endgame.' Markham's eyes were dark pools against sharply etched cheekbones. 'No way out.'

'An' he's got one of ours.'

'Not for much longer.' When Markham spoke in that tone, Noakes knew the die was cast.

* * *

The sun was no longer shining as their unmarked car pulled away from the art gallery, snow showing dull ivory against a sullen sky. A vaporous mist wreathed the countryside, spreading through the air in concentric ripples like foamy breakers against the shore.

'Start talking, mate,' grunted the DS, watching Daniel Westbrook in the rear-view mirror as he sat next to Markham. So far, Westbrook had not said a word and Noakes's patience was fast evaporating.

'I'll make it easy for you, Mr Westbrook.'

Markham's voice was colder than the North Sea.

'You knew the killer's identity but chose to say nothing.'

Aubrey Carstone's deputy looked as though he hadn't slept for days, eyes like black pips in the sallow gourd of his face.

'I didn't know anything for certain, Inspector.'

'I believe you got the wind up when your uncle's papers went missing after the first murder.'

An infinitesimal nod. It was enough.

'Helen Melville had talked about a mystery, an unsolved crime from the past. You made the connection with Alex Carter straight away.'

Another nod.

'You figured she was killed because of something hidden in those papers . . . a clue your uncle let slip.' Impassively, Markham added, 'Complicity to murder perhaps.'

Westbrook jack-knifed as though he had been kicked in the stomach.

Nice one, guv, thought Noakes shooting another glance in the mirror. You've got the bastard on the ropes now.

'I knew there were some private things of my uncle's in storage.' Westbrook spoke low and fast. 'Just odds and ends, stuff that had been found in his house and passed to my mother as his executor. They ended up in her attic . . . nobody even remembered they were there.'

'Until you went looking.'

'At first there didn't seem to be anything, but then I found this . . .' Westbrook reached into his jacket pocket and withdrew a small Silvine notebook. 'He must've used it as a jotter at some point. There's drafts of letters, scribbles and notes to himself . . .'

'There was something hidden in there,' Markham prompted. 'Something that shook you to the core.'

'I suspected he and Aubrey had been lovers at one time. Some of what he'd written confirmed it.'

'No big deal these days,' piped up Noakes from the front, very much man of the world.

'There were these sketches of a child too. Over and over.'

Westbrook's breathing was very rapid now. Despite the cold, he looked clammy and feverish.

'Some were labelled "The Lost Boy." Others had the initials AC or CH.'

Making a visible effort to pull himself together, he continued. 'There were scraps of doggerel too, stuff he'd copied out . . . all about children dying young with their lives before them . . . like inscriptions from a Victorian cemetery.' He shuddered. 'And weird little drawings . . .'

'What kind of weird?' Noakes was watching him closely.

'Stick men in front of a wall with spades and a hammer . . . a rectangular box with a cross on it. Like a grave.'

The DI felt his blood turning to ice water. But there was no sign of horror in his demeanour.

'What conclusions did you draw, Mr Westbrook?'

Markham sounded as chilly and composed as prosecuting counsel.

'Look, Inspector, I *admired* my uncle . . . revered him almost . . .'

'But this made you regard him in a different light.'

Westbrook shut his eyes, his hands clasped tightly in his lap. When he finally opened them and began to speak, his voice was muffled and the words came out very slowly with long pauses between them.

'I realized there was another side to my uncle . . . a whole world I'd never even guessed at.'

'Go on.'

'It was clear he was haunted by something . . . some experience he had shared with Aubrey. He'd had to compartmentalize himself to cope with it, but it all came spilling out in this . . . this horrible little cache he'd squirrelled away.'

'Murder,' Noakes said bluntly. 'You thought him and Aubrey killed that little lad . . . that they were in on it together.'

'No!' It was jerked out of him. 'My uncle wasn't capable of that. He was wonderful to me and my brothers. Never a hint of anything untoward.'

'But you said you didn't really know him.' Markham was inexorable.

'If something *did* happen,' Westbrook looked at the DI helplessly, 'he must have got sucked in . . .' With rising passion, he added, 'I'll never believe he deliberately hurt a child. *Never.*'

'Is that why you didn't tell us?' Noakes asked belligerently. 'To protect your uncle's precious reputation?' His face as it glowered in the rear-view mirror looked apoplectic. 'Two more innocent people died cos of you being a fucking gutless wimp.'

'Keep your eyes on the road, Sergeant.' Markham made no comment on his subordinate's swingeing denunciation, but something in his eyes told Noakes the guvnor agreed.

'I didn't know what the hell to think.' Westbrook's voice was hollow now, defeated. 'And when Charles died, I began to doubt myself . . . decided I must have got it wrong.'

He passed his hand across his face from top to bottom in a curious gesture, as though by that means he could wipe the page clean.

'Charles had a complicated love life, you see . . .'

'An' you loved Charles.' Noakes was matter-of-fact. 'Even though he gave you the run-around.'

'You could say that.' Westbrook's face was bleak. 'But those two women — Melville and Summerson — were like a pair of fucking corkscrews, he had no chance against them . . . didn't know whether he was animal, vegetable or mineral by the end of it all . . . I suppose I latched on to the idea that this couldn't have had anything to do with Aubrey or my uncle . . . I even suspected Summerson of getting a hitman to kill them.'

'*A hitman!*' Noakes guffawed.

Westbrook flinched.

'I wasn't thinking straight, but it seemed to me she might've wanted to take her revenge on both of them . . . Melville left her for Randall after all.'

'Did you speak about any of this to Aubrey Carstone?'

'Not about the things I'd found . . . not about him and my uncle. I *couldn't*. It would have seemed so disloyal . . . so *ungrateful*. A total rejection . . . I mean, they practically brought me up between them.' He stared unseeing out of the car window. 'Donald had dementia towards the end of his life, which could account for him going to pieces and imagining stuff . . . And anyway, it didn't make sense. Aubrey was just the same as ever. There'd have been some sign, wouldn't there? If he'd committed murder . . . there'd have been a giveaway?'

'Not with a psychopath.' Noakes spoke with the authority of one who had personal experience of the breed.

There was an appalled silence during which Westbrook seemed to shrink into himself.

'On the afternoon of Helen Melville's funeral, you were overheard shouting at someone,' Markham observed calmly. 'Who was that?'

The other appeared startled at the change of direction. 'After the funeral?' He sounded dazed.

'That's right. You were shouting at someone to get away from you.'

'I don't remember,' Westbrook replied. 'Look, I was in a kind of fugue state or something . . . like I was cracking up.' His eyes narrowed on Markham. 'You think it was Aubrey, don't you?'

'I think it may have been.'

'Like my subconscious was accusing him . . .'

'Yes.'

Beneath Westbrook's frozen immobility something was stirring.

Remorse.

'I was a coward, Inspector,' he said. 'A fucking coward. I couldn't face the truth . . . tried to rationalize it away . . .' He covered his face with his hands. 'But I couldn't get the echoes out of my head . . .'

'What echoes?' Noakes was intrigued.

'Footsteps coming towards me incessantly . . . they kept coming . . . going . . . breaking off . . . then stopping altogether . . . I could never see whose they were . . . but they kept bearing down on me . . .'

Jesus, thought the DS with a wary eye on his passenger, looks like this one's headed to the funny farm before very much longer. *Footsteps?*

'Course the guvnor looked as though it all made perfect sense, though as far as *he* was concerned Westbrook might as well have been speaking bleeding Esperanto.

'Perhaps it was the footsteps of Truth, Mr Westbrook.'

'More like the Furies, Inspector.'

Noakes didn't understand what the fuck they were talking about, but at least the mad look had gone out of Westbrook's eyes. For a moment back there, he thought the bloke was going to try something stupid . . . like fling himself out of the car.

If Westbrook fancied he heard footsteps, happen it didn't have owt to do with echoes or the Furies, whoever they were. P'raps it was the ghost of little Alex Carter playing Grandma's Footsteps. The DS smiled grimly. Now *that'd* be poetic justice all right.

The lodge at Greygarth House in the hamlet of Troutbeck showed no signs of life when they crunched along a gravel drive towards it, and the electronically-operated gates were closed.

'Sunday,' grunted Noakes. 'With all the budget cuts, they likely don't bother putting anyone on at weekends unless there's an . . . event.' The last word being pronounced with a distaste which gave that noun the force of an offensive epithet.

'Aubrey Carstone no doubt has his own means of access,' Markham replied quietly. 'Ah, there's Doyle's car.'

The young DC came crunching across the snow towards them. An interrogative quirk of Markham's eyebrows elicited a subtle shake of the head.

So, Kate's here, then.

It was what he had been expecting, but nevertheless his heart sank.

I should have kept her safe, he thought. After what happened last time, I should have made Noakes stick to her like superglue.

The DS was looking at him, great leonine head cocked on one side as if he knew exactly what his boss was thinking.

We *both* got it wrong, guv. Both of us.

'Constable, I'd like you to look after Mr Westbrook in your car.'

Doyle looked crestfallen. He wanted to be in at the close, the DI thought ruefully, remembering his own early days in plain clothes.

But he just couldn't risk it. Couldn't go in mob-handed.

'Kid gloves, I understand boss,' the other said quietly, giving a half-salute before escorting their passenger to the other vehicle. Noakes smiled approvingly after his retreating figure. Like a proud parent, Markham thought with a flare of amusement.

It was quickly extinguished as he looked through the gates at the Queen Anne building. With the blinds down, it brooded in the distance, blank and inscrutable.

'Where d'you reckon he is, guv? I mean, there's two potential kill sites.'

Wreaths of mist spiralled into the air and drifted upwards like dank exhalations.

And what seemed corporeal melted, as breath into the wind.

'I think he's in the place where he disposed of Alex Carter.'

'Not the mausoleum thingy?'

Markham shook his head.

'That was dismantled and the coffins moved, remember. The site with most meaning for him will be the room on the ground floor . . . the one Mrs Yately pinpointed for us . . . the library and snug.'

Noakes sensed there was more.

'The place where he killed Charles Henry a second time.'

The DS blinked at this elliptical statement but put his faith in the guvnor.

'Righto,' he said rubbing his hands. 'I'm ready when you are, boss.'

As they came nearer to the low, wide portal, they saw the front door was ajar.

'Looks like Carstone's expecting us, guv,' Noakes muttered as they passed through the pillared portico into the glass-in entrance hall. 'No frigging bread crumbs, though.'

To Markham's eyes, Greygarth didn't look much like a house from a fairy story, though its long drive, with the snow lying deep and crisp, gave the place an aspect of melancholy solitude. No wind stirred the sentinel elms at its rear, while the mournful sound of a dog baying in the distance only seemed to emphasize the building's blank repose.

Later, he found himself unable to recall the interior clearly, save for a blurred impression of frescoed ceilings, balustrade staircase, large gracious rooms with high double doors, walls covered in olive green silk, curtains of brocade hanging stiffly from tall windows and elaborate knotted lace curtains shutting out any glimpse of the snowflakes that were starting to whirl about outside.

Under the strange influence of his surroundings, the DI moved towards his goal as though some gravitational pull at the heart of the house drew him inexorably towards his destination.

With Markham leading they advanced along a bow-windowed corridor lined with thin-legged chairs and occasional tables boasting miniatures of ladies and gentlemen in the powdered wigs of a bygone age. Noakes looked about him askance, as though this preference for ghostly unsymmetrical passages crammed with spindly furniture over solid corporate comfort merely confirmed his darkest suspicions about high-falutin interior designers.

And suddenly, there in front of them was the library, dark and womb-like with its massive mahogany floor-to-ceiling bookcases and the panelled snug lying through a pilastered alcove beyond. Eighteenth-century portraits stood on varnished easels, while other pictures peppered the brocaded walls as thickly as though shot out of some ancient cannon. Yet more occasional tables, elaborate inlaid chairs and strange little footstools with twisted legs were strewn across a luxuriously thick carpet that deadened all sound.

It was a density of effect that made Markham feel as though he must suffocate . . .

Sitting primly in one of two red velvet armchairs over by a window looking out onto the stone terrace was Aubrey Carstone. 'Like he was at a vicar's tea party or summat,' as Noakes described the bizarre scene afterwards to Doyle, 'but with a pistol on his lap 'stead of the cucumber sarnies. Fucking *surreal*.'

Kate Burton occupied the other armchair behind which stood Bill Hignett, looking for all the world like a footman poised to wait at tables.

Markham locked glances with her. She looked worn and wan, as though she had been up all night, but was otherwise unharmed.

I'm all right, boss, she telegraphed silently. Don't worry about me. *Just bring him in.*

Scrutinizing the brittle conker-brown bob, dishevelled and lustreless, framing the serious little face with its myopic hazel eyes, the DI felt as though he could never let her out of his sight again.

Noakes too seemed oddly affected, giving her a clumsy thumbs up which, most uncharacteristically, she shyly returned to his evident confusion.

'You took your time, Inspector.'

The tone was civilized, ironical.

Aubrey Carstone, in his pinstripes and waistcoat, was the same dignified and imposing presence of yore.

But for something wrong with the eyes, thought Markham. Those were not the same.

'And before you ask, yes, I did for them all, gentlemen.' He sounded almost bored.

Markham measured the distance from where he and Noakes stood by the fireplace. Carstone would have the pistol to Kate's head before they could lay hands on him. And notwithstanding the vacancy of Hignett's expression, there was a vigilance about his posture which suggested he would be quick to spring to his mentor's defence.

A twisted smile, as if their quarry knew exactly what he was thinking.

'I suppose you want me to tell you how it was.'

Humour him.

'If it's not too much trouble.'

Markham motioned to Noakes to sit on a fragile chair which stood on one side of the hearth, himself taking the other. Gingerly, as though apprehensive it might disintegrate under his weight, the DS complied.

'Such a pity Helen fancied herself a sleuth,' Carstone said gently in a tone of mild regret. 'Such a pity.'

He might as well having been discussing a change in the weather.

'From her researches in the archives, she guessed your secret,' Markham said quietly. 'The secret of little Alex Carter abducted all those years ago from the gallery and brought here to Greygarth.' His eyes were infinitely sad as they lingered on the wainscot and panelling behind which he knew a child's skeleton had long since mouldered into dust.

'Poor foolish Helen. Rabbiting away to Rebecca Summerson about crimes and mysteries without a thought for consequences,' the other said with chilling disdain as though Markham had not spoken. 'Presumably she thought to unveil her discoveries with some *éclat* . . . but alas, fate overtook her.' This was accompanied by a sardonic curl of the lip which imparted a look of treachery and cruelty to the whole countenance.

'And what of Charles Randall?' Markham forced himself to remain calm. 'Why did he deserve to die?'

'I believe young Mr Randall may have had it in mind to blackmail me, though he never expressly formulated anything so crude, you understand. It was more a case of hinting that he'd cottoned on to something his inamorata had come across while she was playing detective.' There was nothing of civilized urbanity in those eyes now. They were flat, empty, devoid of humanity.

'At any rate, I couldn't take the chance.' Carstone emitted a high-pitched titter which was shocking in its unexpectedness. 'Another second-rater bites the dust.'

'And Ned Chester?' Watching the sly, cruel features — how was it he had never noticed their latent guile? — it felt like profanation even to pronounce his dead friend's name. But somehow he managed it, though his tongue felt swollen and nerveless in the utterance.

'Mr Chester, now there's a *genuine* loss to cultivated circles.'

Christ, thought Noakes at the look on Markham's face, the guvnor's going to lose it.

He half rose from his chair.

That slight movement brought the DI back from the abyss and the red mist receded.

'As you were, Sergeant.'

Aubrey Carstone watched the interaction as dispassionately as a vivisectionist might contemplate his specimens on the slab.

'Your journalist friend would not let the past alone,' he said. 'A risky path to take.'

'So, you got Lurch here to smash his head in,' growled Noakes. 'An' then you stuck him in that suit of armour like the Man in the Iron Mask, you sick fuck.' Now it was the DS looking dangerous.

Carstone's face twitched.

The face of a man who fetishized concealment and fled the light.

'You had a brother,' Markham said.

'Charles Henry.' It was a child's shrill piping voice. Markham felt the hairs rise on the back of his neck. 'Charlie left and never came back.'

Carstone's eyes were suddenly glassy, unfocused.

'I never stopped looking, and then there he was one day at the gallery in front of me . . . recalled to life. I only knew that I had to bring him back to Greygarth . . .'

And that was where the fantasy broke down, thought Markham, leaving him with a little corpse to dispose of.

Suddenly he remembered how Daniel Westbrook had described his state of mind on the afternoon of Helen Melville's funeral. 'I was in a kind of fugue state.'

Fugue. A dissociative disorder. Characterized by breakdown of personal identity and amnesia.

Whatever had happened with Alex Carter in this room, there had been no recalling to life. Charles Henry was irrevocably gone, and it was possibly this realization breaking into Carstone's guilt-ridden fantasy which led to a final terrible eruption of grief and murder.

'Donald was with me that day.' The shrill treble broke into his thoughts. 'Donald helped after I closed his throat . . . Donald helped . . .'

Closed his throat.

As a child, Aubrey Carstone was caught with his hands round his brother's throat. And decades later, in the room where they were sitting, those same hands had fastened like talons about another child's neck.

It was likely they would never know the trigger for Carstone's murderous aberrations. Was he the victim of childhood abuse — some trauma which left an indelible scar? Was sibling jealousy at the root of it all? Or had something in Aubrey Carstone simply closed off at six years of age? Markham recalled a lecturer at Bramshill saying the psychopathic personality emerged as early as three years old . . . Was that the case with the man in front of him? To outward appearance a successful academic and art critic, but inside a hollow shell.

Along with the revulsion, there was profound pity.

'So, you chucked him in with the rubble, you and your mate, Donald?' Noakes enquired gutturally. 'In a bin bag, was it? Or did you root out a cardboard box?'

'The artists' group was helping with renovations.' Carstone's voice was monotonous now, as though he was sleep-walking. 'We laid him in the wall cavity.'

A makeshift coffin, like the one depicted in the Silvine notebook.

Noakes's normally florid complexion was now floury white.

Sick fuck. Sick fuck. Sick fuck.

The words tolled like a mantra in his head. As if they could somehow obliterate the image of that pitiful grave a hand's breadth away behind the room's ornate gilding and stucco.

'What about Basher Bill . . . where does he fit in? Jus' helps you out whenever you have a spot of bother, like?' Furious sarcasm spewed out of Noakes like lava.

Carstone's eyes softened.

'Cathy and Bill have always been part of my life,' he said. 'They were the family I never had.'

At these words, Bill Hignett moved closer to Carstone's chair, as though answering the tug of an invisible leash.

'Let my sergeant go.' The DI did not trust himself to speak Kate's name. 'She's bought you time, now let her go.'

Lazily, Carstone stroked the handle of the pistol on his lap. His eyes — no longer cloudy but filled with implacable purpose — were riveted on Markham's face.

Then he released the safety catch.

The two policemen tensed in their seats, ready to spring.

In a single fluid movement, Carstone held the gun to his temple and gave a deep shuddering sigh.

Then his eyes widened and fixed on some spot on the wall to the right of the fireplace.

'Charlie,' he said with the eagerness of a lover, and pressed the trigger.

EPILOGUE

'I guess after the Bulger case we understand so much more these days about childhood trauma and whatever it is that leads to children killing . . . the fact that kids don't see good and bad or death the same way adults do . . .'

Kate Burton sighed and continued gently, 'But it was a very different world when Aubrey Carstone was a child.'

'D'you think his mum and dad figured it out?' Noakes was intrigued despite himself. 'As in worked out that Aubrey had summat to do with his twin brother's death? I mean, his mum hit the bottle, didn't she?'

'We'll never know for sure, sarge.' Burton's forehead lifted and knitted itself into an expression of perplexity that was more and more common with her these days. 'But I think Aubrey *did* have something to do with it. Egged Charles Henry on or even pushed him through that opening in the mausoleum, then left him there.'

The team was sitting with Olivia in The Grapes four weeks after the conclusion of what became known as 'the gallery case.'

The quaint, resolutely unfashionable little pub was a favourite resort of 'Markham's gang' once investigations were concluded. Denise, the formidable landlady and a dead ringer for Corrie's Bette Lynch, always made sure they had the back room to themselves on such occasions and safeguarded the DI's privacy like a tigress. A subdued hum of conversation floated through from the front lounge, which had all the quirky charm of a ship's brig with its extensive array of antique nautical instruments and other seafaring paraphernalia accumulated over decades, but nothing disturbed their peace in Denise's back parlour where a log fire crackled cosily, casting shadows over the uneven wooden floor that Noakes always said made him seasick just to walk across.

'So, it all came down to jealousy when Carstone was a kid.' Doyle sounded bewildered.

'As Kate says, it's unlikely we'll ever know the truth of what went on.' Markham was resigned. 'But whatever happened, I suspect Aubrey lived in denial and the people round him supported that instead of helping him to understand himself and come to terms with it.' The DI looked at his friends gathered about the table in their comfortable inglenook. 'A terrible tragedy for all concerned.' His eyes fell to the table. 'Aubrey Carstone was a severely disturbed child who needed intensive therapeutic intervention. His mother may well have realized the truth and eventually cracked under the weight of that knowledge. It probably led to her alcoholism.'

'Nobody thought of him as a child who had murdered,' Olivia put in softly. 'So nobody foresaw a future explosion or breaking point.'

'Donald Lestrange had some idea,' Noakes said, eyeing his empty glass.

Doyle knew his cue. 'Same again, sarge?'

'Aye, lad.' The DS might as well just take his ale intravenously, thought his young colleague suppressing a grin. He was always the same when it came to these inquests.

'What about you, sir? Kate? Olivia?'

The others were only halfway through their drinks. 'Nothing for us,' Markham said with a swift interrogative glance at his lover and Kate. 'But be sure to get one for yourself and put it on my tab.'

Doyle headed to the lounge with alacrity.

Noakes continued making vigorous inroads on the pork scratchings.

'What d'you reckon happened with Lestrange?' He addressed the question to Burton, his tone almost deferential.

Olivia smiled to herself. This *was* a turn up for the books. The old war horse seeking psychological insights from the university-educated whippersnapper!

But she thought she had detected signs of a genuine rapprochement between the two and gave silent thanks for it. Whatever their personal idiosyncrasies and rivalries, they were Markham's twin towers.

Kate Burton's eyes rested on her old adversary with something close to affection. 'Again, sarge, I don't think we'll ever know the whole story.'

Not if DCI Sidney had anything to do with it, she might have added.

'But Lestrange was there in the gallery with Carstone the day of the abduction,' Noakes persisted stubbornly.

Kate's eyes were misty as she tried to unravel it all.

'I think it may have been a spur of the moment thing. Aubrey snatched the child on an impulse then panicked. Lestrange and Hignett could've helped him smuggle Alex out to Greygarth afterwards.'

'Alex's mum said she smelled summat sharp and spicy on that corridor where the lad was taken . . . could've been some sort of chemical cleaner. An' she talked about seeing white hands. Everyone thought she was out of it at the time . . . but Carstone worked in restoration.'

'That's right, sarge. Curators use fluids all the time, and white cotton gloves. Plus, there was a private staff staircase behind that alcove on the archives corridor.' She made a sleight-of-hand gesture. 'It would have been a matter of seconds.'

'But did Carstone figure Alex Carter as a replacement for Charles Henry, or what?' It sounded as though Noakes's bafflement would be immune to any amount of beer.

‘If he had a mental crisis . . . some kind of episode where he was reliving that childhood rage, George . . .’

Anything Markham’s ethereal-looking girlfriend said was generally gospel to Noakes — much to his wife’s ill-concealed irritation — but in this instance, he looked pretty much floored.

‘You’re not suggesting he couldn’t help hisself, I s’pose.’ Suspicion of bleeding-heart liberalism ran through Noakes like a stick of rock.

‘I think there must have been some kind of pathology which would have led sooner or later to violence.’ Olivia never talked down to him. ‘We’ll never know for certain, what with Donald Lestrange being dead.’

The DS blinked hard as though to clear his vision.

‘That gorilla of Carstone’s sure ain’t giving us anything,’ he muttered.

‘Bill Hignett,’ Markham corrected him with a faint note of reproof. ‘I doubt he’ll ever be fit to stand trial, Noakesy.’

‘One more for that crowd at the Newman to work on.’ The DS’s tone left no doubt that he didn’t hold out much hopes of the wretched man’s rehabilitation. But then, he had never been a fan of Bromgrove’s mental health unit and its ‘trick cyclists.’

Doyle had returned to their table with fresh pints for himself and Noakes, who smacked his lips appreciatively.

‘I wondered if p’raps Bill was Carstone’s love-child or something.’

‘*You what?*’ The DS boggled at the youngster.

‘Well, it’d explain Carstone always protecting him.’ Doyle sounded affronted.

Markham made haste to pour oil on troubled waters.

‘An interesting suggestion,’ he said diplomatically. Then more seriously, ‘I hope in time we can learn more from Cathy Hignett. Who knows, possibly the bond between Aubrey and Bill was cemented by something else . . . some common experience of childhood abuse . . . a recognition of shared trauma . . .’

'Or mebbe the pair of 'em were just evil bastards.'

Noakes looked sideways at Kate Burton as he said this.

'I'm all right now, sarge,' she said, laying a timid hand on his arm. 'They didn't lay a finger on me. Just kept me shut up in a bedroom while they were . . . doing whatever it was downstairs.'

'What d'you think they *were* doing all that time?' asked Doyle wide-eyed.

'God knows,' grunted Noakes. 'Voodoo an' black masses I shouldn't wonder.' He took a huge swig of his drink. 'Gloating over little Alex Carter's grave . . . or mebbe they popped down the churchyard for a quick peep at Charles Henry.'

'Well, at least in the end you were able to reclaim "The Lost Boy" and give him a proper funeral.'

The group fell silent at Olivia's words, recalling the poignant ceremony at Greygarth Parish Church which had preceded Alex Carter's interment next to the other little victim.

'Do you reckon they'll find other kids there, sir?' Doyle asked thinking of the Cold Case Unit which had discreetly taken over occupation of the estate.

'I think it's possible, Doyle, given the length of the association between Carstone and Hignett.'

'Sidney'll lay it all at Hignett's door, you c'n be sure of that,' grunted Noakes. 'No chance of his precious gallery being dragged through the tabloids.'

'Speaking of which,' Olivia said lightly. 'What news of the team there?'

'Still pretty much shell-shocked.' Burton took up the baton. 'Though, it's amazing how many of them claim to have sensed something dodgy about Carstone all along,' she concluded wryly.

'Interesting what Benedict Bramwell said about there having been a spat between Carstone and Helen Melville.' Doyle contemplated his Foster's ruminatively.

'What kind of spat?' Noakes enquired curiously.

'Well, he just said it in passing.' Doyle was clearly pleased to be the imparter of information. 'Something to do with plagiarism or taking credit for other people's work. Y'know, her and Randall muscling in on those *aediculae* or whatever they're called.'

So, the childhood jealousy never went away, thought Markham. Carstone carried that 'vicious mole of nature' to the very end.

'Ms Melville and Randall played a dangerous game,' he said aloud.

'In their book, *they* held all the aces,' Noakes put in. 'An' they thought Carstone was just this feeble old fella . . . never twigged the connection between him and Hignett.'

'I reckon Melville imagined she could get him to confess . . . that would've been the icing on the cake. *Ta-da*!' Doyle was motoring now. 'As it was, she couldn't be totally sure . . . didn't see where Lestrange fitted in . . .'

'With Randall, it was blackmail.' Markham thought sadly of that desperate father waiting to keep his rendezvous with the son who was already dead.

'But he knew Carstone had killed his girlfriend, sir.' Doyle looked round the table. 'So why didn't he turn him in?'

'He planned to extort money from him . . . use the knowledge as a bargaining chip for career advancement—'

'Mebbe deep down he was secretly glad to be shot of Melville,' Noakes interposed. 'Figured old Aubrey had done him a favour.'

'God that's *sick*, sarge.'

'That's life, lad.' A stentorian verdict.

'Randall's motives were probably mixed,' Markham said with decision. 'Like Helen Melville, he no doubt looked up to Carstone . . . hoped Aubrey would be able to explain away past sins even as he planned to manipulate the knowledge of them for his own ends.'

Use every man after his desert and who should 'scape whipping.

'What'll happen to Daniel Westbrook?'

'That's for the CPS to decide, Doyle, though privately I'm inclined to think he's suffered enough.'

'I s'pose that slime ball Marcus Traherne won't get his comeuppance,' Noakes said morosely.

'He will if I have anything to do with it, Noakesy.' Markham winked at him, tapping the side of his nose in time-honoured fashion. 'Ways and means. Ways and means.'

* * *

Much later, Markham and Olivia walked arm in arm along deserted pavements now free of snow that rang to the sound of their footsteps.

'What happened to the pictures?' she asked suddenly. 'You know — the ones Aubrey Carstone stole from the gallery and hid in his flat at Greygarth?'

'Safely back where they belong, Liv — in a new exhibition space devoted to *aediculae*. Eventually destined to house the Ned Chester Collection.'

And with that simple statement, she knew Greygarth's evil legacy, the house within a house, was finally redeemed.

THE END

ALSO BY CATHERINE MOLONEY

THE DI GILBERT MARKHAM SERIES

Book 1: CRIME IN THE CHOIR Book 2: CRIME IN THE SCHOOL Book 3: CRIME IN THE CONVENT Book 4: CRIME IN THE HOSPITAL Book 5: CRIME IN THE BALLET Book 6: CRIME IN THE GALLERY

FREE KINDLE BOOKS

Thank you for reading this book. If you enjoyed it please leave feedback on Amazon or Goodreads, and if there is anything we missed or you have a question about then please get in touch. The author and publishing team appreciate your feedback and time reading this book.

We're very grateful to eagle-eyed readers who take the time to contact us. Please send any errors you find to corrections@joffebooks.com